Blue Tide Rising

Clare Stevens

Inspired
Quill

Published by Inspired Quill: March 2019

First Edition

TW: This book contains mention of rape, drug use and depression.

Blue Tide Rising © 2019 by Clare Stevens
Contact the author through their website: clarestevens.com

Chief Editor: Sara-Jayne Slack
Cover Design: Valeria Aguilera
Typeset in Adobe Garamond Pro

Paperback ISBN: 978-1-908600-81-3
eBook ISBN: 978-1-908600-82-0
Print Edition

Printed in the United Kingdom
1 2 3 4 5 6 7 8 9 10

Inspired Quill Publishing, UK
Business Reg. No. 7592847
www.inspired-quill.com

To JP for your love and encouragement
throughout and to Jane who loved the idea
for the story but sadly never got to read it.

PART ONE

Balmoral Street

Chapter One

"THERE SHE GOES. Likkle Pixie in har big coat." The Man stands by his railing where he waits, when it's dry, watching the world. I force a smile out from under my hood.

"Ah she smiling now," he says. "A smile from Pixie-girl goes a laang way."

I scurry on by.

My route to Lidl takes me beyond Balmoral Street onto the main road, past the corner where two girls are out. Past the bookies, the boarded-up pubs and the bright, brash, payday loan shops. Past the old Post Office, its windows plastered with faded posters, signs of a battle to keep it open, lost long ago. Past the Methodist Mission, with its giant poster telling everyone to 'Keep calm and follow Jesus'. There are people outside there, handing out leaflets. I keep my head down, hood up and hands deep in my pockets. It starts to rain again.

There's a song playing on repeat in my head. A Smiths song from the 80s about rain and Manchester. It's been in my head for weeks, the soundtrack to my life. As it plays on I curse the fact that all my earworms still come from the Iain Carver period of my past.

People don't choose to come to Balmoral Street. It's not listed in the student literature or the brochures they give to tourists. People fetch up here like flotsam. That's what happened to me. I washed up here after I lost the baby – precisely how that happened is hidden in a Diazepam haze. I guess I fit right in among all the other misfits. Immigrants arriving from warzones around the world. Girls, younger than me, working the street corner, shivering in bare legs. Kids looking for gear, or cigarettes, or change. The social worker calls them 'hard to reach.' Hard to avoid, more like.

"You look down you see shit, you look up, you see de sky," The Man told me. Most people here look down, me included.

When I get back, he is talking to another black man, someone whose clothes don't fit the weather. Someone with that guarded, hunted look of the new arrivals. They live in the houses no-one else wants. Barrel Woman says they should go home, but I reckon it must be bad where they come from if they think this is the promised land.

"He from Somalia," The Man says. Isn't that where the pirates come from? Do I want people like that living near me? But the immigrants are mostly ok, keeping to themselves. It's the spice-heads and pimps and other crazy characters who are the problem.

I nod at the two men and turn towards my building, but

The Man calls me back. "Somebody looking for you," he says.

I feel a jolt of something shoot through my veins. Something that makes me stop, makes me swing round to face him, makes me speak.

"Who?"

"Young mon."

Young? Not Iain then, although it's just possible that to The Man, even Iain might seem young.

"Tall," he holds his hand up above his head to indicate someone at least six foot tall.

Definitely not Iain.

"Very fair. Slim."

Not Howard Carlotti either.

"Dreamy boy. I seen him around here before. But not for a laang time."

Who the…?

Chapter Two

"**B**ITCH."

Psycho-Boy sits on the stairs, blocking the route to my attic.

"What da fuck. DA FUCK!" He's shouting at someone who isn't there. I cower on the landing, just out of sight, pulse racing. Somehow I have to get past him.

"Fucking BITCH!"

I prefer it when he's comatose. I can step over him then.

I tap on Barrel Woman's door. No answer. I brace myself, working up the courage to appear in Psycho-Boy's line of sight. He has one tree-trunk leg splayed out to the side, one stretched in front of him. His hairy belly folds out over his jeans. He smells, as usual, of weed and piss. He doesn't flinch as I appear, doesn't seem to notice me. I size up the situation. He's taking up most of the stairway, but I might just be able to squeeze past. I breathe in, as if that will make me even thinner, then make my move. He looks up through unfocused eyes and bats his hand in front of his face like he's swiping at a fly, then carries on muttering. I make it.

Psycho-Boy lives in the flat below me. Whatever he's on makes him shout a lot. He's a white boy who talks like a black boy and plays hip-hop loud and late. He has visitors through the day and night, and if they can't get in downstairs they throw things at his window. Their aim isn't always that good; once they cracked Barrel Woman's glass. His presence doesn't help my stress levels, especially now, with him blocking the stairs. I reach for the Diazepam, and dive under the duvet.

I don't know what time it is when I surface. Here, day and night merge into a perpetual grey – the window in the roof lets in too much light at night and not enough in the daytime. I'm in the in-between state between sleep and consciousness, half-woken by a hint of outdoors air, like someone's left a door or window open. That's when I notice someone standing at the foot of my bed. An indistinct figure, shrouded in a large Parka. Dream? Or real? Hard to tell, these days. I have no energy to think about him. He doesn't look dangerous. In any case, I've got nothing left to lose.

When I wake again the figure is still there and the smell of the outdoors is stronger. It reminds me of something. Pieces of the past float through my mind. Stanlow on a summer evening, the fishermen's nook down by the river, me and Iain cocooned in our secret love, out of sight, while across the water shouts went out from the party people on the green and the band played on.

But it's not quite that, this aroma. It's something else. Maybe even... but I can't go there. It's locked away. Unreachable.

The figure gets nearer, and clearer, as he moves into the patch of light below the window. I can now see his face. Young, wide, pale, with big intense eyes, brown, I think, and even in the gloom I can see the lightness of his hair. Most of the faces you see around here are ugly. They show the ravages of chaotic lives. This one is gorgeous. Maybe that's why I let my eyes rest on it and do not banish it from my bedroom. There's something almost familiar about the face. Has he been here before, in this room? Is he here every night? Perhaps I saw him at the hospital. Sometimes I think I'm back there. There were plenty of strangers around me then, but surely, none this beautiful. He could even be a girl. I can't make out his shape underneath the Parka, but sense he is insubstantial.

"Amy."

He knows my name.

Chapter Three

"WHO ARE YOU?" my voice sounds strange and laboured.

"Me?" he says, shrugging slightly, as though his identity isn't important. "They call me Jay."

His voice, rich and deep, contrasts with the androgyny of his face.

He stands, hands in the pockets of his Parka, and looks around him. "Hasn't changed much," he says. "I used to live in this room."

"When?" I feel a stab of fear. Has he come to reclaim his room? I sit upright, now wide awake. The slats in the headboard dig into my back.

"A few years ago, but don't worry, I've no desire to move back in again."

It's like he's read my mind.

"So how come you're here now?" I say.

"I thought maybe you could use someone to talk to."

I rack my fuddled brain for some explanation, some category to put him in. Not an addict – they find their way up here sometimes looking for money or stuff to nick. Not another resident – they do the same. Since the break-in, when someone forced the lock on my door, all it takes is a light shove to gain entry to the room.

Then I remember something the social worker said months ago, or it might have been the psychiatrist. What did they call it? Mentoring, befriending? Some meaningless social-worker bullshit.

"Did someone send you?" I say, pulling the pillow behind my back. "They said they were sending some random person round to see me."

He chuckles, perching himself on the table near my bed. "Random. That'll be me."

"But I don't want to see anyone," I say, tired of the new demands speaking is making of me. "I just want to sleep."

"And can you sleep?" he says. "You seem to spend a lot of time in bed, but I'm not sure you sleep."

I shrug. "No. Not really. And when I do I have weird dreams."

He stares straight at me, like he's actually interested in what I'm saying. "What are your weird dreams about?"

It's none of his business, of course, but something makes me want to keep him there.

"There's like a line of faces, and I have to walk along the line, and they're all looming out of the walls at me. They're people I used to know, then they morph into monsters."

"Hmm," he says. "Recognition. That's what that's about. No longer recognising yourself or others. You feel betrayed. Am I right?"

"You a shrink or something? You interpret dreams?"

"Something must have happened to turn everything ugly," he says.

"Everything *is* ugly," I say.

He moves away then, into the shadows near the door.

"I have to go now, Amy, but listen, I'm glad we made contact. I'll call by another time, if it's all right with you? Probably after Christmas."

"Whatever," I say, sinking back into slumber.

I wake to see a thin shaft of daylight breaking through the grey. He is gone.

Chapter Four

I DON'T KNOW what day it is when I venture out. I wonder why the streets are so quiet. I've been conscious of the build-up, of course – tinsel hanging outside Speedy Cash, carols floating out from the Methodist Mission, Christmas songs from the one remaining pub. The temporary fireworks shop has morphed into a temporary Christmas shop. Someone has even hung a few lights on the section of road between Ladbrokes and the pharmacist.

The debris of the season lies all around. Soggy wrapping paper, discarded tinsel, bottles on the street, more vomit than usual. I walk all the way to Lidl to find it shut. I'll have to make do with something from the corner shop.

On my way back I see The Man striding down the street. Very rare to see him away from his post. He looks smart, in a brown overcoat. He's wearing his Trilby. He reminds me of my granddad dressed for Sunday.

"Here she is on Christmas day." He says, holding his

arms out wide. I tense up, in case he's going to hug me, but he sidesteps then continues on his way. He must have somewhere to go.

"Merry Christmas luv," a man swigging from a can of extra strong lager and trailing a length of purple tinsel lurches towards me. I duck.

Coming back over the threshold of the house, I see Psycho-Boy, crashed out in the hall, a pair of antlers round his neck.

"So this is Christmas!" I say to myself as I step over him.

Later, I hear a familiar footfall on the attic stairs, and the wheezing of someone with bad lungs hauling themselves up to my landing. I open the door to Barrel Woman, her face smeared with glitter, a pair of flashing Santa earrings setting off her usual stretch leggings and outsize jumper dress. Black and orange stripes today. She looks like a bee. The pink dye she put in her hair a couple of months ago has mostly grown out and she's back to grey, with flecks of glitter that glint like dandruff.

"Merry Christmas gel!" she thrusts a bottle of Tesco Finest blended whiskey at me.

Barrel Woman's real name is Mary, and she comes from London, which she calls 'Landin'. For her, Balmoral Street is a step up; she's spent a lot of her life in institutions. "I booked meself in for the winter, back in 89, but they wouldn't let me out so I escaped, got on a National Express up to Manchester and I bin 'ere ever since." Barrel Woman has done drugs with Amy Winehouse, gone on drink binges with George Best and hung out with the Beatles. I've no idea how old she is. She's the closest thing I have around here to a friend.

Today we dine on pizza and baked beans, and she dines out on tales of life on the streets and celebrities she's known. We sing along to TOTP2, using the ketchup bottle as a microphone. She produces a pack of cards and teaches me to play Blind Don. I don't smoke, but I have five of her cut-price cigarettes that afternoon. At some point in the proceedings, we go out to the corner shop and buy two-for-one bottles of QC. The rest is oblivion.

On Boxing Day I wake up with the mother of all hangovers and resolve not to entertain Barrel Woman for a very long time.

Chapter Five

THE NEXT DAY, the snow comes. It falls heavily for two whole days, then turns to slush. The slush freezes over and patches of frost and ice hang around for days, lurking on roads and pavements, to catch the unsuspecting. The fog that hangs permanently over Balmoral Street is now freezing. The central heating doesn't work. The electric fan heater makes little difference unless you sit right in front of it. All good reasons to stay in bed.

Sometimes as the meds wear off, I start to feel a scream rising up in me again. I don't want the scream to come. It's a terrifying sound. So I reach for the packet of pills to dull my senses for a few more hours.

Twice, I think I glimpse Jay in the half-light, but he doesn't speak, and when I resurface he's not there.

My life now is full of petty irritations. Trudging up the two flights of stairs to my attic, the light goes out before I reach the middle landing. The bulb at the top has blown and nobody's replaced it, so I fumble my way up in darkness. Inside the room, there's mould on the curtains. A damp patch is spreading across the wall and ice is forming on the inside of the skylight window.

According to The Man, this place was once one big house, now it's 'studio apartments.' Crummy bedsits more like. 'Part furnished,' means a sagging bed, a flimsy chest of drawers and a wardrobe with doors that don't shut properly. The social worker got me an Ikea chair from somewhere, it has light wooden handles and a cream cover. When you sit in it, it rocks. She got me a table too, big enough to have a dinner party, she said. I don't have dinner parties. The only person I ever entertain, if you can call it that, is Barrel Woman when she makes her way up here, uninvited, brandishing a bottle, and we'll spend an alcoholic afternoon together. It takes weeks to get rid of the stench of her cigarettes.

It's too far to walk to Lidl in this icy weather, so I eat beans on toast or pasta with sauce or pot noodles from the corner shop. What does it matter anyway? Nothing tastes of anything.

Washing is torturous. Taking all my clothes off to get in the shower is usually too much effort. The showerhead mostly trickles cold except when it decides to spurt scalding water.

Judith's voice is a constant in my head, telling me I've 'let myself go'. When I catch my reflection in the rusty mirror I'm met with a freakish apparition, my hair a mess of unkempt black (my straighteners, like everything else, went in the burglary), my face a ghoulish white.

"HELLO AMY."

Jay is back, sitting on the table next to my bed, this time clear and distinct. I didn't notice him arrive.

"Oh it's you," I say.

He laughs. "You're conscious!"

"Did you come before?"

"I looked in on you a couple of times."

I'm surprised he bothered.

"Why?"

"You interest me Amy, and anyway, I have time on my hands right now."

He looks more relaxed than the first time I saw him. He's even unzipped the Parka.

I haul myself up into a sitting position, wrapping the quilt round my shoulders.

"Why d'you always come at night?"

He shrugs. "I'm kind of nocturnal, at the moment. So what have you been doing?" he sits on his hands and swings his legs.

"Nothing," I say.

"Nothing?"

"There's nothing *to* do."

"Nothing to do in this cosmopolitan city? Top of the student popularity league? Heaving with nightlife?"

"Like I can afford to go out."

He laughs, briefly, then says: "Money's just a concept, Amy."

I snort. "Tell that to the bank."

"Ha!" he says. "Financial institutions know that better than anyone. That's what they trade on. A concept."

I yawn. "Whatever. I haven't got enough of this *concept* to pay for a night out. And I've got no-one to go with."

He thinks for a moment then says: "Let me guess. You have a commentary going on in your head the whole time, telling you everything's shit. Am I right?"

"My life *is* shit," I say.

"Hmm," he says. "One word to sum up twenty-four years?"

How does he know my age?

"Everything I touch turns to shit. I lost my parents when I was ten. I lost my job. I lost the next one. I lost my man. I lost my baby. Everything I have, I lose."

He leans forward, hands on his thighs, and says, "well, to quote Marilyn Monroe, things fall apart so things can fall together."

"Great," I say. "And look what happened to her."

Jay laughs again, a quick explosive laugh. I can't tell if he's laughing at my wit, or taking pleasure in my despair. Then he says, "this voice in your head, that drowns out everything else, it's not your voice. It's an imposter."

"So what do I do about it, Freud?"

"You need to tell it to fuck off. It's time to kill the commentary before it kills you."

I feel the salt sting in my eyes and my lungs tense as I try to force the tears back down. It takes several laboured breaths before I'm able to speak.

People are surprised when they hear my voice. Posh girl, they called me at school, when I moved up from down south. I use big words. Old words. Words I got from books, when books were my companions, or words from Iain. You can't spend that long with someone twenty years older than you and sound like a normal twenty-four-year old. But here, in Balmoral Street, my voice has all but disappeared.

Now it sounds alien to me as it comes out strangled by sobs.

"Like it's that easy! I can't even do the things I used to do any more, can't walk down the street without freaking out, can't look anyone in the eye. Can't remember the last time I had a conversation with anyone, except you."

"So don't I count?"

"No, not really. I don't know who you are or if you're just proof that I've totally cracked up. Even if you *are* real, you're never there in the morning!"

Jay backs away a little, eyebrows arched, then gives a sudden snort of laughter.

"Nothing worse than a man who's gone when you wake up in the morning!"

"Glad you find it funny!"

He stands up, no longer laughing. "You wanna get out of this? Want to change your life? I can help you."

"How?"

"I'll give you stuff to do. Nothing difficult. Just small challenges. And if you do them, I guarantee you'll feel better. But you have to trust me."

I stare at him. I should just tell him to get lost. Haven't I got enough challenges in my life without him setting me more? Isn't continuing to exist day by day challenge enough?

Then suddenly I'm transported back in time to a

different life, to my eighteen-year old former self.

Iain and I had had our first major argument. I was feeling lousy, my innards all churned up. Hannah, sensing something was wrong but obviously not knowing what, dragged me out to some club in town. We met Stacey there and a couple of the others.

Hannah tried to get me to dance, but I wouldn't. Stacey said, "leave her Han if she wants to be miserable," and they turned their backs on me and carried on dancing while I sat at the side, drinking myself numb.

Then I realised there was someone in my bubble. A dark, cute face, leaning in towards me. One of the Italian boys who'd come over with the twin town exchange was talking to me through my fog. Although I ignored him he kept talking, leaning closer, grabbing my hand.

"Dance with me," he said, and I thought, what's there to lose? So I got up and danced with this Italian guy. We threw ourselves around to the music, giving it all we'd got. The floor around us cleared, everyone was watching us. It was like the dance scene in Pulp Fiction. My mood shot from the floor to the sky in the space of seconds.

I look at Jay now, beautiful and intense. I breathe in the smell of the outdoors that accompanies him and reminds me of something I still can't place, and I want to dance to his tune.

"So where do we start?" I say.

He smiles, like he knew I'd comply. "You can start by telling me your story."

Chapter Six

WHERE TO BEGIN? No point in trying to recall the early years, there's a thick dark cloud obscuring them. I suppose I should start with the day it all changed, the knock on the door. Me sitting on the sofa watching My Little Vampire with Ruby the child-minder and Oscar the cat curled up between us. I was ten.

Then came the voices in the hallway and the feet. Two pairs of shiny black lace-ups, with uniformed legs attached. I heard the word 'Police.' Neighbours filled the house. Ruby held me, her eyes red, her face blotchy. Because she cried, I cried, although I didn't know why we were crying. Then Aunt Judith came to take me away.

I clung to Ruby. But Judith's angular face looked down at me, disapproving, and everyone said I should go. It was for the best.

I'd only met Judith a couple of times, now I was supposed to live in her house. The village she lived in,

Stanlow on the outskirts of Derby, was miles from anyone I knew. She didn't want me there. There was no space in her organised life with her brilliant academic career in biochemistry, her trips to the theatre and her boring intellectual dinner parties for me and my grief.

"Her parents were hippies living some idealistic fantasy down in Somerset," Judith lowered her voice on the phone in her study, but I could hear every word. "Completely skint. The house was rented. Nothing decent to sell. The animals they kept were worthless."

I missed the animals. Nobody had told me what happened to them.

"He was always a romantic fool, my brother. He got worse when he met that crazy Haitian woman. Met and married with a sprog on the way within six months. Madness!"

I learnt through that overheard phone call about the massive burden of inconvenience my parents' death had caused Judith, the legal minefield she had to navigate because they hadn't made a will, the money hassles, and of course, the biggest burden of all – me. She took me in because it was her 'duty'.

Duty-bound summed Judith up. Upright and uptight.

At Judith's the sound of my breathing or moving around made too much noise. My mouth clammed shut, my body permanently tense, every muscle taut, every nerve on edge, waiting for her disapproval. I shouldn't be in whatever room I was in, I shouldn't be doing whatever I was doing, or touching whatever I was touching.

I shouldn't exist.

I should have died with them.

That first summer at Judith's, before I started at the local school, went on forever. I had a permanent, twisting pain in the base of my stomach. The painkillers Judith gave me didn't touch it. She took me to a doctor, demanding anti-depressants. The doctor wouldn't give us any. He suggested counselling, but Judith didn't believe in counselling. She only believed in science.

Her home, like her lab, was clinically clean. It smelt of chemicals. She had a small square garden with a perfectly manicured lawn, each little weed blasted out of existence. I couldn't see the point of a garden where things weren't allowed to grow. I was used to a house full of neighbours and noise and other people's kids. At Judith's once you closed the door behind you that was it. Except on the occasions she invited boring academic colleagues round to dinner, no-one came.

Later, I started to take comfort in small acts of rebellion, like letting the local tom-cat in to spray the place and scratch the furniture, or walking mud all over her pristine carpet. When a certain comedian came on the TV Judith immediately switched channels, saying "I simply cannot stand that man," so I downloaded all his shows and put pictures of him on my walls. And when she said, "this stuff has no musical credentials," I made it my mission to get into rap music.

'Passive aggressive', is how I heard her describe me to her friends. "I think she could be trouble."

Books were my saviour. There was a little bedroom in Judith's house she called the Library, and in among all the books on biochemistry I found literature. Nothing for kids, but all the classics. Brontë, Hardy, Dickens – you name it, I read it that summer. This suited Judith; it meant she didn't have to talk to me.

MY THROAT IS hoarse from speaking. My vocal cords physically ache. Jay sits, taking in details a succession of professionals tried and failed to draw out of me. Jay is different. You can almost *feel* him listening.

Chapter Seven

JAY HAS GIVEN me instructions. I'm supposed to start talking to people. Strangers. But there aren't many people around Balmoral Street it's safe to talk to. He suggested the man in the corner shop, who I see most days, but when I go in, there's a queue of people and I bottle it. I manage 'hello', but that's not enough. I have to 'initiate a conversation.' Jay says I need to re-learn how to connect, to rediscover who I really am. This introvert person I've become isn't the authentic me, apparently. God knows how he knows. Sometimes I think he's full of bullshit.

I call by the pharmacy to pick up my pills. Some days there's addicts queuing up for their scripts but today the place is empty. Maybe I'll initiate a conversation with the pharmacist guy. He's a quiet, non-threatening Asian man. But it's not him who comes to the counter, it's a girl, about my age. I think she's his daughter. Maybe she'll do.

"Hello," I say, my heart thumping, my face hot. I hand

over my repeat slip. "Hey," she says, looking at the prescription. She has thick dark hair almost down to her waist.

"How you doing?" I mumble when she comes back with my tablets. She doesn't answer, just peers at the paperwork. Not only am I invisible, I'm inaudible too.

Then she looks up and smiles. "I'm so tired today," she says. "Yesterday we had a *big* party." She has huge brown eyes, long lashes and a tiny, glinting, red nose stud.

"Was it good?" I say.

"Yes. It was for my sister's engagement. A family party. Lots of food and dancing. It went on late." She draws out the word 'late'.

I could leave it there but I'm on a roll. "When's your sister getting married?"

"Next year, next April."

"Will it be a big wedding?"

Am I asking too many questions?

"There'll be lots of family coming from India. Lots of preparations."

"Do you like your sister's fiancé?"

This could be the wrong thing to say. What if it's a – what do you call it – a forced marriage?

"Yes, he's lovely. She met him at University. Sometimes in our culture people have marriages arranged for them, but my sister found her own groom."

"Awesome," I say. "I'm Amy by the way."

"I'm Dvinder."

ARRIVING BACK ON Balmoral Street, two Police officers are

outside, talking to The Man. He hails me over.

"Dey asking about Mary," he said. "You seen her?"

He means Barrel Woman.

"Not since Christmas," I say.

"And you are?" the Policeman takes my name.

TRUDGING BACK UP to my room, I stop and tap at Barrel Woman's door. There's no answer. I sniff the air. The lack of tobacco fug on the first-floor landing suggests a prolonged absence. Maybe she's in one of her institutions.

An hour or so later I hear boots on the stairs. I tense, fearing a visit from some of Psycho-boy's friends, then someone shouts 'Police' and there's the thump, thump, thump of a door being beaten down. I sneak a look down the stairwell. It's Barrel Woman's door.

The Police don't like us round here. They assume everyone's on drugs. When this building got broken into they barely bothered to list what was taken. Contrast that to when Fiona Carlotti had her handbag lifted in a swanky café in town, the Police bent over backwards to help her. Money talks. I lost everything in the break-in here; my straighteners, my leather jacket and my phone which I'd left on charge while I nipped out. It took them less than fifteen minutes to ransack the place; they must have been watching the house. They also took the emergency supply of Diazepam I got off the Internet. Rumour had it the girl in the ground-floor flat, who Barrel Woman says is a 'high-class tart', had £750 cash stolen that day.

When I go out later there's a piece of chipboard nailed across the smashed-in door.

"Do you know what's happened to Barrel Woman?" I ask Jay later.

"Mary?" he knows who I mean. "I see someone's kicked her door in."

"The Police did it," I say. "Do you know where she is?"

"Have they tried the Gallagher brothers?"

I laugh. "Are any of her celebrity stories true?"

He shrugs. "Reality is subjective. The main thing is she believes them and they entertain people. But you don't need to worry about Mary. Mary will look after Mary. It's your story I'm interested in. Tell me more."

Chapter Eight

"ARE YOU GOING to introduce us, Judith?"

A woman with bleached blonde hair and a jacket that didn't quite go around her middle stopped us in the street. Lynda Carver was one of those women who bustled around and knew everyone. She organised the Stanlow carnival, the village garden party, the picnic in the park. Judith thought Lynda was 'interfering'. She mostly was, but that day she threw me a lifeline.

"Amy, you must come to ours and meet my daughter Hannah. When you start school you'll be in the same class." So I was spared the ordeal of turning up on the first day of term knowing nobody. Hannah adopted me like some exotic stray kitten. And Hannah, like her mother, knew everyone. Under her protection, I escaped the bullying that might otherwise have come from these alien kids with their flat Derbyshire vowels. Despite my freakish looks and southern accent I was accepted by association.

Iain Carver walked into my life one day in September. Hannah's mum picked us up after school and took me to their house for tea. I was sitting on the sofa with Hannah and Nellie, her West Highland Terrier, while her younger twin brothers wrestled on the floor. Nellie was climbing all over me, licking my face. I was trying to push her away, giggling.

Iain, Hannah's dad, came in, carrying a briefcase, which he flung down, then shouted, "Nellie come here!" The dog trotted off to him. He got down on all fours in his suit and rolled around on the floor with Nellie, tickling her, making her growl, driving her mad. Hannah and I and the twins howled with laughter. Then he stood up, brushed himself off and walked towards me. "Hannah who's *this*?"

Right from the start he made me feel I mattered.

After that, I went to Hannah's after school most days. This suited Judith, it meant she could work long and late in her lab. It suited me too, I felt much more at home in the organised chaos of the Carvers' house. It became my second home, with Iain a protective father figure.

Second Dad. That's how people described Iain. And when it all came out, that's what caused the most outrage.

WE WERE FOURTEEN when Hannah got her first boyfriend. "He's called Jake the invisible man," said Iain at the dinner table. "And nobody's allowed to meet him, talk about him, or speak to him on the phone."

"*Dad!*" said Hannah.

"Have you seen this elusive creature, Amy?"

"Jake, yeah, he's in our year at school."

"What's he like? Is he hideously deformed or pathologically shy?"

"Er, no, he's just normal."

"So why aren't we allowed to meet him?"

"Dad!" said Hannah again. "This is why – you'll show me up."

Then Iain said, "Have *you* got a boyfriend Amy?"

"Not at the moment."

"Good for you," he said. "Take my advice, save yourself. Don't just go with anyone who can wear a baseball cap backwards."

"Dad's always going on about you," Hannah said later. "'Amy's so intelligent.', 'Amy's going to be a stunner.' I think he wishes you were his daughter instead of me."

He did seem to notice me more than the others. We were a group of six by the time we were 14 – Hannah, Charlotte, Lucy, Stacey, Sinead, and me. We'd meet at Hannah's house before heading out to the teen club-night in town. We'd jostle for position at the bathroom mirror putting on makeup and hairspray, then troop downstairs to where Iain waited by the people carrier. I sensed him looking me up and down and sometimes he'd say things like: "Nice outfit, Amy," as I got in the car.

Once, Sinead said, "Hannah's dad fancies you." She said it quietly, accusingly, so nobody else could hear. My face burnt.

Iain looked and acted younger than the other dads. He still had all his hair. He had a cool chinstrap beard. He was slim. He dressed well – sharp suits for work and designer jeans at home.

He managed the car showroom at the edge of the village and got to test-drive different vehicles. Once he gave me a lift home in a Porsche 911. The car was very low with plush seats. He looked at me sideways and said: "You look good in a sports car."

I scrabbled around for the seatbelt. He reached across me, found it and plugged me in, his hand brushing against my body for a nanosecond.

"Mind if we go for a little spin on the way home?" he said. "I love driving this thing. Want to give it a proper run."

So off we went up the A6 into Derbyshire, Iain and Amy in an open-topped sports car, burning up the road, attracting glances.

"Fancy an ice-cream?" Iain parked up outside a bikers' cafe in Matlock Bath. He watched me step out of the car, then said: "You know Sloane rangers have lessons in how to get out of a sports car wearing a short skirt, but you're a natural, Amy,"

I puffed up with pride at everything he said.

And I've tried, looking back, to remember the exact moment when I started to have feelings for Iain. When indeed?

At fifteen, watching the village fireworks with Judith, conscious of someone approaching from behind, squeezing my shoulders. Thrilled he'd spotted me among the crowds.

At fourteen, brushing past each other on the landing on the way to the loo. A moment of contact. A frisson.

Aged thirteen, on the trampoline with Hannah, bouncing high. Iain climbed up there with us. Hannah said,

"Get off Dad, you'll break it." Iain pushed her off, but he and I carried on jumping then collapsed together in a giggling heap. I felt giddy and breathless from laughing.

And there was the ice-skating trip when we were 12. Iain took me, Hannah and the twins. The others had been before, they knew what they were doing, but I clung to the edge.

"Come on Amy I'll take you round." He coaxed me out onto the ice. And before long we were gliding together across the rink. He was little and lithe and graceful, and I was graceful next to him.

We fitted. Even then.

Chapter Nine

TASK NUMBER ONE: talk to new people. Initiate conversations. Task number two: do something different. Go somewhere new. Deviate from my normal route. Take in some culture.

Jay's told me to go to an art gallery. He's obsessed with art. There's galleries in town, apparently. But I'm not ready to face town. He told me about some heritage centre nearby where they've got an exhibition on. I don't know where it is and I don't know who to ask. I have a battered A-Z map book someone left in my room. I find Balmoral Street and scour the page but I can't see anything that says heritage centre. Then I notice patches of blue on the map not too far away. Blue means water. I have a sudden longing to be near water. I decide to try and find the place.

For once there are clear skies over Balmoral Street. It's cold but bright. My route takes me in the opposite direction to my usual beaten track, off the main road, away from the shops. I tread carefully, eyes peeled for danger, but the buildings and the spaces I walk past are indifferent. And with each step I grow bolder. It's almost as if I have a right to be here.

A few streets in, there are allotments bordering onto the road and the outline of hills in the distance. The houses are built of the same red brick as the ones on Balmoral Street, but they're smaller and have little gardens at the front with things like children's buggies and bikes and plant pots in them. There are even snowdrops peeping through in a couple of them. I'm not sure where I am. There's staples on the bit of the map I'm walking on. I see a gravel path leading off between the houses. This could be the way to the lakes. But I stop in my tracks. What if I meet some psycho down there?

"Shut up!" I shout to the voice inside my head, the one that would have me crawl back to Balmoral Street and die there. Tell the voice to fuck off, Jay's always telling me. The voice falls silent, allowing the crisp air to filter through to my senses. I stand a little taller and breathe in.

A middle-aged woman trudges up the track, two fat Labradors in tow.

"Hello luv, what a beautiful day!'

She's got that salt-of-the-earth Manchester accent. Dour but honest.

"Are there some lakes around here somewhere?" I say.

"You want the ressies? Just follow't lane, there's one either side. We've just walked all't way round and it were beautiful."

The sight of the water lifts me. It's hard to believe I'm

only twenty minutes away from Balmoral Street. This is a different country. Down by the lakeside there are parents with children in buggies and people walking dogs, not the bulldogs you see on Balmoral Street, but Westies and Collies and Spaniels. There are windsurfers at the far end. I watch the coloured sails glide across the water. A little terrier runs up to me, and sits, panting, at my feet. I bend down to pat it. Its owner, a very old man, leans on his stick and tells me it's a Jack Russell cross called Freddie and he got it from a rescue centre. It feels good to drink in daylight and greenery through tired eyes, to connect with strangers.

Perhaps it is the sight of blue sky, the feel of sunlight on my skin, or the relief of telling my story to Jay by instalments, that makes me feel almost alive. It's a fleeting feeling, more of a memory, but it's here.

Chapter Ten

I WAS SEVENTEEN, it was the start of the summer holidays, and I was walking through the village. It was a hot day. I was wearing a short red dress which brushed my thighs. I liked the feel of the dress on me. I wasn't thinking about Iain. I was thinking about money, and what I could do to earn some. Iain's car drew up. He lowered the window. "Hello stranger! Want a lift?" and I got in, even though I had no particular place to go.

I hadn't seen Iain for some time. Since going to college and studying different subjects, I saw less of Hannah. Now, sitting in his car, feeling him eyeing up my newly confident seventeen-year-old self, the teenage awkwardness gone, I felt a power shift.

"What you up to?" he said.

"I'm looking for a job for the summer."

"Look no further," he said. "It just so happens I need a receptionist."

It was fate.

I started at the showroom the next day.

"You'll meet and greet customers," he said. "You'll be the first line of sales."

Seeing him every day, in his position as boss, my crush on him returned big time. What happened was inevitable.

It was a Friday. The sales team were leaving. I was packing up to go, and Iain stopped by my desk: "Not shooting off just yet, are you, Amy?"

He turned the latch on the showroom door, went to the fridge and brought out a bottle of Champagne and two glasses, saying, "Come up to my office, let's have a celebration."

So I followed him up to his office on the first floor, and he poured us both a glass.

"What are we celebrating?" I asked.

"Sales are up, and that's partly due to you, Amy."

We clinked glasses. I took a sip.

"I've watched you with customers. You really are fucking good, if you'll pardon my French."

"I've heard worse," I said.

"To us!" he said, raising his glass, then added almost as an afterthought, "to Stanlow Motors and all who sail in her."

"To us," I said, and met his eye, already giddy with the fizz and the intensity of the moment.

He took the flute out of my hand and pulled towards him. We kissed. I felt him pressed against me, hard. He said: "What are you doing to me, Amy?"

He wanted to know how many boyfriends I'd had. I mentioned Alex, a boy from college who I'd seen for a while and he said, "I heard about that, I was insanely jealous," then he said, "Have you ever been made love to by an older, more experienced man?" and pulled me down onto the couch.

This was different from the fumbling encounters I'd had with boys my age. Iain knew what he was doing. He took control.

Afterwards he said, "this is our destiny."

He drove me home, his hand on my knee the whole way, and said: "Can you get in early tomorrow? I can't wait that long to see you again."

That's how it started.

I'd get to work at seven, we'd have sex in his office before the showroom opened. I'd stay late, we'd have more sex. Sometimes we'd sneak off at lunchtime to some secluded spot and have sex in whatever car he was driving. He said he liked to christen them.

Nobody was supposed to know, but they all knew. I'd catch the sales staff glancing when Iain and I left together. I liked the feeling of being talked about.

I was living off adrenaline. That heady mixture of lust, euphoria and guilt. The thrill of secrecy.

Hannah said, "You're seeing someone, aren't you? I can tell. Who is it? Is it someone at the showroom? Is it Steve, the new guy? He's quite fit."

She was my best friend, but I had to lie to her.

I never went back to college after the summer. I carried on working at the showroom while everyone else got their A levels and went away to university. I was happy in my bubble with Iain.

Until it all turned toxic.

Chapter Eleven

J AY SITS AT the end of my bed until I've gone to sleep, like my granddad used to. I remember Granddad sitting, very dark and still, humming softly, until he thought I was asleep. Then he'd kiss me on the head and say, "sweet dreams little darlin'."

Although my parents' faces are obscured behind a cloud, I can still see Granddad, watching over me. With him there, I felt safe.

He used to visit us on Sundays. We'd meet him at the station, me sitting on my dad's shoulders, looking out for him. I'd spot him by his trilby. Once, my mother and I went to see him in Bristol where he lived. We found him in the back room of a pub in the afternoon, playing dominoes with a group of men. They slammed the counters down on the table so hard it frightened me. Granddad looked different then, kind of scary, but when he saw me his face creased into smiles and he held out his arms for me to run to him.

He died when I was little. Mum still lit candles for him on his birthday and we'd have cake and talk to him like he was still alive. But my memory is messed up because I'm sure I remember him sitting at the end of my bed right up to the time when my parents died.

I once asked Judith when my granddad died. She said: "I know nothing whatsoever about that side of your family."

I found a photo in a drawer at Judith's from my parents' wedding. She'd either hidden it from me or never bothered to put it up. I stole it from her room and kept it. I still have it, kept in an envelope that travelled with me to the Carlottis and the Chorlton flat and now here to Balmoral Street. Granddad is on the photo, exactly as I remember him. Everyone else looks faded, like ghosts. My mother wears a brightly coloured dress and matching turban, flowers in her hair.

She's got a bump. Me.

My dad has long wavy hair, and a beard. He looks like Jesus.

"Your mother was of white American and Haitian descent," Judith told me. That makes her mixed race. Me too. Dual heritage, the social worker called it.

People didn't know what to make of me in Stanlow. Thanks to the influence of certain celebrities in popular culture, mixed race was actually quite cool. But my skin is pale. I pass for white. And my hair's not proper afro, just thick and frizzy and impossible to get a comb through.

"So what are you? A quarter black?" the girls at school asked me, disbelieving, after Hannah told them about my heritage, "like Sinead's a quarter Irish?"

They then proceeded to inspect me. "Look at her bum. She's got a black girl's bum."

Judith once cooked up a scheme with Hannah's mum to introduce me to a token black family in a nearby village. They had twin girls my age. Lynda told Judith I ought to have some contact with people from 'my culture'. But I had nothing in common with Leticia and Shakira and none of us knew what I was doing there. I never went again.

Here in Balmoral Street, with people of all colours of the rainbow around me, I ought to fit in. But still I don't. Here I feel posh and very white. I'm destined to always be a freak.

Chapter Twelve

"WHERE'S STEVE?" I asked Jim, one of the sales team.

"Haven't you heard? Boss had him moved to Derby."

"Why?"

Jim shrugged. But I later heard that Iain thought Steve and I were getting too close.

I liked Steve, he was closer to my age than the other showroom staff. We were mates, that was all. I challenged Iain about it.

"I run the showroom," he said. "Staffing is not your concern. You do your job, Amy, and I'll do mine."

That was the moment the loved up feeling I had at the beginning began to turn into a slow burning resentment.

Iain was a married man. A family man. So there were lots of times when he couldn't see me, or cancelled at short notice.

Weekends were the worst. I'd drift around at Judith's,

waiting for texts.

My week was the wrong way round. Normal people count down to the weekend and dread Mondays. I'd long for Monday mornings, when I'd see him again. But more and more often the week would start with angst – and interrogation. Where had I been? Who had I been with? Why hadn't I returned his messages? Iain didn't like me going out without him, in case I met someone.

I began to feel like I was a toy he kept in a box, to be taken out and played with when he felt like it, to be wined, dined and sixty-nined then put away till next time.

I started to rebel.

I looked up some old college mates who were still in the area and started going out to clubs and picking people up. Nothing serious, just one-night stands. Iain would get suspicious, we'd have a massive row, then make it up again.

He said he loved me and wanted to be with me. "So leave your wife," I'd say.

Then one day Hannah, home from Uni, came clubbing with me on a Thursday night. I met a boy who was half-decent who I arranged to see again. I knew it would get back.

The next day, Friday, Iain was out at a conference all day. All the sales team had gone home. I was about to lock up and leave when he stormed into the showroom. "In my office, now!" he said as he marched through reception. I followed.

"Give me your phone," he said, grabbing my arm.

"No, it's private."

"I paid for that bleedin' phone, now I'm asking for it

back. Where is it, Amy?"

He had hold of my arm and was going through my pockets, but I'd left the phone downstairs.

"You've got no right to do this, Iain."

"Hannah says you've met someone,"

"So? What's it got to do with you?"

"It's killing me!"

"We're finished, Iain."

"We'll never be finished. Don't you understand?' He held both my arms and shook me. "We can never end what we've got. It's too powerful. We need each other."

He looked at me and I knew he was right. Neither of us could ever end it. We were fated to go round and round in ever decreasing circles, locked together in misery.

"I can't live without you," he said. "You're an addiction."

He pulled me towards him and started to rip off my clothes. He lifted me up onto the two-draw filing cabinet and fucked me hard. Always, after a row, the sex was highly charged, but this had an extra energy.

I'd got most of my clothes back on when a wave of despair washed over me and I started to sob. "Come here, Amy," he said, folding me up in his arms and sitting down with me on the couch.

"I know I'm a shit. I know I've behaved appallingly and you don't deserve it, but I'll make it up to you," he said. "It's been torturing me all day, picturing you with someone else. We can't go on like this. I will leave Lynda, I promise. I just need to work out a timescale."

At that moment, Lynda Carver walked in.

We'd forgotten to lock the showroom door.

Iain sprang away from me, his face drained of colour, but all I felt was euphoria. This massive build-up of tension had finally burst. At last we could stop pretending.

I watched as Iain hopped from foot to foot in front of her as she stood silent, her face frozen, like she'd been turned to stone. "Lynda, it's not how it looks. I can explain. Amy's upset and I was comforting her."

As he trotted out clichés, I realised, as if I needed telling, that he would never leave her.

For a few seconds, Lynda said nothing. Then she looked at the floor and saw my tights lying there.

"Comforting her with bare legs? You must take me for a bloody idiot. And as for you, Amy Blue, you little slut. After all we've done for you over the years."

I'd never seen Lynda so angry. She was shaking. She gripped the office chair and for a second I thought she was going to ram it into me, but she turned round and walked out.

Iain ran after her, shouting: "Lock up, Amy, and go home."

When I rang his mobile later Lynda answered and told me to "stay away from our family you little whore."

When he didn't get in touch that night or the next day, I packaged up the garage keys and posted them through the showroom door.

The rest is a blur. Trying to contact friends and having them hang up on me. Being blanked in the street. Getting hate mail. The Facebook page someone set up called the 'Amy Blue Appreciation Society,' its purpose to hate on me.

After that I deleted my social media accounts and changed my number.

For the next few days, I shut myself in my room, Judith oblivious. Then on day three she called me into the living room.

"Is it true what I've heard about you and Iain Carver?"

No words would come. Just tears.

"You stupid, stupid girl. You've broken up a family. You've lost your job and your friends and you've brought disgrace on me," she said. "I've always known you were trouble. I can't stand the sight of you. Just get out."

She never even asked if I was ok.

I had to get out of Stanlow. I searched the Internet for au pair jobs – I'd had some work experience in a day nursery. That's when I saw the job working for the Carlottis in Manchester.

"ANOTHER STORY FOR another night," says Jay, bringing me back to the present, and we sit silent for a while. Then he says, "It wasn't your fault."

"What wasn't?"

"Iain Carver. He controlled you. He'd been working on you for years."

"But I wanted to be controlled."

I planned it. I invited it. I was an equal partner. And nothing even happened till I was seventeen.

Chapter Thirteen

I RUN INTO Dvinder at the bus stop, on her way to University where she's studying pharmacy so she can join the family business. She asks me if I have a job, or am I a student? I feel the heat rise up my neck. The trouble with re-entering any kind of normality is people expect you to do normal things, like work. I mumble something about being off sick.

"I love your scarf," she says, probably to change the subject. It's just a bog-standard red floral scarf I got from Primark. "It really suits your colouring. You are so pretty Amy." She hails her bus.

"D'you see yourself as pretty?" Jay asks later when I tell him about it.

"No."

He studies me for a moment, then says: "You're a pre-Raphaelite."

"A what?"

"Has anyone ever told you, you look like a pre-Raphaelite model?"

Iain used to say I could be a model, which was rubbish as I'm nowhere near tall enough.

"What's a pre-Raphaelite?"

"Dante Gabriel Rossetti, Edward Burne-Jones, William Morris. They painted thin pale girls with masses of curly hair like you."

"I hate my hair."

He smiles. "Of course you do."

"I used to straighten it but my straighteners went in the burglary along with everything else."

"Good," he says, standing up and pacing round the room. "Girls who straighten their hair all look the same. You look different." There's an edge to his voice today, like he's losing patience with me.

"I don't want to look different," I say.

He shrugs, and perches on the side of the table. "Anyway about the pre-Raphaelites. They were stunning looking and mostly consumptive."

"What?"

"They had consumption. TB. It was terminal in those days. And a lot of them were addicted to laudanum. That's an opiate, like heroin."

"So you're telling me I look like a dying junkie?"

He sighs. "They were the super-models of their day, Amy. Perfect bone structure, striking features, gorgeous, voluminous hair. Like you." He says it with no sense of involvement, like he's commenting on a painting.

I wonder if any of the Pre-Raphaelites were dual

heritage.

He grabs the Ikea chair and pulls it close to the bed, in front of the table. He sits with his knees pulled up to his chest and rocks. The chair knocks the table each time he rocks back in it. The sound grates.

He picks up the blue and green pill packet which is lying on the table.

"Why d'you fill your body with this shit?" he reads the label. "Ten milligram, four times a day. Fuck that's a large dose," He pulls out the information print-out. "Memory problems, motor problems, muscle twitching," he does an exaggerated twitch. "Breast enlargement in men," he laughs, then carries on reading. "Delusions, nightmares, hallucinations… no wonder you're fucked-up."

He grabs the box with both hands and pretends to crush it.

"Stop! What are you doing?"

"Why are you even on these things?"

"Told you, they're keeping me sane."

"They're the only thing holding you back," he says, springing up out of the chair. "You ever want to move out of this shithole? You need to ditch the Diazepam." He drops the box, intact, on the table.

"Who said I wanted to move out?"

"So you want to stay in the lovely Balmoral Street for the rest of your life? Christ." Then he adds, more to himself than me. "I've never met anyone so passive. Why did I have to pick someone so passive?"

"So fuck off then," I say. "I never asked you to come. Why are you even here?"

I watch him stand up, shrug and walk out.

I'm supposed to wait till morning to take my next tablet. I take one anyway. When I wake up, I take another. Fuck Jay. I've allowed myself to think he cared. I don't suppose he'll visit me again.

I pick up the Diazepam instruction sheet, lying where he left it. I look at the list of rare but possible side effects. Delusions. Nightmares. Hallucinations. I no longer know what's real. Jay is dreamy, beautiful, ethereal. Have I dreamt up this vision of perfection? And If I've made him up, can I equally easily destroy him?

Chapter Fourteen

IT'S CLOSE TO midday when I surface. My brain is a fug. My body feels like it's chained to the bed, my limbs like lead. But somewhere in me a scream is rising. It starts in my stomach, forcing its way up through my body, until it pushes against my skull. I contain it, just. My arms and legs feel heavy as I move, but my insides are on fire. I've slept in my clothes. I probably stink. I pull on my hoodie and drag myself down the two flights of stairs to the outside.

The Man hails me. "Sun is shining today," he points at the sky. I look up between the buildings and see blue. As I do so my hood falls back off my face.

"You looking better Pixie, not so pale," he chuckles, the sound comes from somewhere deep within his chest, like a mountain spring gurgling. "It must be your young mon."

"He's not…" I start to say, as the heat rises up through my body, but The Man continues. "She got colour in her cheeks now little Pixie."

I want to tell him, Jay is not my young man. And anyway he walked out on me last night. I doubt he'll be back, but The Man seems so happy for me I don't want to disillusion him.

"He a good boy, your young mon. He paint you yet?" He beams, "he live around here two, three years ago, he paint everything. He paint me once, standing here," he taps the railing.

Walking to the shops, I get a sense of some forgotten feeling trying to force its way up through the drugs. I am young. I want to spend time with friends, hit the town, watch a film, go to a club, do whatever people of my age are supposed to do. Then I remember, I have no friends.

I go into the chemist, to see if Dvinder is there. But it's her dad behind the counter. "Can I help you?"

"I… I want some advice."

I don't know where this has come from.

"Yes?"

"So I'm on Diazepam. A high dose. I want to stop taking it."

"You should talk to your doctor," he says.

"But, what if I can't get to see my doctor for a week? Would it be ok to, like, cut down?"

He advises me to do it gradually. I could reduce from four tablets a day to three, evenly spaced out throughout the day. But really I should see my doctor. I thank him and leave.

The sun is still out. It's cold, but there's a freshness in the air. The door to my building is wide open, and the freshness continues up the two flights of stairs. It makes a change from the usual fustiness or stink of weed or fags from the first-floor flats. When I open the door to my attic the first thing I notice is a shaft of brightness, angled in from the skylight, throwing a circle of light onto the table, like a spotlight. On the table underneath the light is a piece of paper, or card. I get nearer. It's a pencil drawing of a girl, wearing a long, flowing robe with flared sleeves. She's leaning on a piano, gazing moodily out of the picture. Her hair, cascading loose, fills the frame. There's expression in her eyes. Intense. Interesting. Devastating.

It's a picture of me.

It's beautiful.

I pick the picture up. There's no signature. I turn it over. In pencil, on the back, in flourishing, elaborate handwriting, it says. 'Amy Blue, the undiscovered Pre-Raphaelite'.

I lift the drawing up to the light, turn it over, read the writing again. I pace around the room, still clutching the picture. It should be framed, hung on a wall. I hold it up against the yellowed wallpaper. It's too beautiful a thing for a room like this.

There's strange sensations shooting through my body, like electricity. Normally in this state of agitation, I'd take a Diazepam. This time I don't. I continue to pace, and let the feelings come.

How has he drawn this? From memory? Did he sketch me one day when I was asleep? Did he sneak a photo of me? I've never seen him with even a phone, let alone a camera. But I feel a surge of hope. Maybe I haven't driven him away.

I want to show the drawing to someone. Thinking of

The Man, I grab the picture and walk downstairs with such speed that I almost collide with someone coming in through the front door. It's the girl from the ground floor flat. The 'high class tart.' I get a whiff of some exotic perfume. Usually I would rush past, avoiding eye contact. This time I look at her, and we do that dance that people do. This way. That way. We apologise, the English way, we laugh, we let each other pass.

I stand in the doorway. It's starting to rain and The Man's gone in. I don't want to get the picture wet, so I head back into the building. The girl's still there, rooting through the mail in the hall. This is the closest I've ever got to her and the first time I've really looked at her. She's tall and unnaturally thin, almost model proportions, with long legs. She's wearing skinny jeans, a short black leather jacket and studded ankle boots with four-inch heels. Her hair is thick, shoulder-length, black with red highlights. Her eyes are enormous, outlined in heavy black kohl, her face is dirty.

I wonder if she's a pre-Raphaelite too.

"Hey there," I say.

The girl looks up, eyebrows arched, then with a hint of a smile says, "Hiya darlin' how's things?"

She's got a lilt to her voice I can't quite place. Not Manchester.

"I'm good thanks," I lie. "You?"

"I'm sound. Expecting an important package."

Scouse maybe.

"Can be risky getting stuff sent here," I say.

"Someone better not have filched it. Seventy quid it cost me. Ann Summers top of the range!" She laughs. A musical, infectious laugh.

I laugh too.

"I'm Amy," I say. "I live in the attic."

"Tania," says the girl, and holds out her hand. A swirling tattoo snakes out from under the sleeve of her leather jacket. We touch hands for a second. Walking back up to my flat I feel a sense of triumph. I've just initiated another conversation. With a 'high class tart'.

When I get back to my room the Jay smell is back, stronger than before. And there's a note on the table, scribbled on a torn-off bit of paper. It says: 'Hope you like the portrait. Got stuff to do so may not see you for a few days, but remember the tasks. J.' How come I didn't notice this earlier? He can't have been back up here in the time it took me to walk downstairs and back. It doesn't make sense.

Chapter Fifteen

"YOU NEED A change of scene,"

Jay's voice jolts me out of a dream in which I'm running through the park in Stanlow with Hannah's dog. It takes a few seconds to re-orientate. He's sitting upright in the Ikea chair, and wearing a light jacket instead of the Parka. He's looking pleased with himself.

"You?" I say. It's been weeks since I last saw him.

"Nice to be welcomed!"

"Where've you been?"

"Oh around. Had stuff to do. Plus you told me to fuck off last time. So I did."

"So why'd you come back?"

He smiles. That smug smile again. "I thought you might be missing me." Then he leans back onto the chair and looks at the picture, which I've Blu-Tacked to the wall.

"Glad you like my sketch."

"It's good." I don't know what else to say.

"So what's going on, Amy?"

"I've been doing more than normal. I've got a bit more energy since I stopped taking so many Diazepam. I'm down to two a day."

"Good idea of yours, giving them up, wouldn't you say?"

I scowl.

"But living in this shit-hole isn't good for you. You need a change of scene,"

"What, like a holiday?"

"Like a move to the country."

I laugh. "Like that's gonna happen!"

Today he seems thoughtful. He doesn't immediately pull me up on my negativity.

"How did you feel when you walked round the reservoirs?"

I don't recall telling him I did.

"I liked breathing the air. I almost felt like I wasn't in Manchester, but back in Derbyshire or somewhere."

"The countryside does you good," he says. "The town drags you down."

I wonder if he knows he's mis-quoting from my old earworm.

"Are you suggesting I buy some walking boots and head for the hills?"

"Why not?" he says. "Manchester is surrounded by hills, if you hadn't noticed."

On a clear day, you can see the outline of the Pennines in the distance from the end of the street, but they look bleak and uninviting.

"Walking boots cost about sixty quid."

"Try the charity shops."

"Is this, like, one of your instructions?"

"Why not?" he says. "You've been doing the other stuff, and it's helping, isn't it? So I'm right, aren't I?"

The annoying thing is that, so far, he *has* been right.

"Listen," he says. "I know a place where you could go, to get right away from all this. Somewhere you can forget the past and start again. You like water. This place is by the sea."

"Really?"

"Yes. I'll need to go away and sort things out. It'll be in a couple of weeks. So we haven't got much time. In the meantime you can finish telling me your story."

"I told you everything."

"The baby. You said you lost a baby. Was it Iain's?"

"No. Iain'd had the snip."

"So whose was it?"

Chapter Sixteen

I GOT AN email back from the Carlottis inviting me for interview. I found it kind of weird that instead of going to the house and meeting them both, Howard Carlotti wanted to see me on his own in some random pub. I met him in the Mark Addy, down by the river, near where he worked. He was standing at the bar when I arrived. "Ah, Amy," he said, standing too close, crowding me. He'd just finished work. He was sweaty, and his gut hung over his pinstripes.

We sat opposite each other at a table by the window overlooking the water. I watched the swans glide by, so I didn't have to look him in the eye.

"My wife and I are both professional, busy people. We have a hectic work schedule and social life so we're out a lot. We need someone we can trust to just get on with it." Howard looked me up and down. "D'you think you can handle it?"

I said I was used to responsibility and that I'd often been in sole charge of the showroom.

"You'll do. You're hired. Start Saturday."

If I hadn't been desperate to get out of Stanlow I might have thought twice, but there was no time to think. It was back to Judith's to pack a bag, then I was off.

Howard met me off the train at Piccadilly. He drove an Aston Martin Vantage, fast. I think I was supposed to be impressed. On the way he told me, "most of this city is a slum, but we live in Wilmslow, the leafy des res of Greater Manchester, as you'll see."

He turned in to a driveway with remote-controlled gates. The house was massive, with a brand-new Alfa Romeo and a Range Rover parked outside.

"Come and meet my wife, Fiona," said Howard, leading me into a spacious kitchen. A woman in her late thirties sat at the table, talking on a mobile and looking at a laptop. She looked up briefly as we came in, then carried on with her phone call.

"I'll leave you two to get to know each other," said Howard, winking at me. I pulled up a chair, which scraped across the tiled floor. The woman glared at me.

"Have you seen the proofs?" she was saying. "Are they ok? Why not? We need them signed off by Monday." She had a clipped, middle-English accent.

Fiona was a study in black. Black trousers, black shirt, black ankle boots, heavy black mascara. She had thick, shiny blue-black hair, long and hanging loose. Every so often she'd flick it, angrily, out of her face. Her clothes looked tailored and expensive. I felt extra conscious of the cheap leggings and t-shirt I'd turned up in.

She was obviously on a very important phone call. It seemed to go on for ever, and while she spoke she stared at me, with no flicker of welcome, no gesture to put me at ease. I looked around for signs of the child I'd been hired to look after. There were none. I sat rigid, waiting for release.

When she eventually came off the phone she didn't say hello. She just said, "Has Howard shown you the nursery?" Did people in this day and age have nurseries in their houses? I felt like I'd walked onto the set of some period drama.

Fiona's induction was brisk. She marched me through the house, pointing out rooms, her heels clipping on the varnished floorboards. The nursery was on the first floor of the split-level house, opening out onto an area of decking at the back. It was a fully equipped safe play area, big enough for about ten kids. They had all this just for one four-year old boy.

"Can you drive?" Fiona asked.

"Yes" Although Iain robbed me of my education he did provide driving lessons.

"Good. You can pick Daniel up from his grandmother's in the morning."

"So he's not here?"

She gave me a withering glance, as if to say 'obviously', then said, "he stays over at my mother's every Saturday," like I was supposed to know that.

"Has anyone offered this girl a coffee?" Howard asked, when we got back to the kitchen.

"Help yourself," said Fiona, jerking her head towards a

high-tech coffee machine. "I've got to get back to work."

"I'll show you how to operate it," said Howard.

Mercifully, that evening, they both went out, leaving me to acclimatise. Before they left, Howard said: "D'you cook?"

"A bit."

He opened cupboards and showed me jars of pasta, rice and spices. "Kitchen's all yours, cook yourself a sumptuous feast if you like," and winked.

I looked at the gleaming hob and the spotless Aga. Eventually I found myself a frozen lasagne to microwave.

The next day, I drove Fiona's Alfa Romeo to Altrincham to collect Daniel, the child. He looked like a miniature Howard. He was a nice enough kid. All he wanted to do was watch videos in the nursery.

"A bit quiet, isn't she?" I heard Howard say from the next room.

"I don't care, as long as Daniel likes her."

"I prefer them with a bit of personality," he said. "This one's a little mouse."

"God, Howard, what does it matter if she's an introvert?"

SOME PLACES GET easier with time. Some people drop their guard, reveal their softer side. Not Fiona.

Her face was frozen into an expression of contempt. She wore boots and dark suits and strutted angrily across rooms. I'd hear her heels on the floorboards and I'd tense up. It was floorboards everywhere, and expensive rugs from Persia or Turkey. Rugs you had to keep Daniel away from in case he dropped biscuit crumbs or spilt juice.

She had designer clothes, designer shades, designer furniture. She dripped labels.

From day one I was convinced she was setting me up to fail. She'd say things like: "You'll have to leave the key for Ralph so you need to disable that bit of the alarm." I didn't know who the hell Ralph was – turned out he was the gardener – and nobody had shown me how to do the alarm.

On the ground floor there was a huge open-plan living room leading out into a large conservatory and a dining room, and off that was Fiona's office. The place was like a show-home and apart from the nursery it was hard to tell there was a child there at all.

The gang of cleaners who descended on Tuesdays made every surface gleam. But although the house was spotless, Fiona swooped through it, running her finger over the furniture, looking for specs of dust. And the times when she handed over the keys of the Alfa Romeo for me to ferry Daniel around, she'd examine it afterwards for scratches.

Unlike Fiona, Howard made some effort to be matey, but I had nothing in common with him. He'd been to public school. He had dark, thick, floppy hair, and rubber lips. He was big and sweaty. There was a picture on the wall of Howard from his uni days when he was in the Oxford rowing squad. His team won the boat-race that year. You could see the contours of his body then, the muscle-tone in his legs and arms and shoulders. I suppose some people might have called him good-looking. But he still had those rubber lips.

Now all that muscle was lost in fat. Apart from the odd round of golf, most of his activities involved sitting down.

They suited each other, Howard and Fiona, they believed in the same things: money, status, branding.

Howard liked his food. And every few weeks when they entertained, Howard would take over the kitchen. I mostly avoided those occasions, except that once.

Chapter Seventeen

"YOU LOOK SMART," I say as I pass Tania in the hall heading into her flat. She's dressed in a trouser suit, like a business woman.

"Been on jury duty," she says, watches my face for a second then laughs. "Imagine that Ames, I'd be like 'excuse me your honour, don't I know you from somewhere?'" She lowers her voice. "There's an important case on at Crown Court. Some big shot lawyers in town. One of my clients is a high court judge, likes a bit of punishment himself, as it happens." She nudges me and giggles. "Fancy a cuppa?"

I follow Tania into her flat. Although it's morning, she doesn't open the curtains, instead she puts lamps on around the place. As my eyes adjust to the gloom, I notice the walls are purple, and there are various tools of the trade hanging around. A pair of heavy-duty cuffs looped over the bed-head, a whip on the wall, a leather strappy basque hanging from the wardrobe door.

"D'you have clients here?" I ask her.

"Only me homeys, I call them." These are people she's known for a long time and trusts. Mostly she works for an agency and they send her to meet men in hotels and things. She talks about her work like it's a job in a shop or an office, something she's doing to save up to go to University. She tells me several times that the agency boss is a woman and she's not controlled by any man.

"You see Ames, what I do is my choice. A means to an end. It's worlds away from the kids on the corner. They're recruited from their kids' homes, hooked on heroin and pimped out from the age of twelve. What a life!"

The flat is smaller than mine, and smarter. I think she's brought her own furniture. It's just one room, really, with a kitchenette in the corner. We sit on tall bar stools as we wait for the kettle to boil.

"How long have you lived here?" I ask.

"Year or so. Not my choice of neighbourhood really but it's a stop-gap."

"Did you know a guy called Jay who lived in my flat? Tall and blond? He's been back a lot recently. Comes to see me."

She looks blank, and shakes her head. "A lot of people come and go in a place like this. Can't say that description is ringing any bells. Black coffee all right for yous? I forgot to get milk."

She starts ladling instant coffee into mugs.

"One of me homeys was asking about you, actually," she says, "Wanted to know if you were interested in any business. I said I didn't think so but I'd pass it on." She hands me a mug. "Don't look so horrified Ames. This fella, he's about seventy. All he wants is to be stroked all over with a feather for half an hour then you have to finish him off by hand. He even puts a condom on so as not to mess up the sheets. And for that, he pays two hundred and fifty quid. Think about it."

As I digest this information she adds. "And he's got the tiniest cock you've ever seen Ames, he's like, a one-incher!" She holds her thumb and forefinger an inch apart. We both laugh.

"Two HUNDRED AND fifty quid for tossing off a lonely pensioner," Jay says later. "You could do worse." But he doesn't mean it. He says I wouldn't be able to detach myself in the way that Tania does. According to Jay, Tania is a sociopath. She can emotionally detach. God knows how he knows. He's never even met her.

He's still on about this opportunity he's working on for me. A sort of job, I think, a 'project'. Says he can't say too much about it, yet. But it's near the sea, and it's going to happen soon. He even gives me a departure date, which means nothing to me as I don't know what day it is. It seems like fantasy to me. A long way from here.

In the meantime I carry on telling him my story.

Chapter Eighteen

"HOW MANY HAVE we got for dinner tomorrow?" Howard rooted around the kitchen, opening cupboards, tapping into his phone the items that needed buying. I was making myself a drink. Fiona sat at the kitchen table, busy with her laptop.

"It was six but Marsha can't make it," said Fiona, not looking up.

"So it's five."

"Correct."

"Can't we get another female to make up the numbers?" Howard caught my eye and winked. I winced.

"It's too short notice so it'll just have to be uneven," said Fiona.

"We need someone for Charles to play with." Howard was still looking at me.

"What happened to that bimbo he brought last time?"

"She ran off with a footballer," said Howard, adding,

"Amy, fancy joining our little soirée tomorrow?"

Fiona looked up, eyebrows raised. I willed her to come up with some reason why I shouldn't go. But Howard kept on. "Daniel's at his granny's so there's no problem there. What d'you reckon Amy?"

"Um… I'm not great at dinner parties."

Fiona laughed, a harsh staccato. "All you have to do is *eat!*"

I wondered if Fiona ate on these occasions; I'd only ever seen her pick at her food like a sparrow.

"Go on," said Howard. "Bit of vino to loosen your tongue, you'll be fine."

"What's she going to wear?" Fiona looked me up and down. "I could lend you something but you're so skinny even my stuff would look like a sack on you. You must be, what, a size zero?" Fiona could turn a compliment into a criticism.

"She'd look all right in a sack," said Howard, winking again. Fiona shot him a look, then turned back to her laptop.

Howard fished his wallet out from his jacket pocket and pulled out some notes, pressing them into my hand and whispering, "clothes allowance." There were two fifties. I bought a little black dress from H&M which cost twenty-seven pounds. I kept the change.

I'd witnessed these events from a safe distance. I'd seen the cars. Jaguars, Range-rovers, Lamborghinis, the odd Porsche. I'd heard the voices – loud and getting louder as the evening progressed. I'd seen the preparations. Howard cooking up great vats of pasta, 'It's my Italian heritage,' guzzling red wine while he cooked. Fiona strutting around, checking, stressing. I wondered why she bothered with these occasions, they seemed, like everything else, to annoy her. I'd seen the debris the next day, the plates, the wasted food, the bottles. How could six people get through *that much* alcohol?

I waited till I'd heard the guests arrive before making an appearance. I was conscious of being sized up when I walked into the room wearing my H&M dress. I'd been briefed, so I knew their names: Piers and Penny, Hugo and Sophia, and Charles. Hugo and Sophia I'd met before. They had a little boy the same age as Daniel. Sophia was almost kind.

"Advance your glasses!" Howard poured Prosecco. "By the way everyone, this is Amy. Amy looks after Daniel."

Charles leered at me. He was wearing a paisley waistcoat slightly too small for his belly. He had wispy, gingery hair and bags under his eyes. "What are you, private tutor? Governess? Au pair?"

"Governess?" Penny snorted. "What century are you from Charles?"

"Nanny," I said.

"How delightful," said Charles. "How do you do it H? You always manage to recruit eye-candy for the task."

"That's because Fi lets Howard do the interviewing," said Penny.

Howard beamed, and ushered everyone to the table. I was wedged between Piers and Charles, with Howard opposite. Piers had platinum blond straight hair, receding slightly, and a face that seemed to lack pigment.

"Piers is a world-renowned surgeon," Howard said,

looking at me. "Of the plastic variety. Want a new face, he's your man."

"Now *she* doesn't need one," said Charles.

"Not *now* she doesn't, but ten, twenty years down the line, who knows?" said Howard.

"Not even that," said Penny. "Half his clients are under twenty. Tell them about that girl the other week."

"God yes, H. This girl, said she was eighteen, looked more like twelve. Came in wanting Scarlett Johansson lips and a Kim Kardashian arse."

"And what did you do?"

"I obliged, of course. We have to keep the customer happy."

"Some people have more money than sense," Sophia chipped in from the other end of the table.

"This girl was dating a premier league boy," said Piers. "It goes with the territory. WAGs" he said, looking at me. "WAGs are my livelihood."

"WAGs and hags!" said Howard. Guffaws all round.

Mercifully, the wine was limitless, and Charles saw to it that my glass was topped up.

"Seriously though," said Penny. "It's where the money is. It's an absolute gold-mine."

"What? Playing on people's insecurities?" said Sophia.

"Helping people look as good as possible for as long as possible," said Penny. "Talking of which, Fi, you *must* give me the name of the woman who does your injectables."

"Shh!" said Howard, "No-one's supposed to know."

"Oh come on!" said Penny. "Nobody can keep such an alabaster skin into their forties without a bit of help. You can't tell though; this woman is good."

"You get what you pay for," said Fiona. "You should see some of the people who go for cheap fillers. They look like stroke victims."

After that they started to talk about the stock market.

I was grateful for the food, because it gave me something to do. Starter number one was little thin pieces of toast, with bits of anchovy. Starter two was asparagus and something. Then there was a pasta dish, tagliatelle, I think, with some kind of meat, and a salad with Parma ham, then strawberry tart with cream.

I kept one eye on the clock throughout.

"So," said Charles. "You been to University Amy or are you fresh out of school?"

"I didn't do Uni. I worked for a few years. I used to sell cars."

"Oh," said Charles "Who for?"

"It was an independent garage. We sold second-hand luxury cars."

"Would you buy a used car off this woman Piers?"

Piers snorted. "Ok sell me a car. C'mon. Let's hear your patter."

My mind went blank. Of course, technically I didn't do the selling. Although Iain always said I was the first line of sales.

"What's the classiest car you sold?" said Charles.

I told them about the old red XJ6, my favourite, with its cream leather seats and walnut dash. Iain took me up to Edinburgh in it, it seemed to just waft along. Now I *did* sell that one.

"What d'you get for it?"

"Not much. No-one wants those gas guzzlers any more," I looked around, and wondered if they even noticed the price of fuel.

I drained my wine. Charles topped it up. He seemed to have a bottle of red permanently to hand. Perhaps it was the wine, or the fact I was finally on home ground, that made me eloquent. Thanks to Iain, cars are something I know about. I expounded the virtues of the XF versus the Mercedes E-class. They nodded, and threw in their opinions.

"There were a lot of BMWs of course. They were easy to sell. Spot a BMW driver a mile off. They're all tossers."

It was a risk, but I was pretty sure I hadn't seen any BMWs on the drive that evening.

Charles and Piers shrieked with laughter. Piers banged the table. "Hear that H? "BMWs drivers are tossers. Hear it from the used car saleswoman."

Howard glared. His face grew purple.

Charles rescued me. "Howard always had BMWs before he discovered the Aston. But I'm with Amy on this one. It may be a cliché but it's true. You get someone up your arse driving like a complete maniac, you can guarantee it's a BMW driver."

Howard didn't acknowledge Charles, he looked directly at me, and he wasn't smiling. "I'll give you a BMW driver up your arse," he said. And there was something about that look, something that cut through my safe haze of alcohol, turning it to chilling sobriety.

"Howard, bring out the cheese," said Fiona.

Chapter Nineteen

I'M BROWSING ROUND the charity shops looking for walking boots. I can't find any. People are poor round here and the quality of donations not great. There's one more shop to try, past the main shopping area. As I walk, something catches my eye. A little further down the road is a house I've seen from the bus. It stands out because it's got window boxes, and someone has painted the woodwork – a splash of colour among the drabness. It's a big house, like the ones on Balmoral Street, but this seems to still be one property. Outside there's an old Rover and a vintage VW campervan. I have never had the curiosity to walk up to it, until now.

There's a woman outside watering the hanging baskets and a sign in the front window which says: 'Garage Sale.'

"Round the back!" says the woman. Is she talking to me?

"Pardon?"

"If you want the sale, it's round the back."

I walk round to the back of the house and join a handful of people browsing through piles of junk. The woman follows me.

There are toys, children's clothes, bits of engine, radio equipment, the usual junk you get at these things. Then I notice a table done up like a sort of shrine. There's a big banner with photos of a young woman with jet-black hair in a short bob. The banner reads 'celebrating Sian.' On the table there are some pieces of musical equipment, amplifiers, a couple of guitars, various items of black or purple clothing and five pairs of Doc Martens, one red, one yellow, one multi-colour. I pick up a pair of standard black ones, they look almost new. "What size are these" I ask the woman.

"Four – what size are you?"

"Four."

I try them on. They feel snug round my feet.

"I haven't got much money," I say.

"Fiver?" says the woman.

"I can just about manage that!"

They belonged to her niece, the woman in the picture. She died in a light aircraft crash aged twenty-seven. She was lead singer and guitarist in a band.

The woman hands me a cutting from a local newspaper. There's a picture of her niece on stage at some festival wearing black shorts and fishnets and doc marten boots. Possibly this very pair.

I keep the boots on and walk back in them, and when I reach Balmoral Street I carry on walking, back to the reservoirs. And it's like, with the boots on, I've taken on the persona of the previous owner, a feisty singer, rather than a pathetic drugged-up mess.

When I get back I don't feel like going back to my flat yet. Jay has told me there's a garden at the back of the house. It's for everyone, but the only person who ever uses it is the guy from Flat Five.

I've seen the sign to Flat Five, pointing down the alley at the side of the house. Although it's part of the same building it has its own entrance. I've glimpsed the man who lives there. A middle-aged guy who's up and about early in the mornings. I think he even has a job.

I venture round there. It is just a yard, really, hemmed in by high walls, but there are plants growing in pots lined up inside the fence, and the sun is shining right in. There's a plastic table and two chairs encrusted with last autumn's leaves. I wipe one off with my sleeve and sit on it. On the table is a battered paperback copy of *Under Milk Wood* by Dylan Thomas. There's no sign of the resident of Flat Five.

It's ages since I've sat in sunlight. I'm wrapped up in my coat, as it's still cold, but the high walls shelter me from the wind. I shut my eyes, lifting my face to the sun, conscious of something starting to give within me, of muscles suffering from a winter of constriction beginning to relax.

Then someone clears his throat near me. I open my eyes. He's here, standing in front of me, the man from Flat Five. I brace myself to move then I notice he is smiling.

"Well hello," he says. "I have a visitor."

He looks old. Forties or even fifties. His voice is posh, but his clothes are shabby. A tweed jacket which has seen better days. Jeans sagging at the knees. A tatty canvas man-bag over his shoulder. He has pale hair, thinning on top, and deep furrows in his forehead.

"I live in the attic," I say.

He walks up to me and holds out his hand for a formal handshake. His fingers are stained deep orange. His hand is sweaty.

"Barnabas," he says.

I stifle a giggle. Barnabas is the name of a converted double-decker bus in Chinatown that gives free soup to dossers – Barrel Woman goes there sometimes to freeload on food. I didn't know people could be called Barnabas.

"I'm Amy."

"Welcome to my terrace, Amy."

"Sorry to intrude," I say.

"Don't be," he says. "This space is for everyone. But I'm the only one who uses it now, so I've made it my own. See those?" he indicates the row of pots. "That's my Scarborough Fair garden."

I think for a moment then say: "Parsley, sage, rosemary and thyme?"

"You've got it!" he says. "In that order. That's how I remember which is which. You can help yourself to a bunch or two to sprinkle in your cooking."

"Thanks," I wonder if a sprig of fresh parsley will enhance my pot noodles.

"Would you care for a cup of tea?"

He unlocks the door to his flat, disappears inside for a while and emerges with two mugs. My mug is chipped and stained.

"Have you got a job?" I ask.

"I work at the Royal Mail sorting office in town."

"What's that like?"

"I like elements of it," he says. "I like the fact I go there early, finish early, and have the rest of the day to myself. I like the fact that I can leave it behind at the end of the day and pick it up again the next morning. Nothing carries over."

He pulls out a tin from his pocket, opens it carefully, takes out rolling papers and tobacco and starts to roll a stick-thin cigarette. I notice he has three perfectly rolled ones already in the tin.

He offers me one. I shake my head.

"What do you do Amy?"

"I don't work, at the moment, I'm kind of... recovering from something."

"Aren't we all?" he says.

He's drinking very dark coffee out of a mug even filthier than mine. He draws deeply on his super-thin roll-up as we sit in the sun. There's something comforting about the smell of it.

"I like sitting in the sun," I say.

"Well you must come again," he says. "In all the years I've lived here very few of the other tenants have ventured down here."

"Did you know someone called Jay?" I say. "He used to live here, in my flat, a couple of years ago, I think."

Barnabas furrows his brow.

"Jay?"

"Yeah, blond bloke, tall, young."

His expression changes. "Ah. I know who you mean. He lived here about three years ago. An art student. How do you know about him?"

"Oh, I've seen him around. He said he used to live in my flat."

His eyes widen. "He came back?"

"Yeah. He comes and goes."

Barnabas stubs out his roll-up and stands up.

"Well I never thought he'd come *back*. Excuse me a minute." He dives into his flat again, emerging wearing a beanie hat and scarf with his tweed jacket, locks his door and shakes my hand again.

"I have to go now, Amy, but it's a pleasure to make your acquaintance. Stay as long as you like, and don't forget to take some herbs."

I stay a while longer, turning to feel the sun on my back.

Chapter Twenty

IT WAS THE Monday after the dinner party. Fiona had gone to her Mum's, taking Daniel. It was around six in the evening. Howard didn't usually come in till gone seven. I appreciated having the house to myself. Although I never felt relaxed there, it was better when they were out. I was downstairs, fixing myself some food. I'd just put something in the microwave when I was conscious that someone was in the room. I swung round to see Howard striding across the kitchen towards me.

I said: "Howard I didn't hear you come in," but he didn't speak, just kept coming nearer till he was close enough for me to catch his whiskey breath. He pressed his finger on my lips. "Shh," he said. "Can you keep a secret?"

I pressed myself into the cupboards, hoping this was just some game. He reached into his pocket and pulled out a wad of notes. "My winnings. I've been to the casino," he said in a loud stage whisper. "Fiona mustn't know." He backed away, replacing the notes in his pocket and humming a little as he opened the drinks cabinet.

"This calls for a little celebratory tipple, don't you think?"

I didn't answer. I felt frozen to the spot as I watched him take out two cocktail glasses, rub lime and salt around the rims, drop an ice cube into each then pour in a generous portion of clear spirit, adding a slice of lime and a little umbrella to each glass.

"Here you are, a Carlotti special."

I didn't really want a drink with Howard, but it seemed rude not to now he'd done all this, so I took the glass he offered me. Anything to ease the awkwardness.

It smelt like the tequila slammers we used to have when we went for happy hour in Derby.

"Is this tequila?" I said.

"Close," he said. "Mezcal, Tequila's big brother."

I took a sip. The strong sweet liquor warmed my innards.

"C'mon! Down the hatch." Howard drained his glass. I took three gulps to swallow mine. He whisked the glass out of my hand and took it away to refill it.

"Thanks Howard but I don't want any more," I said weakly. Already the strength of the alcohol was making my head spin.

"Don't be a lightweight. You need to let your hair down more often," he said, tuning round to face me. "You were a hit at the dinner party!" I watched as he mixed us both another drink, this time pouring from a bottle of light green liquid and adding some clear rum.

"This one's like nothing you've ever tasted." He said handing it to me. "Have a sip and tell me what flavours you get."

I played along. "Aniseed". I said. "Rum. With a twist of lime?"

"Absinthe," he said. "*la fée verte.* The drink of the bohemians. Down it in one and you'll get a fabulous herbal aftertaste."

I knocked it back. My head now giddy, my vision starting to swim. He took the glass away again, smiling.

"It's what made Van Gogh cut off his ear," he laughed. "It was banned in the UK 'til the 90s."

I felt unreal. Like my body was separate from my mind. Somewhere in my psyche, a voice urged caution. But another, stronger voice, said 'What the fuck. Get drunk with Howard. What's to lose?'

So I took another glass of the absinthe potion. Then another. And I looked at my fingers in front of my face and thought, with wonder, *these are mine.* And my voice came out strange and disconnected. Then from somewhere within me a voice of reason cut through. *Stop*! It said. *Stop drinking. Leave, and go to bed.*

So I said, "thanks Howard, but I seriously don't want any more." I put the glass on the work surface behind me, but it was too late. I hung onto the worktop as Howard moved closer.

"Maybe you deserve a bonus if you're good." He pulled out the notes again and fanned them in front of my face. His face was huge in front of mine. For a second I saw two of him. "D'you think you deserve a bonus, Amy?"

I shrugged, hoping the spinning in my head would stop. Hoping this game, whatever it was, would soon be over. He then rolled up a couple of the notes and pressed them down the front of my top. They scratched my skin. Then he leaned in to kiss me. I turned my face away. He grabbed my shoulders and turned me round so I had my back to him. "You know you want this," I felt his hot breath in my ear as he marched me into the living room, pushed me down onto the couch, pulled my leggings down and was into me. I don't know if the weak little 'no' I formed on my lips ever came out.

My lower half was numb, all sensation lost. My upper half felt crushed. The rough serge of the sofa pressed into my face, my hands pinned under my body. I tried to push up my chest to give myself space to breathe, at the same time forcing back vomit. I felt something like rain fall on my neck. I realised it was Howard's sweat.

All I could think of was, let this be over quickly. And it was, mercifully, within minutes. He rolled off and hissed into my ear, "not a word." I listened to him leave the room before I dared move.

I got up from the couch, my head now suddenly clear. Mechanically I walked up to my room, locked the door and pulled my clothes off, surprised when two twenty-pound notes fell out of my top. I'd forgotten about the money.

I took a long shower. Like that would wash what had happened out of me. What *had* happened? I looked at the notes. Forty pounds for ten minutes' work. Was this some unwritten part of my contract?

I put the clothes I'd been wearing in a plastic bag and

chucked them in the bin. Acting on automatic, I packed my case, stowing it out of sight behind the bed, just in case, then sat at the window looking at the gate. I knew what I had to do.

Some time later I heard Fiona return with Daniel, and sounds filled the house. Normality resumed, but not for me. Fiona came to check on me, which was unprecedented. "Are you okay? Howard says you didn't eat anything tonight." She said it in an accusatory way, not a hint of concern in her voice.

"I'm okay Fiona," I forced a smile, hating myself for it. She left the room. I felt sick.

That night, I lay fully clothed on top of my bed, waiting for morning. It was a warm night, but I shivered like someone with a fever. I booked a cab for five am, then crept out with my case in the dark, carrying rather than wheeling it down the drive. I waited at the corner for the taxi, which took me into town. I'd left Howard's forty pounds on the dressing table in my room.

Chapter Twenty-One

I CAN'T TELL what Jay is thinking. Is he, like me, silently blaming me for not putting up a fight?

"Say something!" I say at last.

"I don't know what to say Amy. Groomed by one older man, raped by another. No wonder you're messed up."

"Was it rape?' I say. "I didn't fight. I didn't even say no. I was pathetic, wasn't I?"

He looks at me for a moment, like he's sizing me up. "Howard Carlotti was an ex Oxbridge rower. I'm guessing he wasn't a lightweight?"

"He was big, like rugby-player build."

"You'd have stood no chance if you'd tried to fight him off."

I nod.

"So this wasn't your fault. Any more than Iain Carver was, okay?"

"Okay" and then the sobbing starts, slowly at first, then

in great waves that engulf my whole body.

Jay sits, still and serious. Gone is the smugness. And I tell him through my sobs how I sat in an early morning café at Piccadilly scouring the Internet for rooms. How I got myself a flat-share with two girls in Chorlton. How I held it together, sort of. Still acting on automatic, amazed at my ability to function, I even walked into an agency and got myself a job.

How I started to unravel.

The two girls, nice enough, would invite me out with them into town, but I preferred to stay in, and they stopped asking. My confidence shot, I began to doubt my ability to do even the low-level tasks my employer asked of me. The whole time, I felt as though a scream was building up inside me. To stop it escaping, I kept my mouth firmly shut, trapping it inside. I became once again the mute child I had been on arrival at Judith's.

And then the bombshell: I found out I was pregnant.

It was Howard's. I should get rid of it. But some perverse thing in me wanted, just for once, to nurture something. I wavered wildly between terminating the pregnancy and keeping it, indecision driving me insane.

I worked up the courage to phone Howard, getting through to his secretary, half hoping he'd be out.

"You?" he said. "What do *you* want? After you left us in the shit?"

I could hardly speak. There was so much venom in his tone. My voice sounded weak as I said: "I'm pregnant... after... after what happened."

"Christ that's all I need. Aren't you on the pill?" He

barked the words at me. Like being on the pill was a condition of my employment.

"You'll have to get rid of it," he said. "How far gone are you?"

"A few weeks," I lied. I was close to eleven weeks by then. Of course he could have worked that out.

"Not too late to get rid of it then," he said. "Go private. I'll pay. A grand should do it."

He got my address to send me a cheque, then said: "After that I never want to hear from you again. Understood?"

Click.

It wasn't so much that I decided to keep it, more like I persisted in indecision. I wanted to keep it because Howard told me not to, but also because it was a life, and it was mine, and bringing this life into the world was something I could do – I'd failed at everything else. I felt an affinity to it. We were both alone and unwanted. Against the world.

A cheque for a thousand pounds arrived two days later. I decided to use the money to buy things for the baby. But that day I got ill, overwhelmed by a pain so consuming I doubled up on the sofa in agony, then I felt the thick, congealed clots running down my leg and realised I was losing it. I blacked out.

My flatmates got me into hospital.

That's when the scream finally came out.

I lost the plot as well as losing my baby.

I came out of hospital after the miscarriage, swallowed sixty aspirins and went straight back in. They pumped me clean and sent me home. I overdosed again and this time they put me on a psychiatric ward. I don't know how long I was there. Weeks, possibly even months.

At some point the girls from the Chorlton flat came to the ward. They brought my stuff packed up in my case and said they needed someone who could pay the rent. That was the last I saw of them.

And the really shitty thing is, I never cashed Howard's cheque. At some point between going into hospital the first time and ending up at Balmoral Street I lost the bag the cheque was in. The girls could have nicked it but I don't think they did. Anyway, it went.

Someone got me a social worker who sorted out my benefits and brought me here, to Balmoral Street.

"SO DID THEY section you?" Jay asks.

"No. I went quietly. I was so out of it, I didn't have the energy to argue."

He muses for a minute then says, "*I* was sectioned."

Weird! He never talks about himself.

"You? Why?"

"They thought I was bi-polar. I wasn't of course. I had highs and lows but I was perfectly in control. It was an interesting experience." He chuckles. Like he's proud of it.

"And do you still have mood swings?"

"Not any more. I had a knock on the head which cured me."

"Maybe I need one of those."

He shakes his head. "You don't want to go there. It fucked my memory. Some of it's come back but there's whole chunks of stuff I can't remember."

It's the most he's ever told me about himself.

Chapter Twenty-Two

I DON'T SEE Jay for a while. He has stuff to do. He's sorting out this 'situation' for me, apparently. For the rest of the week it rains, so I don't go back to the garden, or the lakes. I do, however, go to the doctor and get a lower dose prescription, plus a plan for withdrawal.

The rain turns to sleet and it's like a return to full-on winter. People are talking about the coldest winter since records began. More snow on the way, they say. As I walk down Balmoral Street the chill hits me right in the chest. I turn the collar up on my jacket and pull it round me, regretting not wearing my big coat. Just then I see The Man, unusual to see him when it's not dry. He is standing under a big black umbrella. He beckons me over.

"Pixie I been watching for you. I hope you all right with dem boys around." Boys? I haven't noticed any. "Anyway. You seen dis? I want to show you someting." He has a piece of paper. It's flapping in the wind and hard to see what he is pointing to. "It's from de church," he says. It seems to be some sort of newsletter. I focus in on what he's showing me, and there on the page is a grainy photo of Barrel Woman. Then I notice the headline. 'Memorial Service for Mary Mulholland.'

"Oh my God!" I say. "It's her!"

"Yes, Mary. Dey held a service for her at de Catholic church. I pick this up to show you."

"So she's...." I can't bring myself to say it.

"She gone to the Lord," says the Man. It's the first time I've heard him say anything religious.

"But.. but... how?"

"You take dis. Read all about it."

I grab the paper and turn back towards my building. The door is open and there are two youths running in and out, shouting. They run up the stairs to Barrel Woman's flat. They've taken off the piece of chipboard which has been there since the Police kicked the door open. Psycho-boy's door is open too and I can see him, lying on an unmade bed. A stained, coverless duvet and a sheet half-covering the mattress. He's calling to the youths. I scurry past to the relative safety of my room, clutching the newsletter.

I shiver as I read.

We held a memorial on Thursday for Mary Mulholland. Mary (pictured) was a regular at our Wednesday drop in and a familiar face at the St Michael's Food Bank. It was with great sadness we learnt Mary had died in a fire at a house where she was staying. May her soul rest in peace. Here's what some of our volunteers said about Mary.

"She'd have us howling with laughter at her stories. She always had a smile on her face and a tale to entertain us with," says Margaret Burke, food bank volunteer.

"I last saw Mary on Boxing day when she dropped in for a mince pie and a cup of tea. She said she'd had a lovely Christmas, which she spent with Lily Allen! Mary was popular at the centre and she looked on all her friends as celebrities."

I sit, staring at the paper for some time. I turn it over. I read everything on it. It's called St Michael's Messenger. Most of it is stuff about church things and there's bits from the bible. I never knew Mary went there. I never knew half of what she did or where she went or any of the friends she stayed with. I stare at the photo. It's been taken on a phone and badly reproduced, but it's all I have of Barrel Woman. She's sitting in front of a plateful of mince pies and cake and smiling up at the camera. She's wearing the same bee-stripe outfit she wore on Christmas day. I sit, shivering and reading and re-reading the words.

I'm shaken out of my thoughts by the sound of feet on the attic stairs. 'Dem boys' who have been kicking off on the landing below are now apparently coming to pay me a visit. I freeze, hoping they'll go away. But one of them pushes the door open.

"Shit man," he says when he sees me. He's stick skinny, wearing baggy trackie bottoms, the crotch half-way down his thighs, and a hoodie. His face is gaunt. I think I've surprised him by actually being here. "You got any…?"

I shake my head. "I got nothing." He shuffles a few feet into the room and starts looking around, sniffing, then a shout from downstairs alerts him and he leaves. I put my big coat on and sit shaking, then reach for the Diazepam. I have a new prescription. Lower dose. But this calls for something stronger. I wait till the commotion dies down and go downstairs. There's no sign of the youths. Psycho-boy's door is firmly shut. Mary's door is wide open. I venture inside.

I have only been here once before, but it's unrecognisable. The room is all tipped up. The boys, or the Police before them, have rifled through everything. Her clothes are strewn on the floor, I see several of those garish jumper dresses she was so fond of. Piles of leggings, black, multi-coloured and spangly. The Santa earrings she wore on Christmas day still rest on the bedside table. Mary's 'studio', like the others in the house, is no more than a glorified bedsit. Because I have the attic, my room is bigger as it spans the width of the house. Mary's is tiny. When I came here once before I remember it full of fleecy throws from the pound shop, layered up on the bed and covering every piece of furniture. Now everything is strewn about in a heap. There's empty bottles of cheap sherry. A bin on its side overflows with cigarette packets. The wardrobe, one door hanging off its hinges, spills out clothes onto the floor. The drawers have been pulled out and heaped up or overturned on the floor. Cheap jewellery falls out of one drawer, gigantic underwear another – huge lacy knickers, massive 'harness' bras. A Halloween skeleton costume hangs freakishly from a hook on the wall.

Next to the bed, stripped of its duvet, is a small wooden

bedside table. It alone seems undisturbed. The bed sags beneath me as I sit. I see a pile of photographs, not in frames, from the days when people still had prints. There's one of two little girls on a sledge, muffled up against the snow. The colours are faded and I'm guessing it's several decades old. I wonder if one of the girls is Mary. There's another, this time black and white, of those same two little girls in a church, one of them dressed in some sort of miniature wedding dress, white, with a veil. Then there's an even older black and white picture of a couple. Dressed in 1940s-style clothes. Mary's parents probably. I never knew how old she was. Looking at these pictures, I still can't work it out. There's one more recent picture. A printout of a digital snap, and it's Mary with some woman from Coronation Street outside Granada Studios. The only other thing on the table is a chain of wooden beads with a cross on it. I pick it up along with the photos and put them in my coat pocket.

Perhaps it's seeing the sherry bottles that makes me head for the off-licence. I need to raise a glass to Barrel Woman. I buy a litre of her favourite brand sherry and go back. It's dark by the time I return to Balmoral Street and the youths are outside, kicking over wheelie-bins in the sleet.

Back in my room, fearing a repeat visit by my friend from earlier, I drag the chest of drawers in front of the door, spread out the pictures from Mary's flat on the table, next to the cutting from the church newsletter, and pour myself some sherry. The only glass I have is a tumbler. I fill it full.

"Cheers gel!" I say, imitating her voice, and feel the sweet liquor slipping down my throat, warming my insides.

Chapter Twenty-Three

I T'S SEVERAL HOURS later, and the bottle is empty. I'm
tempted to go out and buy another. That's what Barrel
Woman would have done. But the thump, thump, thump of
the hip-hop beat from the flat below and shouts above the
volume suggest Psycho-boy's mates have taken up residence
in Barrel Woman's flat. I'm glad I rescued her photos. The
clock says half past midnight. Time to sleep, surely, but
those below are only just getting going.

I stand on the table, opening the skylight to its full
extent. You have to hold it open otherwise it could swing
back and knock you out. I look out over the rooftops of East
Manchester. I think of Barrel Woman. Her life. Her lies.
Her death, mourned only by a bunch of do-gooders who
didn't even know her.

And then it hits me.

I wouldn't even have that.

If I just climbed out here, onto the shiny, slippery roof, I could make a swift exit. They'd find me in the morning. Maybe Tania and Barnabas and The Man would go to my funeral. I stand a while, looking out at the glistening rooftops. The sleet has stopped, at least. The threatened snow has not yet come. It's only the insistent ache in my arm that brings me back down, where the thump of the noise downstairs seems to fill the room, fill my soul.

Partly to warm me up, partly to drown out the sound, I put the fan heater on, right next to my head. And it seems to speak to me. *You could just do it. Go on. Bow out now. There's nothing to live for. That bloke Jay. He wasn't even real, was he? And if he was, he was full of shit. You'd do everyone a favour. You just bring trouble.* The voice morphs into Judith's. "I've always known you were trouble."

A packet of Diazies on top of a bottle of sherry. That should do it. You've got some paracetamol in the cupboard. Take those too, just to be sure. Don't believe this bullshit about starting a life somewhere else. Somewhere in the country. You'd do us all a favour. Everything you touch turns to shit. You know that. You've even killed Barrel Woman off.

I go to the sink, fill the beaker with tap water, and sit down. I pull all three strips of tablets out of the packet and lay them out in front of me. I need more than this low dose to shut up the voice. I take one, swig it down. Not enough. I can still hear it. I take another. The voice is louder now, insistent, I reach for another...

"Amy – let me in!"

He's pushing the door but it won't open because there's a chest of drawers in front of it. I go to the door and haul it out of the way. Jay shakes water off his Parka leaving a pool by the door, then looks around him. He clocks the empty sherry bottle, the pictures on the table, the tablets all lined up.

"Looks like I got here just in time," he says.

"Where the hell have you been?"

"Never mind me. What's going on, Amy?"

"I …I.. was just going to …"

"Going to what, end your life? For fuck's sake Amy, I leave you for two minutes and you become a wreck again."

"Two minutes? Two weeks, more like. And Barrel Woman's dead!"

I pick up the cutting and shove it in his face.

"And so will you be if you don't get out of this place."

"What are you on about?"

"Tomorrow Amy. Tomorrow's the day you're due to leave, remember?"

"What?"

"The day you start your new life."

"Like that's gonna happen. I can't. I'm in no fit state."

Jay looks me up and down again. "I get it," he says. "You'd rather stay here and mourn your sad bitch of a friend and listen to your psycho junkie neighbours having a party in her old flat. You'd rather stay here and swallow all your tablets all at once so somebody will come and take you to hospital again. Is that it?"

I'm sobbing now. "You weren't here for me Jay. And you *lied*."

"What?"

"You said Mary would be okay. You were wrong."

"I said, if I remember correctly, 'Mary will look after

Mary.'"

"So you were wrong."

"How so?" he says. "Mary looked after Mary right until the time when Mary decided it was time to go. Mary died in a squat in Gorton with her mate Billy. They'd scored some smack. They found the oblivion they were seeking then someone put a torch to the place. Believe me Amy, that's how it happened. Anyway, she was a good age. Fifty-seven isn't bad on that kind of lifestyle."

"How d'you know how old she was?"

"I was around at her funeral."

"You didn't tell me about it. I might have wanted to go!"

"It was family only."

"But..she never mentioned any family. And how come you went? You're not related to her are you?"

"I didn't say I went. I said I was around. I got a look at the service sheet. Mary did have family, they'd disowned her years earlier, but they all came to say goodbye. The church was packed, actually. That's Catholic funerals for you!"

"So Mary was Catholic?"

"With a name like Mary? Duh! So as I said, Mary will look after Mary. There'll be enough people praying for her soul. And, who knows, maybe she even had time to repent just before she went," he laughs. "You, however, are not going to go the way of Mary. Unless you want to that is. And if you don't want to, you leave tomorrow. So listen up, I haven't got much time."

I write down his instructions, because he says he'll say them only once.

"Pack your stuff in a rucksack. Ditch the Diazepam. Hand in the key at the agents, cancel the rent, and leave. Get the bus into town. Get off at Piccadilly. Go to the ticket office. Ask for a one-way ticket to Bangor North Wales."

"But. Wait a minute. How much will the train ticket be? How am I supposed to pay for it?"

"At a guess, about forty quid. But don't worry about the money. The money will come. Trust me."

He reels off instructions. What bus to get from Bangor. Where to get off.

"Walk up a slight hill, past a big white-gated property. Carry on until you see a gate set back a bit from the road and a sign which says Môr Tawel. Here, this is the place."

He hands me a battered business card with a drawing of a wigwam on it near the sea and a web address.

"Môr Tawel?" I read off the card.

"It means 'Quiet Sea', which is a misnomer 'cos it's bloody noisy sometimes. Anyway, go through the gate and walk down the lane for about a mile. It's like a farm track, quite overgrown. Eventually you'll see a house. Tell the woman there you're looking for accommodation and work experience on a farm. Don't mention me or say you've come from Manchester."

"What am I supposed to say if this woman asks me?"

"Say you're from Derby or wherever you came from originally. Just don't say anything to the woman or her husband about Manchester and whatever you do don't mention my name. Okay, you got that? I need to go in a minute."

"But…"

"But what?" says Jay. "If you follow those instructions all will be well. And don't worry about the money. Okay?"

"But.."

"Take it or leave it. Take it, you change your life. Leave it, you die a slow, painful death in Balmoral Street."

"Will I see you again?" I say.

"If you go, yes you will. Not straight away, but I'll know where to find you. I'll get in touch. If you bottle it, you won't see me again, because I will have given up on you. Got it?"

I nod. He grabs his coat and heads toward the door.

"Oh and Amy,"

"What?"

"Don't forget. Lose the pills. You won't need them where you're going. Now I'm off."

He stands by the door. It all seems suddenly final.

"Jay, is that it?" I say. "Aren't you going to give me a hug or something?"

"I don't do hugs," he says, shrinking away from me. "But I wish you well." He opens the door.

"But Jay…"

"What?"

"This place you're sending me to. What will I find there?"

He looks at me then, with a look that seems to penetrate right to my soul.

"You'll find you, Amy Blue. You'll find you," and with that he is gone. I listen out for his footsteps on the stairs. I hear nothing. Even the psychos downstairs are silent.

PART TWO

Môr Tawel

Chapter Twenty-Four

N EXT MORNING THE sun breaks through the skylight window, rousing me. I wake with a feeling of unreality. Was Jay here? Or did I dream it? The first thing I see is the empty sherry bottle, lying on the floor, then the tablets lined up on the table. My stomach lurches. Sitting up, I see my notebook in a fold of the duvet. I pick it up. The card with the picture of a wigwam by the sea falls out. And there are the two pages of instructions he gave me.

Not a dream.

Get the bus into town. ... Ask for a one-way ticket to Bangor North Wales... don't worry about the money. The money will come.

But how? I pull myself out of bed. It's seven am. I never surface this early. I feel a sense of urgency, like I need to move quickly before the mood has passed. I throw on some clothes, pull on my DMs and go downstairs. No sign of Pyscho-Boy's friends. Instead there's a man in overalls measuring up Barrel Woman's door. I meet nobody else on the stairs. The house doesn't stir till later. Downstairs, I sift through the mail in the hall. Same old junk. What do I expect to find?

"Where's this money, Jay?" I whisper.

The flat to Tania's door opens slowly. I brace myself, in case it's one of her homeys emerging, but it's Tania, yawning, dressed in a kimono. She's got a full face of make-up on.

"Hiya babe," she says.

"Hey Tania, how are you?"

"Doing good kid. Glad I've caught you. Got something for you. Come in."

There's a strong smell of weed mixed with her exotic perfume. The place is in near total darkness.

"Some fella dropped this off last night," she says, "Amy Blue – that's you?"

She hands me a large jiffy envelope done up with gaffer tape. On it is a label with several crossed-out addresses. Someone has scrawled over them 'Try Balmoral Street.'

"Thanks Tania, did you get a look at the guy?"

"Not really. It was snowing. He looked y'know, studenty. It was like three o'clock in the morning. I didn't want to leave it in the hall with them smack-heads about."

"Thanks Tania,"

"Fancy a cuppa?"

"Yeah, that'd be nice. This might be the last time I see you. I'm off to Wales later," telling Tania helps make it real.

"Nice one," Tania yawns again and moves over to the kitchenette. "Aren't you gonna open it Ames?"

I start to rip at the packaging. My pulse racing, I take a peek inside.

"Oh my God! I never thought I'd see this again,"

It's instantly recognisable by its gold chain shoulder strap. I pull it out. It's the bag I lost in transit when I left the Chorlton flatshare. Apart from anything else, I love this bag. Gucci, seventies style, green snakeskin leather.

Tania brings two mugs over. "Black all right?"

My head is reeling and I hardly dare look in the bag. Surely after all this time there won't be any money left in it.

"Mind if I…?" Tania starts to roll a spliff.

"You go ahead," I say, opening the bag, and there, folded where I'd left it, is Howard Carlotti's compliment slip stapled to the cheque for a thousand pounds. And in the zipped pocket there's forty-five pounds cash.

"Bloody hell! The money's still here! How the hell did they find me?"

"Made up for you!" says Tania. She offers me the spliff. I shake my head. "Today's gonna be your lucky day Ames. It's a good omen for your trip to Wales."

"Thank you!" I breathe, as much to the universe as to Tania, then I quickly drain my coffee and leave. I have to pack. I'm going on a journey.

Chapter Twenty-Five

IT DOESN'T TAKE long. I have so few possessions. Anything of any value walked long ago. I take care with Jay's drawing, wrapping it in tissue and placing it at the back of the rucksack to protect it. I place Barrel Woman's photos in the envelope with my parents' wedding picture and I pack her chain of beads too.

Most of the stuff in the room, I can leave behind. Like all the papers the social worker gave me. I start tearing them into pieces and stuffing them into a bin liner. I spot a leaflet with the words 'Mentoring and Befriending' on it. It's from something called the Amistad Trust. This must be the outfit that sent Jay. I pick it up and skim through the pages. In the section called 'Where to meet' it says, '*For the first meeting, we will arrange for someone from the charity to be present. After that, you decide where and when to meet your mentor, but it will usually be in a neutral place like a café or a park. We do not recommend you meet in each others' homes.*' So Jay didn't exactly follow the guidance, barging in on me at night.

I carry on reading. *'Your mentor is not there to offer counselling or therapy. Mentors are not trained counsellors, but many are good listeners. You can tell them as much, or as little about yourself, as you like, but in certain circumstances if they are alarmed by what you tell them they may need to refer to a member of Amistad Trust staff.'* So Jay totally broke all the rules, trying out his amateur psychology on me. But hey, who cares now?

Set into the wall behind where the chest of drawers was there's an old fireplace. I notice a pile of books in the hearth that I hadn't seen before because the fireplace was obscured. In my Diazepam haze I haven't read a single book while I've been here. I stoop to take a look. The books are caked in cobwebs. There's *War and Peace* in paperback, a Bill Bryson travel memoir and a book about philosophy. There's also a hardback A4 notebook wedged in between them. I pull this out. There are drawings, poems and what look like diary entries. All scrawled in a half-familiar pen. Jay's from when he lived here? I briefly skim the pages, but none of it makes sense to me. Stream of consciousness stuff. Names that mean nothing. I start reading one of the poems. It starts:

A suicide stood naked at the dawn
Of understanding,

I think of myself last night, standing on the chair contemplating the rooftops. Is this some sort of message? I shiver. For a second I consider taking the book with me, but some strong instinct says 'leave it'. Items found in Balmoral Street should stay in Balmoral Street. It's a clear voice that's been talking to me all morning. I replace the notebook and drag the chest of drawers back in front of the fireplace. Who knows, some future resident might want to read *War and Peace*. God help them.

A knocking from the landing below breaks through my thoughts. Time to get moving.

I look at the instructions again. *Lose the Diazepam.* My month's supply of tablets are still lined up on the table. I scoop them up, then carry them to the toilet, ready to flush them away. I feel a tug. I am going to the unknown. The jitters might return. Shouldn't I keep a few back, just in case?

I pace around the room, the tablets in my cupped hands. I sigh. Then I get another glimpse of my long-lost Gucci bag, placed next to my backpack ready for departure, and I feel a wave of wonder. So far, everything Jay said has come true. The money materialised. I mustn't break the spell.

I march over to the toilet again, open my hands, drop the entire lot into the pan and flush. I watch the water in the cistern froth up and up. As it reaches the rim of the bowl, I have a sensation of a river bursting its banks, and carrying me away, then the froth subsides.

"Goodbye" I whisper to the room.

On my way out of the building I see the landlord. It's only the second time I've ever met him. He's supervising some sort of clearance of Barrel Woman's old room. This saves me a trip. I hand him the key and tell him I'm leaving.

"You're supposed to give a month's notice," he grunts.

"And you're supposed to fix things like the landing light

and the lock on my door," I say. "I'm paid up till the end of the week, that'll have to do you. Goodbye!" I hardly recognise this new assertive me.

"BANGOR NORTH WALES please, one way."

"Bangor? You'll have a luverley time there," says the ticket clerk. The fare is thirty-six pounds sixty. The money in my purse pays for it with some to spare.

"What time's the next one?"

He looks at his screen. "There's one in ten minutes on Platform Fourteen. If you run, you'll just about make it. Direct train too, there's only about one of them a week."

Platform Fourteen is so far away it takes nearly ten minutes to get there. I arrive, breathless, just in time to step on the train. I collapse into a double seat as they blow the whistle for the off.

"This is it kid," the voice talking to me now is mine.

Opposite are two girls about my age, both blonde, wearing walking boots, talking in a foreign language. The other people in the carriage are mostly lone travellers, engaging with their devices. It occurs to me I have nothing, no phone, tablet, e-reader, not even a book. So I sit back and observe. And the feeling that dogged me on Balmoral Street, the feeling of being watched by hostile, critical, or pitying eyes, suddenly isn't there. A guy in a suit looks my way, catches my eye and smiles before opening his laptop, but most people don't look at me at all.

People on this train actually think I'm normal.

Anxiety is just beneath the surface, threatening to bubble up. My heart-rate quickens. I start to feel lightheaded. The psychiatrist tried to teach me techniques. I've never used them until now. There's the breathing thing, you breathe through your stomach counting to seven, and there's the mindfulness thing where you notice what you can see, hear and smell, at any given moment.

I see the girls in the seat opposite dragging a huge backpack from the luggage area and pulling out foil-wrapped sandwiches and a litre bottle of water, which they pass between them. I smell garlic from whatever they're eating and a hint of diesel oil. I hear the announcer reeling off a long list of station names. Bangor is last on the list.

At Chester, the man in the suit gets off. More people get on. Still nobody sits next to me.

At Flint, also spelt Y Fflint, I figure we must be in Wales, and I feel a weird kind of high. I've crossed the border.

The landscape starts to rise. First hills, then actual mountains, craggy and dark. There's a squeal from the girls when they see the sea. It starts as a thin strip of blue, then the whole view is full of sea. I see the blades of wind turbines elegant against the skyline. A road runs alongside the railway, carrying holiday traffic. Cars pulling caravans, carrying bicycles, or towing boats. A castle looms into view. We plunge into a dark tunnel in the side of a mountain and come out the other side.

Stations come thick and fast and I've lost count, then the train pops through another short tunnel and we're here.

Bangor, the end of the line.

Chapter Twenty-Six

OUTSIDE THE SOUND of seagulls hits me. Loud and anguished.

Just past the ticket barrier stands a man in zipped leather trousers and a red, military style coat. A guy in his late 30s, I'd say, with blond hair tied up in a man-bun. He clocks me with a look of almost recognition, does a half-move towards me, then spots someone behind me.

"Isabella!" he calls, and I turn to see him swooping a petite, Mediterranean looking girl into his arms, kissing her on both cheeks. "Step this way, your chariot awaits," he says, leading her to a waiting car, conspicuous because it's parked in a No Parking bay, and because it's a convertible left-hand-drive VW Beetle painted two-tone purple and white.

We only connected for a second, but as the car revs off, I feel a pang of loneliness, a physical stab of grief that this colourful stranger is not in my life, that there is no-one here to greet me.

My bus arrives. As Jay said it would, it crosses a suspension bridge onto the Isle of Anglesey then leaves the coast and goes 'round the houses'. I am now the sole passenger, and the driver turns round and starts shouting. I can't make out the words, maybe he's speaking Welsh. He sounds angry. I wonder if I've done something to offend him.

"Where you from?" I understand that bit.

"Manchester," I say.

"You been to Wales before?"

I think it's his accent that makes him sound angry.

"Only Swansea, a long time ago," I say.

"If you go to Snowden don't go up on the train, it's a bloody rip-off. It'll cost you thirty pounds!" He swings the bus round a bend, narrowly missing the wall of a house.

"You know where you're going now?" he asks as he drops me at my stop.

"Môr Tawel?" I show him the card.

"That'll be the Lloyds' place, yes?"

I have no idea, but I get off.

The words Môr Tawel are painted on a wooden sign, the lettering decorated with purple flowers, like the gypsy art you see on canal-boats. The gate creaks as I open it and head off down a stony track with a bank of grass in the middle. Trees line the way, making it dark and secluded. It's muddy, due to recent rain, with imprinted tyre marks from some large vehicle. I trudge on as the path winds round to the right. I can't see an end to it. About a mile, Jay said, but how far is a mile? I feel like I've been walking this track for forever.

I'm conscious of birdsong, over and above the persistent, plaintive cries of the seagulls. Quiet at first, then rising to a sort of crescendo until it fills my head. And I have a sense of being removed from the world, in a land without people. What if I really did jump from the rooftop last night, or swallow the pills? This could be the afterlife. I want to join the birds in song, to sing out loud, in this land without witnesses. Part of me wants to walk this path for eternity, and it's with a faint sense of disappointment that I notice signs of habitation.

A row of scruffy-looking door-less sheds lines the track, each crammed full of junk. There are pieces of machinery, a giant tyre and a broken bike in one; an old Mini minus its doors in another, its engine open to the elements. A tractor fills another, a stack of kayaks occupies another. Then, past the sheds, through a clearing in the trees, I see a cluster of old caravans. Fear jolts through me as I remember something I heard on the news. Something about gypsies luring people in with the promise of work then keeping them as slaves.

Vulnerable people, with nobody to miss them.

People like me.

And here I am, in the middle of nowhere, walking right into the trap.

I stop, rooted to the spot and sick to the pit of my stomach.

A tortoiseshell cat stalks up the path, spots me, then scampers back in the direction it came. It breaks the spell.

"Carry on walking," says the clear voice in my head, and something of the enchantment I felt on the path earlier returns to guide me, so I keep on putting one foot in front of the other.

I see a gate to the left, with another painted sign which says 'Cae Sara'. Am I supposed to go through here? But it just seems to lead to an overgrown field. I carry on down the path, past a row of white slatted boxes set back up a slope, then round the next bend is a grey stone house surrounded by shrubbery.

Môr Tawel.

Tell the woman there you're looking for accommodation and work experience on a farm.

Can you really just walk up to someone's house and say that?

As I approach the door, there's a low growl from a brown and white spaniel lying in the yard. The dog gets up, plods over to me, and nuzzles me in the groin. Its coat is matted with sand.

The door is in two parts, like a stable door, the top section slightly open. I knock. I think I hear a voice coming from inside. Did it say "Come in?" or even "I'm in?" Nobody appears, so I knock again. The dog looks up at me from bloodshot eyes, then utters a single bark. I get the feeling he's on my side.

This time, the voice is clearer. "It's open!"

Pushing the door, I find myself in a sort of anteroom, with a strong smell of fish. There are two huge sinks, one full of dead fish still with their heads on. My stomach lurches. There are buckets on the floor containing shells. The wall is lined with hooks on which hang waterproofs and fleeces, and underneath them is a shelf of boots; wellingtons, work boots and waders.

I'm taking all this in when a woman appears. Middle-aged. About my height and build, wearing cropped combat trousers and a T-shirt with a picture of a cat on it. She has short straight hair, platinum blonde, streaked with white.

"Sorry, I was baking," she wipes her hands on her trousers.

"Hello!" I say, trying to remember my lines. "Is this Môr Tawel?"

"Yes love."

"Um. So I was wondering if you had bed and breakfast for a few nights and if you had any, like, work experience here at the farm?"

I stumble over my words. My voice sounds hesitant.

The woman doesn't exactly smile, but her face relaxes.

"Ah!" she says. "I'm Rita. I won't shake your hand 'cos I'm covered in flour." Irish, I think. Mixed with other things, but definitely Irish. "What's your name?"

"Amy," I say.

"Grand," she says. "I'm glad you found us, Amy, because as a matter of fact we do have a room just now and I could use some help in the garden, come in and I'll put the kettle on."

She leads me through the anteroom into a big farm kitchen, its central feature a long, scratched, wooden table, every inch of its surface covered in stuff – stacks of books and magazines, herbs drying on a dish, pots of pickles, piles of papers. In the corner is a stove which I recognise as some sort of Aga, smaller than Fiona's, and yellowed with age. There's a smell of fresh baking, and I suddenly realise I'm hungry. I've barely eaten all day.

"I've just made some scones," Rita turns out a trayful, then places a huge orange teapot in front of me. I take a scone. It melts in my mouth, setting my taste buds on fire.

"So did you find us through the notice?" I don't know what she's talking about, but I nod anyway. "My daughter Catelen posted that. You're the first we've had, apart from the students."

"Does your daughter live here?" I ask.

"Oh no. Cate's in London doing law. She's twenty-six now."

I'm not sure what to say, even though it doesn't seem to bother Rita whether I talk or not. She busies herself in the kitchen while I drink tea, eat more scones, and look around. On the opposite wall is a shelf filled with little brown bottles and jars of vitamins. It looks like a health food store.

"Have you got any other children?" I say.

"We've a son, Adam, he's in Nottingham."

"Oh, that's near where I come from in Derbyshire." This gets over the awkward subject of where I'm supposed to have travelled from.

"Now I don't know that part of the world at all really," she says. "We don't see much of Adam these days, or Catelen, though we did get down to London for our thirtieth wedding anniversary last month. Thirty years, can you believe it?" She looks at me as though she's known me all her life. "Cate and Robert arranged it all as a surprise. They got Charlotte in to look after the farm and they booked us into a great hotel near the Thames. We'd tea at the Ritz and went to see Wicked, you know, the musical."

"Sounds amazing!" I say.

"It *was* amazing! We don't do that kind of thing very often. Tom doesn't like cities."

"Tom?"

"My other half. He's over at Huw Jones' just now. You'll meet Tom later of course."

As I sit in this kitchen, warmed by the stove, there's an almost palpable feeling of time slowing down. I feel I could stay in the presence of this easy-going woman forever. Rita pours more tea when my mug is empty, goes off to do something then comes back.

"I'll show you round in a bit but there's no rush. I hope you'll like it here Amy."

"I'm liking it already," I actually mean it.

"Have you much experience of the countryside?" she says.

"Um. I lived in a village near Derby so that was almost countryside, and when I was young we lived in Somerset and my parents had goats and geese and things and we grew vegetables."

"So what made them give all that up to move to Derby?" asks Rita.

"My parents were killed when I was ten and I went to live with my aunt."

Rita reaches for the teapot and refills my mug.

"You were young to lose both parents."

"It was tough but I'm over it now."

"That must be why you're so independent," she says.

"Am I?"

I don't see myself that way.

"I'd say so, a young girl like you finding your way out here on your own. A lot of people your age can't do anything without messaging their mates every two seconds. I haven't seen you take your phone out once!"

I laugh. "That's because I don't possess one."

"How refreshing," she says. "My daughter's permanently on hers and she complains she can never get a signal and our WIFI's useless. We're in a bit of a technological blind spot here."

"Suits me," I say. "All that stuff is over-rated."

"I can see we're going to get along," says Rita. "Will I show you around now?" She leads me through the kitchen into a dining room at the front of the house.

"Oh my God!" I say. "Look at that!" The room has large French windows opening out onto to a view of the sea.

"Magnificent, isn't it?" says Rita. "Come through."

The house sits at the top of a steep shingle beach. The tide is half-out, and across the strait, on the other side, I can see a row of dark mountains, the highest peaks capped with white.

"Are they the mountains I came through on the train?"

"Yes love. That's Snowdonia."

There's an area of raised decking in front of the house, with mismatched wooden and wicker furniture on it.

"This gets sun most of the day, if you're a sun-worshipper."

"Everyone says I'm pale," I say.

"A bit of this sea air'll put some colour on you," she says.

There's a crunch on the shingle and a man trudges past.

A white guy with dreads wearing waders and carrying a fishing rod. He sees Rita and nods. Close up he looks at least fifty. His face is furrowed and leathery. His eyes somehow lifeless.

"Is that Tom?"

"Oh no, Tom's over at Huw's. That's Bramwell. He's been camping in the top field."

She doesn't introduce me.

"Now I'll show you upstairs to your room."

My room looks out over that same view across the Strait. It's small, and crammed full of furniture. There's a single bed, a bulging bookcase, a pine dressing table under the window and a computer-desk in the corner with an old PC on it.

"This used to be Catelen's. Next door, which was my son's room, is bigger but it's still full of junk. This all right for you?"

"Sure," I say. "I love it."

"Plenty of hot water if you want to take a bath."

Chapter Twenty-Seven

I SOAK IN a stand-alone bath with feet, the sort people with designer bathrooms have, people like Fiona Carlotti. But I get the impression this has always been here. I can't remember the last time I had a bath. This is such a contrast to the scalding, sporadic shower at Balmoral Street. I lie back, the warm water lapping round my neck. Downstairs I can hear the strains of Latino music.

Afterwards, I feel drained, as though all the muscles in my body, so tense for so long, are saying 'Now we can relax.' The hot bath helped with that, now cooking smells from Rita's kitchen whet my appetite.

Rita is preparing a casserole while jigging around to the music. As I walk in she says. "I'm practising my moves. I go to Salsa every Wednesday. You can come with me if you fancy giving it a try." She puts the dish in the Aga, then says: "Now shall we take a stroll along the beach before we eat? We can take Rory." I really don't want to move. My body already aches from the exertions of the day, but I fear this could be a test of my resilience.

"What footwear have you got on?" she looks down at my Docs. "You'll be all right in those. Some people find it a little awkward on the cobbles."

Rory, the spaniel, seems as reluctant as me to shift. "Come on old man," says Rita "He's a bit creaky now, but he still likes a walk."

It is hard going on the shingle, but after a while I get the hang of which bits to walk on, pacing between the bigger rocks and avoiding the sharp stones. The soles of my feet start to feel like they're being massaged.

"We'll just go to the end there," says Rita.

The tide is further in now. We round a bend and see some cliffs rise up at the edge of the shingle. Then I see the shapes. Dark red rock structures loom up from the beach, giving everything a ruby hue, like some lunar landscape. In front of us is an archway, made of the same red stone, through which I can see a cave cut into the rock-face. One huge rock stands alone like a dark, brooding giant.

The dog sits on his haunches and growls.

"That's a sea stack," says Rita. "Rory doesn't like it. This is as far as we usually go."

"Is that a cave through there?"

"Yes, go and have a look if you like. We'll wait here." She perches on a boulder and gazes out to sea.

I walk through the stone arch and a little way into the cave. It's sheltered from the wind. I run my fingers along the side. It's damp and soft to my touch. High up on the wall, someone has carved the initials JAL and SCL.

I feel a pull towards this place, as though the cave is drawing me in. I walk a little further in, conscious of the seagulls' wail up above subsiding.

I feel removed from reality, a bit like the feeling I had walking down the lane, only this isn't so pleasant. It's like I'm in a trance. I try to turn around and leave the cave, but my limbs refuse to move, as though my feet are cemented to the earth. My head starts to thump. My vision blurs and my knees give way. I sink onto the damp floor of the cave.

Rory barks, short and sharp.

I push myself up, my head clears, and my pounding pulse propels me out of the cave to re-join Rita. Seeing her, serene, sitting on her rock, I feel ashamed of my panic.

"Ah here she is," says Rita, as we turn back towards Môr Tawel. "They're interesting geological features, aren't they? You've to be careful at high tide, you can get cut off here."

Back in Rita's kitchen, I'm conscious of someone filling the doorframe. Tom is the polar opposite of Rita. A huge presence. Not fat, just big. Wide shoulders. Muscles hardened from work. A mass of curly, greying hair. He smells of the earth.

"I'll say hello properly when I've cleaned up." He has the bus-driver's accent, but softer. He doesn't seem the least bit surprised to find a stranger in the kitchen. I get a proper look at him when he reappears, scrubbed up for supper. His skin browned by sun, wind and salt. He smiles a sort of half-smile as he sits down. "So you're going to be staying with us for a while?" His whole face seems to twinkle when he talks.

"If you'll have me."

"It'll be good to get some new ideas for the place. We're

getting set in our ways."

He talks like I'm entering a business venture.

We eat in the kitchen, the piles of papers pushed to one side. The meal is a lamb casserole, delicately spiced, washed down with a bottle of Rita's blackberry wine. As we eat they tell me about the farm.

They have nine acres, but rent three fields to a neighbour called Huw Jones, who Tom works for some of the time. They grow veg, keep hens and might be getting goats. Everything's organic, and they have a compost toilet. Rita tells me this several times. She must be really proud of it.

"Don't forget the bees," says Tom. Of course, the white slatted boxes I saw from the lane were beehives. "You won't see them yet though, they're all clustered together for warmth."

Tom looks after the bees, and they sell the honey.

They want to set themselves up as a social enterprise – whatever that is.

I'm supposed to help with the garden and feed the hens and stuff. They also want me to help with publicity. Rita will show me what to do tomorrow. I don't want to think about tomorrow. Surely once they realise they're dealing with someone who can't even keep a cactus alive they'll send me on my way.

Halfway through the meal someone shouts "Yoohoo" from the anteroom.

"Charlotte come and meet Amy," Rita calls. A woman of about thirty with a round face and a round body sticks her head round the door and says: "Nice to meet you Amy, you'll be seeing a lot of me." She's here to collect the fish. I'm glad they don't want me to do anything with them. I'm squeamish about things with heads.

Rita's blackberry wine is powerful and sweet. It lulls me into a dreamy well-fed mood. Tom just has one glass. Rita and I drink the rest of the bottle. Unlike Judith's dinner parties, or the rare occasions when I ate with the Carlottis, I feel comfortable sitting round a table with these people, even though I have no idea what I'm doing here. After the meal Rita brings out three shot glasses and a bottle of cherry liqueur. It's nearly ten pm by the time we make a move to clear up. We pile up the plates in the sink in the anteroom.

"This lot can wait till morning. Tom and I are off to bed now," says Rita, "Stay up as long as you like."

"Do I need to lock up or anything?" I've noticed all the doors are open.

"Ah no, we've an open house policy here," says Rita. "We never lock our door."

"Amazing," I say. "Where I come from if you don't barricade yourself in you're asking to be burgled."

Rita laughs. "Nobody can get here easily and even if they did, they couldn't get away in a hurry."

"Unless they came by boat," says Tom.

Up in my room, I open the window and take in a lungful of sea air. The tide is in almost up to the decking. Jay's right, the sea at Môr Tawel is not quiet, it roars as the waves crash against the shingle. There are lights on the water from boats and buoys, red and green to guide shipping across the strait. And little specks of light glow among the dark mountains on the opposite shore. The thought of houses nestled in among the slopes gives me a cosy feeling.

Less than twenty-four hours ago I was looking out of a different window at a landscape of wet roofs, contemplating suicide.

Balmoral Street seems a million miles away.

In bed, I listen to the waves. There are other sounds too, owls hooting, the rustle of trees in the wind, the rumble of a distant car. A dog barks somewhere along the beach, getting nearer, then I hear the crunch of boots on shingle as dog and owner walk by.

I got here, I tell Jay in my head. *I made it, and, at least for the moment, I'm actually happy.*

Chapter Twenty-Eight

SLEEP, SO ELUSIVE for so long, now comes irresistibly. In the little bed, I feel as though something wraps itself around me. I surrender to it. It feels soft, warm and benign. And in this thing I sleep.

I wake at first light, and wonder if I'll ever get used to the soulful cries of gulls. I pull back the curtains to see a new landscape, the tide now way out, patches of mud visible among the stones, leggy birds picking their way across. Two figures hunch near the water's edge, and closer in, a solitary walker strides, coat collar turned up against the cold, a dog trotting alongside. I leave the curtains open to let in the day, and fall back into slumber.

I wake to a faint tapping. Rita comes into the room, dressed and carrying tea.

"What time is it?"

"It's half past eight, love. I thought I'd let you lie in as you'd be tired from your journey. Did you sleep all right in that little bed?"

"I must have slept a whole nine hours!"

"Excellent," says Rita. "Never trust a woman who doesn't need much sleep!"

Moving over to the window, she sees Jay's drawing, which I've propped up against the dressing-table mirror.

"This you?" she says.

"Yes. A friend drew it. It's supposed to be Pre-Raphaelite."

"Gorgeous," she picks it up, looking at it closely. "You've some talented friends. You should frame this. We've lots of frames downstairs."

She replaces the picture then touches Barrel Woman's beads, which I've also placed on the dressing table. "A rosary?" she says. "You Catholic, Amy?"

I shake my head. "They belonged to someone I used to know," I say.

"I'm Catholic of course, being from County Kildare, but I'm not a very good one!" she laughs. "Take your time and come down when you're ready."

After she's gone, I dress, and look at myself in the long mirror on the landing. Already I look different. Gone is the guarded expression. I meet my own eyes direct. The voice, the critical one, is silent – in its place, a scary void.

What happens now?

My senses, numbed for so long, seem to have come alive. I'm keenly aware of smell, taste and vision. In Rita's kitchen I eat home-laid eggs, toast and blackberry jam. Everything tastes divine. My muscles feel like they've been massaged. And somewhere in my being there is a new sensation, a little shiver of anticipation.

Rita suggests I have a wander round and get my bearings. Later she will give me some jobs to do. I like that word, later. In Rita's world, it seems, there is plenty of time.

A hippy house, I think as I amble around. Wall hangings from far-off places. Plants everywhere, growing on every windowsill and on every spare bit of horizontal surface. I wander into a living room which leads off the dining room. There are two roomy sofas covered with oriental throws. Rory, lounging in one of them, thumps his tail as I walk in but doesn't bother to get up. An ancient record player sits on a sideboard. The only concession to modern life is a small TV in the corner. On the mantelpiece is a picture of a young woman in graduation garb. Tall, big boned, with voluminous dark hair under her cap.

"Is this your daughter?" I ask Tom, who walks in with a bucket of logs.

"Yes, that's Catelen."

"She looks like you!"

Tom twinkles. He starts stoking up the wood burner. "I'll light this, get a bit of heat going. There's a chill in the air," he adds.

There's another room leading off the dining room. I hesitate to go in as the door is shut, but Rita did say to have a look around. The curtains are drawn and my eyes take a few seconds to adjust to the dim light. The first thing I see, resting on a giant easel, is a huge, grotesque painting of a nude, its hips rounded, breasts hanging low like strange fruit, the face gaunt and cheeks hollow. Other canvases are laid out on surfaces or propped against the walls. Some are seascapes, others abstract splashes of colour, garish and surreal.

Without warning my body tenses as a sick feeling lurches in my stomach. My head starts to pound. I feel faint. I slump to the floor, my back against the wall, and try to control my breathing as my pulse slowly returns to normal.

I know what this is, of course, and I don't want it to happen again. Not here, not now. More than anything I fear the return of the scream.

"Ah, you've discovered Rita's art room."

Tom looks round the door at me. I jump up, like a kid caught doing something wrong.

"She said I could have a frame," I say, noticing some empty frames propped up against the wall. "Did she do these paintings?"

"A few of them are hers, most are by our son," he says, and turns tail. I get the impression this room is out of bounds. I pick a frame the right size for Jay's drawing and close the door behind me.

I SIT WITH a supersized mug of tea on the thick stone steps, looking out to sea. Although the breeze is chilling, I'm sheltered by the walls, sitting in a patch of sunlight trapped on the step. The spring tide is high, the edge of the water about ten feet from where I sit. A line of fresh seaweed marks the point it has reached. The tide is just on the turn.

The rhythmic roar of the waves enchanted me last night. Now I watch, mesmerised, the ebb and flow, the highs and lows. Whatever happens to me, I muse, doesn't matter to the sea. The tide will keep coming in and going out, twice a day, every single day, as it has since time began. As long as I can sit here, looking out across the strait at the dark mountains on the other side, everything will somehow work out right.

I shut my eyes, and my world fills with colour. The colour of mango. I bask as it permeates the dark corners of my mind, as, cell by cell, I come alive again.

On the step where I sit, somebody has placed a pebble. I pick it up and run my fingers across its surface. It's not smooth and shiny, as I imagine pebbles to be, but rough to the touch, and mottled, with bits that glint in the light. It fits neatly in my palm. I move my fingers round it. It feels cold. I look at it more closely. It has a pink hue, with flecks of black, a darker red, and grey, and across the surface there are little lines that look like veins. I have never looked so closely at a pebble.

Rita appears behind me. "That's quartzite," she says. "Metamorphic."

I vaguely remember what metamorphic means from school. Something that has changed and become something else, after being exposed to extreme pressure and temperature. I look at the pebble with new admiration. It's withstood a lot, and lived to tell the tale. Its trials have made it more beautiful.

"Can I keep this pebble?" I ask.

"Of course," says Rita. "Plenty more where that came from. Now will I take you to see the hens?"

Chapter Twenty-Nine

RITA LEADS ME round the back of the house onto the lane I walked down yesterday. Passing the gate with the painted sign that says 'Cae Sara' I ask, "What's through there?"

"Oh," says Rita. "It's a memorial to a little girl who died." I would like to have asked more, but Rita quickens her pace and I have to run to keep up. She leads me through a gate into a fenced enclosure. It's a sea of mud.

"These are the girls," she says, pointing out hens. Some of them start to follow us, squawking, as we walk through. "That's Branwen, Bronwen and Heulwen. They all have names."

"Welsh names?"

"They're Welsh hens! Bronwen means white breast. Heulwen means sunshine. And here's Eirwen, which means snow white. And the little brown one over there is Gwen."

"Am I supposed to remember them all?"

Rita laughs, "As long as you feed them they're not bothered. We're getting twenty more next month. You can name those ones." She scatters feed for them. "This will be one of your jobs. Great, here's an egg."

She shows me how to pick it up 'with a soft hand not an angry hand', then leaves me to get to know 'the girls' and hunt for more eggs. I find three in the hen house, all different colours and sizes, with straw and muck stuck to them. One is still warm. Then I sit on the wall in the sunshine, cradling the eggs, and wait for Rita to return.

In Stanlow I knew people who kept hens, but I've never before watched any close-up. The way they move interests me. They constantly wobble their heads around, while taking long, measured strides. How can something be restless and sedate at the same time? Their heads are tiny in proportion to their bodies. They have ugly little faces but beautiful plumage. Creatures of contrast.

I take deep breaths. The farmyard sounds and smells take me to a place I haven't been to for a very long time. A place that I want to go back to, but the shutters come down like they always do. Too much. Too painful. Then Rita reappears with an egg-box.

"Have you found some more? That's grand. D'you want to take them into the house? There's a stamp on the kitchen shelf. We've to stamp our code on each egg. You'll need to wipe the muck off them first. After you've done that meet me back here and I'll show you the garden."

I go in through the back door, locate the stamp and a little wire brush. My hands shake as I pick up the first egg, terrified it'll break. *You'll mess this up,* says the negative voice. *And they'll throw you out.* But I tell the voice to shut up. The new, calm me takes over as I gently brush and stamp each egg then leave the box on the kitchen table, all eggs intact. It's a small triumph, but I've got a feeling this is a taste of things to come. I breathe a deep sigh of satisfaction then pause before going back to Rita. I want to look once more at that amazing view. I walk back through the house to the dining room, to see the sea from the French windows.

It's here that it happens. I'm hit by a scent so powerful I'm convinced he's here. I even call out: "Jay?" and turn around but there's nobody here.

I walk into the living room where the stove is now alight. Then I realise what the smell is. Wood smoke mixed with the salt air of the sea.

Jay's smell.

Despite the heat being chucked out by the wood burner I shiver, and hurry back out to where Rita is waiting.

She takes me first to see the campers' field. The caravans are empty but people stay in them over the summer. They can also pitch tents on the grass. At the top of the field, hidden from view from the lane, I see a wooden wigwam. I recognise it from the drawing on the card Jay gave me. Its pointed roof silhouetted against the sky.

"I've seen a picture of that!" I say.

"Bramwell built it out of driftwood," says Rita, "It's where he stays."

"Isn't it cold?" I ask.

"He's insulated it with mats and sacking he found in the sheds."

I want to get a closer look but Rita steers me away. "I'll

show you the garden now."

She leads me through a labyrinth of paths, past a huge greenhouse, more sheds, a pile of panes of glass and a quad bike covered in mud.

The 'garden' is the size of half a field, divided into beds separated by little waist-high hedges. There's weeding to be done. This will be another of my jobs. Rita points out plants growing in the soil. Kale, rambling and messy, broad beans protected by canes, leeks and forced rhubarb, whatever that is. There are other beds covered in what she calls seaweed mulch, waiting to be planted. I stare at the vast expanse and wonder what I, of all people, can do with it.

I don't voice my concerns; scared Rita will recognise my uselessness and send me on my way. After just one night here I'm certain of one thing – nobody must deprive me of this haven.

So I set to work with the trowel Rita gives me, get down on my hands and knees and start to weed. "Ah you're a natural," says Rita. "I'll leave you to it for a bit and bring you a cup of tea later." Tea punctuates Rita's day.

Being small, I squat effortlessly, the sun warming my back until eventually I shed my hoodie and work in just leggings and t-shirt.

Once more, the smells of the place evoke strong emotion. Somerset, of course. The last time I scrabbled in the mud. The last time I held a trowel.

The sun hits a point mid-way up my back, and I feel a kind of euphoria, as though all the poison of the past few years is being beamed out of me. Already I feel a sense of space, to expand, to be, to shake off years of unwantedness.

Judith. Lynda Carver. The Carlottis. The girls in the Chorlton flatshare. And Balmoral Street, where I hadn't even wanted myself.

THAT NIGHT, I go to bed dog tired. Craving sleep, I long for that magical feeling I had the first night, but it doesn't come. My brain buzzes, keeping my exhausted limbs tense and alert for action. My stomach twists in agonising pain. My heart thumps loud and fast in my chest, a constant drumming. The anxiety I hoped was gone now comes full force. How fast can a person's heart beat before it explodes through their rib cage?

I'm sweating now, my breathing short and rapid. I get up, stumble over to the window and push down the heavy sash, leaning out so the sound of the waves can drown out the pounding of my pulse. It brings temporary relief. Then in the half-light I see a figure on the decking. I tense, with an intake of breath so sharp it nearly winds me. My vision swims. I blink, and try and focus on the figure, then spot the dreadlocks down his back. It's Bramwell, wrapped in a blanket, smoking. A whiff of weed floats up through the window and I'm back in Balmoral Street, creeping past Psycho-boy's door.

So you thought by running away you'd leave all that behind? It's no good. You can't escape.

I need Diazepam.

I shut the window and creep downstairs, in search of something to numb the senses. A painkiller, a shot of liqueur, anything to shut my brain off till morning when I can get an emergency appointment at the doctors. I was a fool to think I could do without the drugs.

In the kitchen I put on the light, and blinking in its glare I scour the shelf, but it's all herbal stuff. Not an aspirin in sight. And I don't know where they keep the liqueur.

There's a thumping sound coming from the corner of the room and I realise it's Rory in his bed, his tail beating against the floor. He's actually pleased to see me.

The kitchen door creaks open. I whip round, terrified, but it's Rita. Hair spiked up through sleep. She wears a huge t-shirt. One of Tom's presumably. It comes down almost to her knees. I notice her legs are all muscle.

"You ok Amy?"

I ask for a painkiller. She picks a bottle of something off the shelf and gives it to me to sniff. She gets me to sit down and asks where it hurts. I clutch my stomach. She takes my hand and presses on a point between my finger and thumb and starts to massage. Bizarrely, the cramp eases. I'm extra conscious that my hands are shaking.

"Are you taking anything?" she asks gently. I tell her about the Diazepam. "I haven't had any since the night before yesterday."

"Did you go cold turkey?"

"No. I cut down gradually over a few weeks, like the doctor told me to."

She picks a book up from the shelf. A thick hardback with a blue cover, and leafs through it.

"Those things are notoriously difficult to come off," she says. "The first seventy-two hours are the worst. You're almost there. You're doing really well."

She makes mint tea to soothe my stomach. We stay up a

while, sipping our tea. Rory, roused from his bed, comes to join us. He rests his head on my knees, looking up at me with big soulful eyes.

"That's the look of love," says Rita.

I feel calmer.

"I was impressed by what you did in the garden," she adds.

"Good," I say. "And sorry about tonight."

"Don't be," she says. "We'll get you through this. You've come to the right place."

Chapter Thirty

THEY SAY IT takes twenty-eight days to form a habit, and within a few weeks I feel as much a part of the place as the brickwork. Like the garlic and asparagus I've planted, I'm putting down roots. The late spring has sprung, we are getting super-moons and extra high tides. Rita says each year they get higher. The house is safe, it's elevated from the beach, but waves lash the decking. The power of the tides thrills me.

Ours is a busy life. Tom and Rita are up at dawn. I'm not far behind them, tending to my jobs, letting the chickens out, mucking out their shed, scattering feed, collecting eggs, weeding, putting out glass cloches and moving plants from the sheds and windowsills outside, harvesting the kale, more weeding, filling up the giant compost containers and rotating them when they are ready. All my clothes are mud-stained now. My docs caked. My fingernails dirty. But I don't care. I work all day, and as the nights get lighter I work in the evenings too. I go to bed tired, and mostly, I sleep.

Tom shows me the bees. It's time to start inspecting them. I put on a suit way too big for me, I have to roll up the sleeves and trousers. He tells me about their life cycle. In their first few weeks of life they progress through different jobs. Nurse bee, wax bee, housekeeper bee, guard bee then foragers. They have scout bees that go out looking for nectar then tell the others by doing a waggle dance. They even have funeral director bees.

"They're so organised!" I say.

They have moods too. Sometimes calm. Sometimes angry.

"You have to tell them when someone dies," Tom says. It strikes me as an odd thing to say.

I get a sense of achievement every time I master some new skill. I've even learnt to drive the tractor, *and* reverse it with a trailer on the back.

I'm proud of the organic principles they use here. I remember Judith bringing in a rotavator to churn up the earth, laying too-green lawn and spraying the paths, freaking out if even a dandelion got through. Here they're 'no dig' and of course, being organic, they don't use weed killer.

Charlotte pops in several times a week to box up veg for the organic veg scheme. We've got a chart up in the kitchen telling us what she needs when. Rita takes produce out to farmers' markets all around North Wales, and sometimes takes me with her.

Mid-morning, if it's sunny, I sit on my spot on the step, where I sat that first day. By now the sun has risen above the mountains and its rays beam straight in to my sheltered cocoon.

As I sit in the sun, time slows and life seems ripe with possibility. My world is filled with sound. The ever-present crash of waves on shingle, the soulful, anguished cries of the gulls, children's voices, distant across the water, the whine of a speed-boat, traffic just audible on the coast road. There is always a breeze at Môr Tawel, but here on my step I'm sheltered, and as the rays hit my arms I have a sense of awakening. Sunshine, so rarely seen in my recent winter of discontent, is abundant here.

Balmoral Street now seems like something that happened in a bad dream. I sometimes wonder which is real; this life, or my life there, which was only half a life. I wonder about Jay. I miss him. I talk to him in my head. *Look at me now, Jay. Look at the difference a few weeks has made to me.*

He knew about Môr Tawel. He must have been here. But how? And when? And why did he ban me from mentioning him? Did he leave on bad terms? His name plays on my tongue many times, while talking to Rita, or Tom, or Charlotte, or other people who pop in. 'I had this friend Jay in Manchester…' but something holds me back. Superstition, maybe? Like mentioning his name will break the spell and all this will melt away.

He said he would come and find me here one day.

Rory has taken to following me around. As I set off in the morning on my rounds, he plods after me, then flops to the ground as I work. I've never lived with a dog, and to begin with it unnerved me, him being always there, hanging on my every movement. But I've grown to love this creature and the total faith he puts in me.

There are cats here too, mostly semi-wild. They sleep in the outhouses and come into the yard to be fed. Unneutered and thin, they remind me of the feral cats that hung around the restaurants in Greece, on holiday with Judith, the ones I used to feed under the table when Judith wasn't looking.

Like the hens, the cats all have names, even the kittens. There's Fred and Frankie and Blackie and Miranda. The current kittens are Sammy, Freda and Lucky Simon. Lucky because he's jet black and is the only one allowed inside the house. He got injured soon after he was born and Rita took him in to nurse him.

Charlotte says the place is full of assorted strays, and that goes for a lot of the people that show up here too.

"Not you," she adds quickly. "I mean people like Bramwell."

We rarely see Bramwell. He doesn't join us in the house or on the decking. Occasionally I glimpse him fishing, or sitting outside his wigwam, deep in meditation. I've never heard him speak.

In my early days here, I got a lot of strange sensations. Headaches, shakes, and violent stomach cramps. Withdrawal from the Diazepam, of course. My mood swung wildly between meteoric highs and abject fear, but when the jitters threatened to take over Rita was always there, helping me over it, never judging, letting me do whatever I needed to do to feel ok again.

"What are you afraid of?" she asked.

"I'm scared I'll scream the place down."

"Scream if you want to," she said. "Go out onto the

middle of the fields and scream where there's nobody to hear. Scream and shout and let it all out. Lord knows I've done that before now."

I looked at her. Hard to imagine calm, rational Rita screaming. I didn't go into the fields, but I did walk some distance along the beach. What came out was more of a wail than a scream, lost in the roar of the water. I went back to my chores feeling a small sense of liberation.

She took me to an acupuncturist in Beaumaris, someone she goes to regularly. This woman stuck pins in my feet and arms and I lay there, feeling nothing. Then she stuck one right in the centre of my chest. That one hit the spot. I felt release.

Rita supplies me daily from her shelf of natural remedies, little bottles of oils and jars of vitamins and other supplements. Iodine, B12, magnesium, potassium, you name it, I'm taking it to build me up.

"I'm not a believer in conventional medicine," she says. It explains why there's not so much as an aspirin in the house and a big pile of magazines called 'What Doctors Don't Tell You' stacked up in the kitchen.

"So many things people pop pills for. Headaches, insomnia, depression. Look at the prescriptions handed out. Billions of anti depressants every year. People spend all day sitting in front of a computer, getting headaches and eyestrain and getting fat, then take pills to counteract all that. Don't get me wrong, Amy, I'm not judging anybody, I just believe you don't have to live like that."

"I took Diazepam for anxiety," I say. "It just made me dopey and confused."

Chapter Thirty-One

TODAY IS SUNDAY, and Rita drops me in Beaumaris where I'm setting up a stall in a mini-market opposite the castle. I'm selling eggs, cherry liqueur, chutneys and honey. While I'm there Rita heads off to the nearby church. "Every now and then I feel the urge to make my peace," she says.

There are only six stalls. Next to me is a man selling watercolours and ceramics, which people look at but don't buy. Other stalls do a steady trade in cheeses, locally brewed beer and bara brith – a kind of Welsh currant bread. Although it's not yet the holiday season, Beaumaris is buzzing. There's a sign across the road which says 'Art exhibition this way.'

My neighbouring stallholder glares at a purple and white VW Beetle pulling up on the pavement next to the stalls. I recognise this car from the day I arrived in Bangor. Out steps the man I saw at the station. He's wearing black leather trousers and boots, a fitted military jacket, open, revealing a leather waistcoat and white lace-edged shirt with a purple cravat. His hair hangs loose and very straight past his shoulders, parted down the middle. He lifts a canvas from the back of his car and walks off with it under his arm. The man next to me says. "It's at times like this you wish you'd see a traffic warden."

"Who *is* that?" I say.

"Local artist," grunts the man. "Lionel Rees-Prosser. Teaches at the college. Thinks he's God's gift. I wouldn't mind, but his art's not even any good."

A few minutes later, Lionel returns, minus the painting. He stops by my stall. He gives me that same look of half recognition he gave me at the station. Picking up a bottle of cherry liqueur, he looks me in the eye and says: "Have you got any of that rowanberry vodka you had last time? That stuff blew my mind!" His accent is Welsh, but less harsh than most of the people round here. It's softer and more musical.

"Sorry – not today," I don't tell him this is the first time I've been here.

"Well I'd better take this then!" he hugs the liqueur to him then fishes for a note in the pocket of his trousers. They fit like a skin, so the note takes some extracting. "Damn, I've only got a fifty!" he says. The man next to me tuts. Lionel leans in towards me. "What's eating *him*?" he says in a loud stage whisper. I notice he has green eyes. I shrug. Lionel walks off, brandishing his bottle like a trophy. As he drives off in the purple and white Beetle he gives two short toots of his horn.

I sell three boxes of eggs, two chutneys and a couple of pots of honey. After the church kicks out trade picks up.

Later at Môr Tawel, after counting up the takings on the kitchen table, I step out onto the decking. Now it's April there's real warmth from the sun. I see a figure in the sea, some way out, head bobbing with the waves. I stand up for a better look. The figure waves. I realise it's Rita. She asked me earlier if I fancied a swim. I thought she was joking. I watch as she floats for a while on her back, then does a strong front crawl back to shore. As she emerges I see she's naked apart from a pair of black swimming shoes. I watch, fascinated, as she runs up the beach, her limbs sinewy, her breasts low. It occurs to me I have never seen a woman her age naked. I'm reminded of the nude in the painting. I look away.

That evening Tom and Rita's daughter Catelen turns up in a four-by-four with her boyfriend Robert. They're on their way to Holyhead to catch a ferry to Ireland. I hear her before I see her.

"Mam the privet's taking over, soon you won't be able to open the gate. What happened to 'I'll clear it after Christmas?'"

"Feel free to have a go while you're here Cate, you know where the shears are!" Rita responds.

"Like I've got time to do gardening! I thought you had someone to help now Mam. Where is she?"

I'm summoned to the kitchen. Cate is a big woman, built like her father. She wears jeans and long boots and a Nordic jumper. She towers over her boyfriend, who says little. They are both barristers.

When she sees me she says: "At last someone to get this place in some semblance of order! I hear you're doing a fantastic job in the garden." Her accent is a mix of Welsh and southern English.

I wonder if I should make myself scarce but it's made clear I'm one of the family. We have a meal in the dining room, with wine. "Pinot Grigio, Mam, to make a change from your home-made poison."

Over lunch we talk about the super-moons, the high tides, and the sensitive subject of the Môr Tawel finances. I've seen the books. I know Rita and Tom are skint. But I still feel awkward when Cate quizzes them about return on investment. Rita makes suitably elusive answers.

"Perhaps now Amy's here you can start to diversify," says Catelen. "Make use of the top field."

"It's overrun with Himalayan Balsam at the moment," says Tom. "That stuff gets everywhere."

"That's why we're getting goats," says Rita. "They'll clear the lot."

"How about alpacas as well?" says Cate. "Alpacas are a thing you know."

I've seen photos of alpacas. Like llamas. Like camels without the humps.

"I suppose you keep them for the wool?" says Rita.

"You can do lots of things with them. You can hire them out for weddings."

Tom laughs, choking on his drink. "What do alpacas do at weddings? Are they the ring-bearers?"

We talk about London, and Charlotte, and other people I've not heard of. Then Catelen says: "Adam's landscape gardening business is really taking off you know." I'm surprised. Rita and Tom never mention their son. I thought the subject was taboo. "And he's teaching horticulture at the University too, he's loving it!"

Rita mumbles: "That's grand" and gets up to clear the plates.

After dinner Catelen takes me to one side and says: "It's great you're here. You can tell Mam really likes you."

I glow.

"Maybe you can get her to get on with things. They really ought to be bringing more money in. Mam loses focus easily and she can't say no to people, but I get the impression you're more focused."

By the time Catelen leaves my head is buzzing with her suggestions for developing the business, like turning the front field into a proper campsite, replacing the old caravans with log cabins, setting up school visits, opening a tea-shop and developing an online presence. And, of course, the alpacas. After she's gone I mention these suggestions to Rita, who just says, "that's Cate for you, always full of ideas, that one."

The house has had little done to it over the years. What investments there have been are to make the place greener, like solar panels on the roof, and the compost loo. I wasn't sure about this at first, now I love using it. It sits in a sort of tree house. You climb steep steps to get to it and do your ablutions from a great height. You then chuck earth over what you've done and it turns, eventually, to compost. Amazingly, it doesn't smell.

I wonder what my former friends would think of me

now, living on the earth and pooing on compost, barely a mobile device in sight. I picture Hannah, Stacey and Sinead, living out their suburban lives filled with petty infidelities and local outrage. It occurs to me that those people, once so important in my life, have shrunk. What I'm doing now is global.

Chapter Thirty-Two

*I*T'S HALLOWEEN, THE *day before my fifteenth birthday. I'm at the Carvers' Halloween ball. Everyone's in costume. I'm a witch. Wearing a Goth dress and lots of kohl.*

Iain sees me arrive. "You look older"' he says. He's angry with me for getting older. Tonight Iain is Dracula with a white face and fangs.

I'm talking to The Joker in the kitchen. No idea who he is. His make-up's good. What you drinking? He says. Cider. I say. Want some vodka in that?

I'm outside, alone, leaning on the wall in the gap between the Carvers' and next door.

I'm round here smoking. Not sure how I got here. Iain is here, he's taken his fangs out. He's still angry. "Don't smoke Amy!" He takes the cigarette from my hand, drops it and crunches it into the ground. Now I'm pushed against the wall and Dracula is kissing me. My brain swirls as his tongue bores into my head. I feel the bile rise within me.

"Amy are you drunk?" My head lolls and I can't stand up. Iain holds me up, propped against the wall. He pulls me to him, his mouth next to my ear and says: "That didn't happen."

He leads me back inside.

Lying at Judith's, watching the ceiling gyrate, I keep repeating. That didn't happen.

"DID YOU HAVE a nightmare last night?" Rita asks.

"Don't remember. Why?"

"You cried out."

"Oh, I hope I didn't wake you up."

"It's ok," said Rita. "Dreams have their purpose."

Only in sleep does my turbulent past play out. Sometimes I wake drenched and breathless after a dream featuring Hannah or the Carlottis or Balmoral Street, or worse – Iain, but one whiff of the salt air brings relief.

Rita never pries into my past. Sometimes she prompts me to talk about my early childhood in Somerset. I want to remember, but I can't. She doesn't push it.

Chapter Thirty-Three

I WAKE TO hear music coming from downstairs. I look at the clock. Three am. Strange. I wonder if Rita left her radio on by mistake. I get up, and make my way downstairs. The door to the living room is open and I stop in my tracks, gawping at the sight. Rita's little radio is on the table and Bramwell is there, swaying to the music, arms in the air, then swooping low. The music isn't Rita's usual Salsa, it's more a kind of wordless wailing, with a tribal drumbeat. I glimpse Bramwell's face through the open door. His eyes are half shut. He seems to be in a kind of trance. I creep back upstairs.

Next morning Rita tells me Bramwell's gone. "He's dismantled the wigwam, taken his things and gone."

"Did he say anything?"

Has Bramwell ever said anything?

"He said, and you mustn't take this the wrong way, he said now that you're here he doesn't need to be here any more. His work is done."

I laugh. Apart from fishing, I've never actually seen Bramwell do anything resembling work.

"I think his work was spiritual," Rita says. "And you know what the weird thing is? I looked up the date he arrived. It was exactly a year ago."

I'm glad he's gone as he slightly freaked me out. I wish he hadn't destroyed the wigwam though.

"How come he came here in the first place?"

"My son told him about us. He met him on his travels."

"So was Bramwell in Nottingham?"

"Not Adam, my other son."

Rita walks away.

Nobody told me she has another son.

Chapter Thirty-Four

I'M OUTSIDE WITH Rita and Charlotte, catching some afternoon sunshine. It's now mid April, and warm enough to sit on the decking. I notice what looks like a procession approaching along the beach. As they get closer I see children of varying sizes, a scrawny dog and a woman with long dark hair and an awkward gait. Their clothes are ill fitting and old-fashioned. They look like a family of refugees.

"Uh oh!" says Charlotte, "Look what's coming."

"Who are they?" I say.

"That's Maria and her tribe," says Rita. "They'll have walked from Menai Bridge."

"All the way with all those children?" I count at least five. "Are they heading here?"

"Oh yes," says Charlotte. "Time I was out of here."

The children range from about four to teenage. The younger ones jump from boulder to boulder, and run to the water's edge. The older ones plod alongside their mother, who is limping.

"People call her walking woman because she walks everywhere. You see her walking all over North Wales," says Rita. "We thought when she had the children she'd stop, but they all walk with her."

Maria is dark, greying, late 30s or 40s, hair half-way down her back. Her face is thin and drawn. She has pupils the wrong size, like the addicts on Balmoral Street.

She doesn't introduce herself, just climbs up onto the decking and finds herself a seat.

"Bella Bella!" she calls out. It takes me a moment to realise she's talking to the dog.

"*Paid â mynd yn rhy bell,*" she shouts at one of the girls who leads the younger kids down to the water. A boy, slightly taller than Maria, stays by her side. "Don't go too far," he translates, perhaps for my benefit. He's dressed in clothes that wouldn't look out of place on a fifty-year-old – chino trousers with a jumper, shirt and tie. He must be about fourteen. The boy turns to face me and does a little bow. "I'm Aneurin. Named after the sixth century prince of poets. But you can call me Nye."

"Hi Nye," I say.

"Cup of tea please Rita and can we have a bowl of water for the dog?" says Maria.

She speaks Italian to the dog, Welsh to the children and English to everyone else, and jumps randomly from one to the other.

"Have you been down Llandudno this week?" to Rita.

"*Bella Bella. Siediti!*" to the Dog.

"*Dos â hi i ffwrdd!*" to a child who brought her a crab's claw.

"Take it away," says the boy.

"Maria, this is Amy," says Rita. Maria looks at me, as if noticing me for the first time. Her eyes are glassy blue. Her pupils pinpricks. She doesn't smile, but says: "Good to see some youth around here again, *yn tydi hynny'n wir, blantos?*"

"Isn't that right, kids?" Nye translates.

Rita goes inside to get some drinks. Maria leans over to me, lowers her voice and says: "She had a terrible time you know, with the children. Terrible."

I have no idea what she is talking about and suspect she might be mad. "What children?" I say. Maria breaks off to yell at the dog then says, "Did you not know? Well I won't be the one to tell you. I've been in enough trouble already. You'd better ask her yourself, but you'll have to pick your moment."

She produces an ancient mobile phone, says, "There's no signal on this damn thing," stands up, holding it up against the wall of the house, walks away with it and comes back to her seat again. Her restlessness unnerves me. I make my excuses and retreat to the sanity of my garden. "Pretty girl that one," I hear her comment, to no one in particular, as I leave.

"So what did you think of Maria?" Tom says later, a smile playing on his lips.

"She's kind of interesting, isn't she?"

He laughs. "Mad Maz, our children call her, though Rita says we mustn't call her that."

"I know what you mean Tom, she's got issues!"

"Social Services bought her a treadmill."

"Why?"

"She's got compulsive walking disorder or something. She's worn out her feet pounding the pavements. That's why she limps."

Tom tells me Maria and her husband live in separate houses but meet up every now and then to create babies. Her husband is a lot older than her and is some sort of landed aristocracy which means money is no object.

This surprises me. "They don't look rich."

"They look like a bunch of urchins, don't they? All dressed from charity shops. She doesn't believe in spending money on clothes. She home-schools all the kids you know."

I wonder what they learn.

Later that evening, when Charlotte returns with the veg boxes, I walk her to her car.

"You know that Maria woman who came earlier?"

Charlotte rolls her eyes. "Mad Maz," she says. "I stay away from her in case she drives *me* mad!"

I tell Charlotte what Maria said about Rita and the children, and ask what it could have meant.

"Oh, didn't you know?" says Charlotte, drawing closer to me, "Rita had two other kids. Twins. A boy and a girl. Both died in tragic accidents. But don't say anything. Rita doesn't like to talk about them."

"Oh my God!" I say. "What were their names?"

"The little girl was called Sara." (she pronounces it Sarra), "The boy was Jude."

"Sara, like in 'Cae Sara'?"

"Yes. It means Sara's field. Rita put it aside as a sort of

remembrance place. Sara was only eight. It was a canoeing accident in the Brecon Beacons. School trip. Tragic! Five children drowned. You probably saw it on the news."

"Oh my God!" I say. "And what about the boy?"

"He died later. He was a lot older. They said it was a climbing accident."

She lowers her voice, even though we are well outside earshot of the house. "Mad Maz is a medium, you know, one of these people who contacts the dead. I think it's a load of old rubbish but anyway, after Jude died she kept on at Rita to have a séance. Said Rita's kids were trying to get through to her. Rita refused. She wouldn't have Maria here for a while. It caused a lot of ill feeling."

As I walk back into the house, my heart goes out to Tom and Rita, so quiet in their grief.

Chapter Thirty-Five

I T'S TOO WET to go out, so I mooch around the living
room. It is not often I find myself here alone. Usually I'm
outside or in the kitchen or dining room. We only really
come in here in the evenings to watch TV.

I stop by the vintage record player. It sits on a glass-
fronted sideboard full of vinyl. I slide open the door and leaf
through the albums. Iconic covers from the 60s and 70s –
Rita and Tom's era. The Bowie one with the lightning bolt
on his face, the Pink Floyd one with the man on fire.
There's other stuff I've never heard of. Some of the artists
have Welsh names.

Then I stop in my tracks. Something about the faded
brown cover tugs at me.

I have seen this before. A long time ago.

There's a picture of an orange globe behind the
lettering, which says 'Harvest'.

I pick up the album and run my fingers along the cover,

rough card, brown, with a dark picture of the band on one side and a blurred, distorted photo of the artist on the inside cover. It is exactly as I remember it.

Just then Tom pokes his head round the door.

"Can I put this record on?" I say.

"Course you can. You like a spot of Neil Young do you?"

"I don't know. I can't remember."

"It's a fine album," he says, moving closer and taking the record from me. "I haven't listened to any vinyl for years, though it's cool again now. That turntable was made in the 60s but it still works a dream."

"Will you show me how to work it?" I say.

He balances the record, pulls the arm across and flicks a switch to make the record drop. Then it plays.

As Neil Young's distinctive cracked falsetto voice launches into 'Out on the Weekend' I stand, transfixed, and transported. Back to a place I have almost forgotten. A place I have blocked out for fourteen years.

The place before the crash.

Running around with the other children who belonged to Mum and Dad's friends. Charging round the house. Dad lifting me onto his shoulders. Dad playing along to this very song on his guitar.

A place where I was happy.

I feel like someone waking from a coma.

They wouldn't let me say goodbye. They bundled me up, frightened and confused and took me to Judith's tidy house, the place where I couldn't breathe. They wouldn't let me go back, to wander through the house, one last time.

Now memories come in a sudden flood, vivid and unstoppable. My eyes swim.

"You ok, Amy?" I almost forgot Tom is here.

"My parents had this record. I haven't heard it since…"

"You ok?" his face is searching.

"I'll be fine," I say, smiling through my tears.

"I'll leave you to your memories," he says.

I remember all the songs, and when it gets to 'Heart of Gold' I turn the volume to full blast and belt out the words.

Later, the rain cleared, I go outside. But I can't settle to my tasks. The memories are still coming, at first fluffy, impressionistic, then clear and vivid.

A lawn full of daisies and dandelions. A border, poppies, big smiling sunflowers. Beyond the lawn, a field with ponies. Runner beans scrambling up poles. Cabbages green and crinkled, close to the ground. Bushes heavy with fruit. My parents working in the garden, me following with a child's trowel, pottering, playing, picking. Splashing in puddles in yellow spotty wellingtons.

They were outdoors people, my mum and dad, and my early years were spent under the sun, the rain, the snow.

My dad was a joiner. The smell of wood sometimes hits me with an unbearable pang. He made furniture and fittings for boats. He kitted out canal barges. And he made things for me. A swing, a rocking horse, a seesaw. When it snowed, I had the best-made sledge in the village.

As I sit on the wall, all these years on, watching the hens with their funny jerky walk, tears well up from some unfathomable source. Sights, sounds, smells – all the senses now bring that other life back to me. And after a long, long time, the tears stop. The well is spent.

"Someone has brought me to another garden," I say out loud.

Rita finds me there on the wall, my face washed out with tears. And I say. "I've been remembering."

I tell her about my parents' place in Somerset, how I'd blocked it out for so long, how being here has unlocked the memories in vivid detail. I tell her how I feel certain that if my parents saw me now, they'd be proud. I tell her she and Tom are a bit like my own lost parents. As I say it I feel the tears smart up again.

"Have a good cry," says Rita. "It's been a long time coming."

I don't even know why I'm crying. I'm happy now, here. But I'm scared.

"I'm scared all this will end like everything else good in my life has ended," I say.

"Everything ends," says Rita. "Life itself is temporary. But you've nothing to fear here, we love having you. You can stay as long as you like."

I hug her.

It's something I've never done before, hugged Rita. She hugs me back, briefly, but her body stiffens, then she pulls away and I see her eyes, too, are glistening.

She says, "God moves in mysterious ways."

"What d'you mean?"

"I've often wondered what unlikely set of circumstances or twist of fortune brought you to our door. Whatever it was, I thank the Universe."

I'm so tempted to enlighten her, to tell her about the

guy who came, night after night to my room in Balmoral Street, who sent me to this place. I want to blurt it all out. But I remember his words, and I stay silent.

Chapter Thirty-Six

I 'M ON MY knees, earthing up potatoes, when Maria visits again, this time alone and approaching from the lane, not along the beach. She cuts through the garden towards the back door. She's clutching a rolled-up magazine.

"Is Rita there?" she brushes past me, not waiting for an answer, letting herself into the house.

After a while she re-emerges. This time she stops and watches as I work. I'm conscious of her eyes boring into me as I mound soil around the leafy shoots and draw it into a ridge, leaving a channel for the water to flow down to the roots.

"We sow what we reap, we reap what we sow," she says. "The law of cause and effect. And we are all under this law. You mark my words." She has the same spaced-out look in her eyes as when I met her the first time and the same capacity to unnerve me. She limps off up the lane.

A few minutes later Rita appears with two mugs of tea.

"Amy love, come and sit down," she leads me to a bench in the sun. She is carrying the magazine Maria had. I sense that something has changed.

I feel my heart thump against my chest, chilled by a sudden dread Rita will tell me they no longer require my services.

Rita opens the magazine, and there, staring up from the page, under a headline 'Missing, can you help?' is a picture of me.

"Oh my God!" I gasp.

"This is the Big Issue, North Wales edition. Maria spotted it," says Rita.

The picture is old, from when I was about twenty, with straightened hair, wearing a blue Topshop coat. It dates from Stanlow days, light years ago. I read the accompanying blurb.

Amy Blue, last seen in Manchester, where she had been working as a nanny. Amy left the house where she was working on September 14th last year and has not been seen since. Her family are concerned about her because she had been feeling depressed. It is thought she may be living in North Wales.

"Family?" I say. "Judith must have put that in."

"So Amy," Rita moves a little closer. "Do you want to tell me what happened? It's ok, I won't judge."

For the second time, I tell my story. Judith. The Carvers. Iain. The Carlottis. Howard. The baby. The breakdown. I give a précised version, skipping over details, the words spilling out of me. It takes two pots of tea to get up to date. At the point where I talk about the baby Rita puts her arm on my shoulders, and again when I tell her about the overdoses. Otherwise she barely interrupts.

"So," says Rita, when I've reached the end of my story. "Are you going to contact your aunt?"

"I sent her a post-card when I first moved here to say I was ok. That must be how she knew I was in Wales. I didn't give her an address. I didn't want her turning up here."

"When did you last speak to her?"

"She phoned me when she heard I quit my job at the Carlottis. It was when I was off my head on Diazepam. I think I blurted out something about the miscarriage. Soon after that I lost my mobile so she had no way of contacting me."

Rita touches me, briefly, on the shoulder. "You're welcome to use the phone here to give her a call, just to let her know you're ok," says Rita. "I know you didn't get on but she must be worried to put this in the Big Issue."

"I will," I say. "I will."

Chapter Thirty-Seven

"WE'VE GOT SOME campers staying tonight," says Rita, "two Finnish girls." They arrive mid-afternoon, weary from walking, and I realise I recognise them. It's the two girls from the train, the ones with the sturdy boots and giant backpacks.

"We worked at the hotel for two months," says one. "Now we are walking the Anglesey coastal path. We saw this place on the Internet!"

"We're not an official campsite," I say, "But you're welcome to pitch a tent in the field and make a donation to the running of the farm." I show them the field, the barbecue on the beach, the compost loo. No shower, just a cold hosepipe or a dip in the sea. The girls take it in their stride. Later, after they've cooked up sausages on the beach, I take them a glass of cherry liqueur and we chat.

After this, it becomes one of my jobs to look after the campers. They come in all varieties, from teenage to geriatric. Some look like they couldn't walk a mile let alone the 200 plus of the coastal path. They come in all nationalities too. And they mostly conform to stereotype.

German women with sturdy boots like to know the rules and stick to them. They also pay handsomely. Australians on gap years arrive in big groups, drink lager on the beach and cook up meat on the barbecue. Americans sometimes move on when they learn there's no shower, others brave out the cold hosepipe or a dip in the straits. A young Spanish student appears one day with a bouzouki protruding from his backpack.

"You look like Spanish girl," he says. He stays three nights and serenades me on the decking in the evening. He wears a chain of wooden rosary beads around his neck. I think of Barrel Woman.

"This is pilgrimage," he says. "Next year, Santiago de Compostela. You know Compostela?"

"Er, no," I say.

"It's pilgrimage. Very spiritual place. I go there next year. You come too, Amy. You come with me?"

They share their food, their music and their life stories with me. I've become the unofficial campers' rep. What starts as a trickle becomes a trail, the word spread by social media.

"Mam you really ought to cash in on all of this," says Cate on her next visit. "This place is becoming legendary. I saw a tweet the other day describing Môr Tawel as the epitome of cool."

"It's cool because it's free," I say. And anyway to start

charging we'd have to comply to health and safety standards and it isn't worth it. Better to keep it like it is. Unofficial. And cool.

Chapter Thirty-Eight

"PHONE CALL FOR you Amy."

"For *me?*"

Apart from Judith, who I wrote to giving my address and the Môr Tawel phone number under strict instructions not to share with anyone, nobody knows where I am.

"Amy, this is Fiona Carlotti."

My first instinct is to put the phone down and run, but that clipped staccato voice still has authority over me. Fiona is not a person to say no to.

"I got your number from your aunt. I need to come and see you. It's important. I need to ask you something. I'll drive up to Wales. When can you get time off?"

The conversation is perfunctory. She doesn't ask me how I am, or what I am doing here in Wales. I put the phone down having arranged to meet her in a café in Bangor on Thursday.

Strange, I muse as I prepare to meet my former

employer, how once you get your life back on track people who disowned you suddenly want to know you again. First Judith, now Fiona.

Fiona phones just before I leave to check the meeting is still on, and it strikes me she sounds almost desperate. Haughty Fiona, who hardly gave me the time of day when she employed me, now, apparently, needs something from me.

It's another glorious day, and I feel ambivalent. Once, I would have worried about what to wear, would have examined my reflection with the same critical eye I expected from Fiona. Not today. I glance briefly in the mirror, see someone tanned and healthy looking back, and skip downstairs to where Rita is waiting in the van.

"You nervous?" asks Rita as we rumble up the drive.

"Not really. More curious to know what she could possibly want from me."

"She might offer you your old job back?"

"No chance. She couldn't stand me. And there's absolutely no way in a million years I'd go back there. I'm happy where I am."

Fiona Carlotti stands out in the café. Her aura of affluence and aloofness sets her apart. She rises as she sees me walk in. I notice she's heavily pregnant. She doesn't smile, but her face relaxes slightly.

"Amy," she says. "Thank you for coming."

As I sit down I realise this is the first time she ever thanked me for anything.

"So how are you?" I say, indicating the bump. "Congratulations by the way."

Fiona flushes. Another first. Can frosty Fiona possibly be embarrassed?

"I'm good. Due in four weeks. You're looking very well," she scrutinises me.

"Thanks, I'm working outdoors now, on a farm, growing organic veg and stuff. I'm living by the sea. I like it."

I feel free. This woman no longer has power over me. I am only here out of good will. I can leave at any time. Fiona says nothing.

"It was a surprise to hear from you, Fiona," I try to hasten the meeting to its purpose.

"It's not really a social call. We owe you money. Three weeks' salary. I have a cheque for you here."

"Thanks!" I say, astounded. "But I never expected you to pay me because I left without giving notice. Hope I didn't leave you too much in the shit!"

Fiona baulks as I recite Howard's words back at her.

"Well, we coped. But I need to ask you why you left."

Her tone is accusing, and my instinct is to walk out, but looking at Fiona I sense something close to desperation in her manner.

"Sorry Amy, you don't have to tell me, it's just…" Fiona breaks off, stifling back tears.

"Fiona are you ok? Has something happened?"

She fishes a tissue out of her bag, pulls herself together, and says: "After you left, we hired another girl. A Polish girl Howard got from the Internet. She was gorgeous, of course. They always are. Anyway after about two months the same thing happened."

"What d'you mean, the same thing?"

"She left abruptly. And she really did leave us in the shit."

"Maybe she went back to Poland?"

Fiona shakes her head. "She's still in England. She's been in touch. She's claiming Howard raped her."

I feel the blood drain from my face.

"She's been to the Police, and now she's threatening to go to the press."

"What did the Police say?"

"They came to the house to interview Howard. They haven't charged him. They say she left it too long before reporting it and there's no evidence. It's his word against hers."

"So what does Howard say?"

"Says he never laid a finger on her."

Fiona stares at the table. During the whole conversation she has not lifted her eyes to meet mine once.

"Well if it's his word against hers and there's no evidence they won't be able to prosecute," I say.

"No," says Fiona, and snivels again.

"What's the matter? Don't you think they'll believe him?"

At last, Fiona looks up, her eyes narrow and dark. "I don't know if *I* believe him."

"Ah," I say.

"That's why I wanted to talk to you. Because I suspected, you see. I've been suspicious for a long time about Howard and the au pairs. The way you left so suddenly. It seemed out of character."

I see my former boss as I haven't seen her before. A person hurt and jaded. A person not at peace. And the power to release her, I know, rests with me.

"Do you really want to know the truth?"

I've never liked this woman, but she's suffering now. She needs to know.

So I tell her what happened the night before I left, while she was visiting her mother in Altrincham. How Howard came in, plied me with drink, then forced himself on me.

I watch Fiona as I speak. I get the feeling that I'm driving a knife in, each word a further thrust.

"Did you consent to sex?"

"No."

"Did you try to fight him off?"

"No."

"You let him?"

"I tried to push him away but he wasn't taking no for an answer. My main thought was to get it over with so I could get out of there."

I watch Fiona grappling with the information.

"He must have thought you wanted it. He must have felt in some way you encouraged him."

This is more like the old Fiona. It has to be someone else's fault. But the difference is, now, I have the power.

"I don't know what he thought, Fiona, but I can assure you I did nothing to encourage him in any way at any time. I felt powerless in that situation which is why I didn't fight. Technically, it may or may not have been rape. I don't know. But I'm not going to prosecute and I'm not going to go to the press so that's one less thing for you to worry about." I grab my jacket and stand up. Fiona motions me to stay.

"Please don't go, Amy. I believe you. I really do. It's just such a shitty thing to get my head around. Did he try and contact you afterwards?"

"He never made contact."

"You sure? You never heard from him again?" She studies my face.

"Well I…"

"Amy I have to know. I need the truth, however ghastly."

"Ok Fiona, but again, you're not going to like it." I tell her about the pregnancy. How I'd phoned him at work. How I thought he ought to know.

Fiona nods, looking directly at me.

"He told me to get rid of it. He sent me a cheque for a thousand pounds."

"And did you? Did you have a termination?"

"No. I decided I wanted to keep my baby. I hung on to the money to spend when it was born. But I lost the baby anyway. I lost it at eleven weeks."

"Oh!" Fiona's voice lifts, then remembering herself says, "But it was probably for the best."

"Things have worked out okay," I say. Then, remembering something, I fish around in my bag and produce a folded piece of paper. In all the excitement of coming to Wales and the busyness of life at Môr Tawel I'd forgotten about the cheque until now.

"Howard's cheque. I never cashed it. You can have it back if you want."

Stapled to the cheque is a compliment slip with a note saying, "As promised. For the procedure. H."

Fiona shakes her head. "Proof, if ever I needed any." She pushes the paper back towards me. "Keep the money Amy. Cash it quick, it'll expire soon. You were a good worker when you were with us and you didn't deserve what happened to you. Keep it and buy yourself some new seeds or a strimmer or whatever organic gardeners need," she looks at me more closely now. "You really do look well you know. You always used to be so pale."

We make no arrangements to keep in touch. There's no point in pretending we will ever be friends or have anything to talk about. As I watch her waddle out of the café in her designer maternity gear I experience an emotion I've never felt in relation to Fiona. Pity.

On my way back to meet Rita I stop at a bank and pay in two cheques. One for my last month's salary at the Carlottis, the other, Howard's blood money.

Chapter Thirty-Nine

IT'S A FRIDAY morning in mid May when Rita gets the call. Her octogenarian mother has taken very ill in her care home in Dublin and is not expected to last the weekend. Tom and Rita both go, leaving me in charge.

It's the first time I've been properly alone in this extraordinary place, and I wander from room to room like I'm seeing things for the first time. I find it hard to settle, so I throw myself into my duties for the rest of the day. It's evening time when, sitting out front in my favourite spot on the step, watching the waves, I hear the rumble of an engine coming down the lane. Rory, sprawled out at my feet, looks up, and trots off to investigate.

Any vehicle approaching the house can be heard some way off. It could be friends, campers, people collecting or delivering, fishermen or winkle pickers taking advantage of a short cut to the beach. Some people take a wrong turning then can't turn round in the narrow lane till they reach the house. Often, they stop to admire the view before turning back.

I hear the engine stop, and wait for the footfall on the shingle, but it doesn't come. Neither does the vehicle turn back again. I begin to feel a slight unease. I haven't locked the doors, of course. Nobody ever does here.

Rory would alert me, usually, if there's a stranger around. He has a single warning bark, or a volley of barks if he sees someone as a threat. But Rory remains silent, and does not reappear.

Should I go and check this out? My sense of unease is growing as it dawns on me I'm alone here, in this remote spot, nobody even within calling distance. To make any move would involve announcing my presence. I can't exactly creep along the shingle beach to see who's there.

For a second I'm back in Balmoral Street, cowering in my attic listening to Psycho-boy's mates marauding up the stairs. It's warm, but I shiver, shrinking into the step.

"This is silly," I tell myself. "This isn't Balmoral Street, this is Môr Tawel. Everyone who comes here is cool." But putting ourselves out there on the Internet has widened the net. More people know about us. This could be anyone.

Still Rory does not bark.

I take a deep breath. Whoever it is can't possibly know I'm here on my own, anyway, can they? I straighten up on the step. Then heavy footsteps approach from behind me, they must have come *through* the house. I whip round, to see a tall figure, wearing motorbike leathers.

And for a second, I think it's *him*. Similar height, blond hair, wide face, but as I look closer I see it's not him, but someone altogether more solid. There are similarities, but this guy is broad where Jay is thin. And older than Jay, the eyes narrower and darker, the face tanned and less perfect.

"Hey," he says. "You must be the legendary Amy." I notice Rory in tow behind him.

Realisation dawns. This must be…

"Adam," he leans forward to shake my hand. "Sorry to intrude!"

I find my voice. "That's absolutely fine Adam, but Rita and Tom aren't home."

"I know," he says. "That's why I'm here."

He smiles. A broad smile that seems familiar yet unfamiliar.

"What d'you mean?"

"I heard the folks are away so I thought this is a good time to come and take a look at the old place." He leans on the wall, his eyes sweeping the panoramic view beyond the strait. "D'you like it here?"

"I totally love it. It's amazing!" I tell him with feeling.

"I know," he says. "Spoilt, weren't we?"

"Don't you miss it?" I say.

"All the time," he says. "There's no sea in Nottingham."

I laugh. "Have you come from there today – all the way on a bike?"

"Yeah, it's a nice run. Perfect weather for it."

I figure he's late twenties, early thirties perhaps.

"D'you want a cup of tea?"

"I'll get you one," He motions for me to sit back down, and walks towards the house. Rory stays with me this time.

When Adam reappears, he's changed out of the leathers

into jeans and a t-shirt. He hands me a mug of tea then sits on the edge of the decking, swinging his feet. He looks younger out of his motorbike gear.

"So," he says. "Cate says you're doing an amazing job and Mam loves having you!"

I swell a little. "Really? It works both ways."

"Says you're the best thing to happen to Mam since J."

"J?"

"My brother. You know about him, yeah?"

"J is for Jude, right?" My heart is beating so fast I feel it could break my ribcage.

"Jude, yeah. But most people called him Jay. Except Mam and Dad. Fancy calling your son after the patron saint of lost causes!"

He goes to take a shower, leaving me reeling. The idea forming in my mind is unbelievable, of course, but I can't move away from it. I have to know. Sensitive though the subject is, I've got to somehow bring the conversation back to his brother.

After his shower, Adam roots around in the kitchen, fixing us both something to eat. He has an easy way about him. There is zero awkwardness. After we've eaten, he says, "Hey, fancy going for a spin on the bike? There's a spare helmet somewhere. Have you been to Penmon?"

"Rita sent me there once on a push-bike. It killed me!"

He laughs.

He unearths a helmet from one of the outhouses and an old leather jacket. The bike is big, a Suzuki 750, red. I haven't been on the back of a bike since riding illegal pillion on Harry Cole's scooter at school.

Adam starts the engine. "Hop on!" he says. I clamber on.

"What do I hang onto? You or the bar?" I shout over the noise of the engine.

He lifts his visor. "Either, but if you don't want to fall off, hold onto me. Tight."

I do so. He then turns round, grinning, and says, "Oh and you lean the same way as me, right?"

"I know *that*."

We trundle up the lane, swing out onto the coast road and accelerate. With my arms around this man, who has appeared out of nowhere, a 750-cc engine between my legs, the wind blowing my hair under the helmet, and the fantastical idea that's been swilling round my brain ever since he mentioned his brother, I feel a scary sort of high, like anything could happen.

We stop at Penmon Point, looking out towards the lighthouse and Puffin Island. It's windy up here and the waves are huge.

"We used to bring the kayaks to Penmon beach," he says. "It was exciting 'cos the waves are bigger here. But it's dodgy 'cos of the currents. You can get chucked against the rocks."

I think of his little sister, drowned on a canoeing trip, and of his brother, killed, they say, falling off cliffs. Despite the leather jacket, I shiver. I look at Adam, and he shudders too.

"Come on, let's go," he says.

Back on the bike, the road climbs away from the coast with a view of a sweeping sandy beach stretched out below. We take a pretty inland route across to Beaumaris. He pulls up outside a pub.

"Fancy a drink?"

The George is old, with low ceilings and black wooden beams. The barman knows Adam.

"You back?"

"Just for the weekend," says Adam. "I'll have a pint of dizzy blonde. What you having Amy?"

We sit in an alcove by a window overlooking the street. We talk about Wales, and motorbikes, and gardening. He's got his own landscape gardening business over in Nottingham and he teaches horticulture. I realise it's a long time since I've been for a drink with anyone approaching my own age.

"So," he says, sinking his lips into his pint. "What's your story?"

"Me? I haven't got a story."

"I don't believe that. There must be a reason why someone like you would opt for voluntary exile in the far north-west corner of Wales! What did Derby do to you?"

"Actually I wasn't living in Derby at the time," I say. "I came here to get away from Manchester."

"I have a personal grievance against the place," he says. "It's where my brother was living before he died."

My pulse starts to race again.

"Really, where?"

"Oh God it was a real shithole. I only went there once, to pick up his stuff after he died. East of the city. Off the road out towards Saddleworth."

"D'you remember the name of the street?"

"Nah. Though hang on a minute. If it's still in my contacts I'll tell you." He consults his phone.

"Balmoral Street, M11."

"I know it," I say, faintly, blood rushing to my face.

"Really?"

"I used to live there, and you're right, it's a dump."

He looks at me intently, suddenly energised. "Hey did you know him, Jay? Is that how come you're here?"

I can feel the heat rising. I must be puce-red. I look away. "I don't think so. I couldn't have – they say he died three years ago?"

"Four, this year."

"It's not possible. I only moved there in December."

"Oh," he says. "So it's just a spooky co-incidence." He's still scrutinising me as my face returns to normal.

"Very spooky," I say, and to break the tension, I add. "I moved to Manchester to get away from Derbyshire 'cos my family and friends disowned me."

"Really?" he leans forward.

"Yeah. Had an affair with my boss who was also my best friend's dad. It didn't end well."

So I tell the story for a third time. Unlike when I told Jay – when I cried a lot – or when I told Rita – when I played down some of the details, this time, I don't cast myself in the role of victim, more the femme fatale. As I talk, I'm conscious of Adam's attention. He laps up the story. He wants detail.

Then I move onto Wilmslow and the Carlottis. "You're not going to tell me you had an affair with him too?"

"Not exactly." Again I play down the victim element, emphasising instead how I insisted on keeping the baby. When I describe how Howard washed his hands of it, Adam mutters "tosser" under his breath. When I reach the bit about losing the baby, he says "hey," and reaches out to touch my arm. My skin tingles.

"Then I washed up on Balmoral Street. Not exactly sure how. It's all a blur. Lived there three months, then came here. So that, for what it's worth, is my story."

"That's epic," he says. "And I'll say this for you. You're hard-core. You've lived through more crises than most people have in a lifetime and you're, what, twenty?"

"Twenty-four, please!"

"Another?" he says.

"I'll get them," I say. "Another Dizzy Blonde?"

He looks at me sideways and says, "Think I'll move onto something darker. Can you get me an extra cold Guinness?"

"Thanks for coming out," he says when I return with the drinks. "I'm enjoying this."

"Me too," I say. "I'd have been on my own at the house tonight if you hadn't showed up. Rory's great company but the conversation gets a bit one-sided."

At that point, Adam spots something or someone on the street outside, and presses himself into the alcove so as not to be seen from the road.

"Hiding from someone?" I say.

"Just… someone I used to know."

I look out of the window, I see a chunky blonde woman retreating down the street.

"Was she a dizzy blonde?"

Adam laughs and drains his pint.

"Better not have any more here. Shall we go back and raid my mam's home-brew?"

Riding back, the wind chilly under the visor, I want this evening to go on forever.

Chapter Forty

AT MÔR TAWEL we sit opposite each other at the kitchen table, leaving the doors open so we can hear the roar of the waves outside. The tide is in and it's only just dark.

"I love this time of year," he says, inhaling deeply.

"Me too."

As we sup blackberry wine out of porcelain goblets, I turn the conversation back to Jay. I have most of the pieces, I just need to be sure.

"Did your brother Jay look like you?" I wonder instantly if this is too trivial a question.

To my relief, he laughs.

"He was much prettier than me. I'll show you a picture. Wanna see a photo of Jay?"

I try to sound casual. "If you've got one. There don't seem to be any on display." I hope he can't hear my heart pounding.

"Mam keeps them hidden away," he says. "Doesn't like to be reminded."

He scrolls through his phone then says, "All the ones I had of Jay were on my old Sim but I'll see what I can find."

He starts rummaging in the cupboard under the stairs, pulling out random items. "D'you play?" he presents me with a stringless guitar. Then he unearths a box full of framed photos and loose prints which he brings to the table. He starts leafing through them.

"That's Jay."

He pushes a picture towards me. For the second time today an icy wave spreads up my spine, for there, looking up at me from the photograph, is the face I saw, night after night, back in Balmoral Street.

"Oh my God!" I say.

"What's up?" he scrutinises me again.

"It's just – he's so beautiful."

Adam moves behind me, leaning on my chair, looking at the photo over my shoulder. I'm extra conscious of his closeness.

"Yeah, pretty boy, our Jay. He's got that angelic look."

"How old was he in this photo?" he looks younger than when I saw him, but not by much.

"About seventeen."

"And how old was he when he died?"

"Nineteen."

"Did he die in Manchester?" could this be why his spectre haunts Balmoral Street? Although that doesn't fit with what they said about a climbing accident.

"No. He came back here to die."

"What, on purpose?"

"I guess so," Adam moves round to the other side of the table and stares at me. "You know *how* he died, don't you?"

"I heard it was a climbing accident."

Adam snorts. "An accident! Is there no end to my mother's denial? It was suicide." He almost spits the word out, and starts pacing around the room. "Jay killed himself, Amy. Threw himself off South Stack cliffs."

"Oh my God! No!"

"Yes, he came back here to die. Saw everyone before he did it. Said his goodbyes, except we didn't know they were goodbyes. He'd planned it all, obviously. Devious little bastard."

"But why, Adam? Why did he do it?"

"Who knows? Only him. And he's not here to enlighten us. He didn't leave a note or anything." Adam is still pacing. "Some people reckon he wasn't really right since Sara died. Like half of him had gone anyway. They were twins, you know."

I nod.

"Here, let me show you a picture of Sara."

He flicks through the box, and shows me a photo of four children on the beach outside the house. Three of the four, I recognise, although they're all younger. The fourth is a little girl with dark curly hair and enormous brown eyes.

"What was she like?"

He smiles. "Sara had a mind of her own. Even when she was three! She was the live wire. Full of energy. Nothing phased her. She looked after Jay. She was the one who did things first. He was the dreamer." Adam goes into a dream

211

of his own as he says this, his eyes fixed on the middle distance.

"Sorry to make you talk about sad things," I say.

"It's ok. We didn't talk enough, when it happened, and when we did, I said all the wrong things. That's why I'm persona non-grata round here."

"And why you wait till they're away to come visit?"

"Yes. Giving you all the family shit to sift over. Sorry!"

"I don't mind," I say. "Your family fascinates me."

We carry on talking as we work through the wine, then crack open another bottle. It's almost light by the time I finally head towards bed at four am.

"I'll crash on the sofa-bed," he says. "That's assuming you don't mind me sleeping in the house?"

"Why would I? It's your house."

"I can sleep in the caravan if you'd prefer not to be alone in a remote farmhouse with a strange man?"

"It's not like I don't know you from Adam," I say. We both laugh.

In bed, I can't sleep. I don't want to. Part of me fears he'll disappear when I do, like his brother used to.

My brain races. When I met Jay, he'd been dead four years. That makes him, technically, a ghost. Everything he'd said at Balmoral Street, how he helped me out of my bad headspace, his disappointment when I nearly overdosed on pills on my last day, now makes sense. He'd been there too. He understood. I have all the pieces, but the enormity of it is mind-blowing. And why send me here, to Môr Tawel? To help his mother? To help me? Or both? I wish I could see him again. I speak to him in my head.

I've met your brother. I understand now. What you said about depression, about suicide. You wanted me to avoid the mistakes you made, and you're somehow using me to help your family.

Jay stays silent, and absent.

I turn my thoughts instead to the brother holed up on the sofa downstairs. I re-run our conversations, and think of more things to say to him. I'm certain of one thing: I want to spend many more hours in the company of this man.

Chapter Forty-One

S LEEP ELUDES ME until about half past seven in the morning. I wake at nine, feeling like I've overslept. The house is quiet. Adam must still be asleep.

It's another glorious day. I pull on a pair of shorts which show off my legs and a strappy red top which sets off my colouring. I take more care of my appearance than I have for months. I even put some make-up on.

I pause a moment by the full-length mirror on the landing. I catch my reflection, the shafts of sunlight glint across my hair. My eyes are bright, my body toned and tanned. I look myself in the eye and remember Jay's words. His words when I asked him, "What will I find there?"

"You'll find you, Amy Blue. You'll find you."

Downstairs, there's no sign of life. The door to the living room is slightly open and the curtains are drawn back to let the light in. "Morning!" I call, but the only response is a faint mew from Lucky Simon, who emerges from the room. Going in, I see the sofa bed's been put back together. Adam's leather jacket is gone from the back of the chair in the kitchen where he left it last night. I go outside. The Suzuki is gone. How didn't I hear him leave? Has he gone for good? Back to Nottingham? Without even a goodbye? Or maybe he's just gone out somewhere and will return. He did say he was here for the weekend.

I tell myself this feeling of loss is irrational. How can I miss someone I've known less than twenty-four hours? But he's sparked some new emotion in me. And as the day passes it looks increasingly like he's just left. I'm late letting the chickens out. I go about my chores half-heartedly, listening for a rumble on the lane that doesn't come. The house, filled with talk and laughter the night before, feels empty, and I'm conscious of my every move within it. Again, I can't settle. I'm even a bit tearful.

Charlotte calls by in the afternoon. She's heard from Rita. "Tom's coming back tomorrow but Rita's staying for as long as it takes," she says. "How you doing here all alone?"

I tell her about Adam. "Not sure if he's coming back."

"You never know with him," she says. "Law unto himself. He upsets Rita every time he sees her."

"He said he was here for the weekend," I say.

"Well maybe he's gone over to see his girlfriend, if that's still on."

"Oh, who's that?"

"Someone he's been with for years, on and off. More off than on, I hear. Lives over in Menai Bridge." Suddenly I want Charlotte to go. I want to be alone.

By late afternoon, I've given up hope of Adam returning. I sit on the step clutching my metamorphic pebble, and I let the tears come. I'm still in this spot when, about six pm, I hear a rumble down the lane, and yes, it's indisputably a motorbike. Just time to rush upstairs and tidy up my face, the make-up I put on earlier now smudged and ugly. He walks into the house. "Anyone home?"

"That you, Adam? Thought you'd gone back to Nottingham." I try to sound casual.

"I'm staying another night if you'll have me." This is a new look on his face I'd describe as sheepish.

"You must have got up early?"

"Yeah, couldn't sleep, so I took a spin round the island. I went up to South Stack to think. It's the best time of day, early in the morning, before the tourists."

He doesn't elaborate on what he's been doing the rest of the day, and I don't ask. I wonder about the blonde I saw walking past the George.

"Hey, there's whitebait in the sea, shall we catch some for tea?" he says. "We can cook them up on the beach."

Just down the beach from the house, there's a small fishing weir made up of a semi-circle of stones embedded in the mud, exposed at low tide. It traps small fish as the tide goes out.

"I've never done fishing," I say.

"It's easy. You just stand there. And you need to put these on," he produces a pair of Rita's thigh-length waders. "Sexy!" he says once I have them on. Adam doesn't bother with waders. He goes in in shorts and crocs. We use nets to catch the tiny, silvery fish. I'm amazed at how many there

217

are.

"Can you catch other types of fish here?" I say.

"There's plaice sometimes, or bass, but you have to go out on a boat to do that. Once in a blue moon Dad goes out with his mate and catches a load of bass." I remember the fish in the sink on my first day.

"Jay used to stand here for hours, bringing back all sorts of stuff. He caught two eels once," says Adam.

We fry the whitebait whole, and eat it with bread and mayonnaise, washed down by Rita's wine.

"Shall we have some music out here?" says Adam.

"You got a means to play it?"

"My phone."

I laugh. "I've been listening to records on your parents' ancient record player."

"So what music d'you like, Amy?"

"My musical education mostly came from my ex and he was forty, so it's a bit retro. When I was a teenager I was into rap!"

"Hmm," says Adam. "Take a look at my collection," handing me his phone.

"What's this? Indy through the ages? Quite retro yourself."

"It spans six decades," he says.

"What's this Welsh band? I never heard any Welsh music."

"They're from near here. Absolute genius. There's a whole Welsh music scene, you know. We're a musical nation."

We listen to music on Adam's phone, sitting on the

beach.

"Reckon we'll get complaints from the neighbours?"

Adam laughs. "Dad says this sounds like the tinny transistor radio he had when he was a teenager. He used to listen to it under the bedclothes at night. Pirate radio broadcast from a ship. That's how cool my dad was."

We talk till dawn again, moving inside once it gets cold. Here the conversation turns to more sombre subjects.

"My family's been here for generations you know," he pours me a glass of wine. "My dad grew up at the farm, and his dad before him. When we were little my nain still lived with us."

"D'you think you'll carry it on yourself?"

"Hard to say," he says. "That was always the intention. That was the idea behind me studying horticulture. Jay was never a contender. He wasn't much practical use."

"Good at fishing though?"

"Fishing. Art. Poetry. Philosophy. Amateur psychology. Good at ambling around. Sometimes he could spend hours on end doing nothing. Other times he was totally manic. I'm convinced he was bipolar, though it never got diagnosed. Mam refused to believe there was anything wrong with him. After he died she refused to accept it was suicide."

"I liked the photos you showed me," I say, hoping he will find some more.

"Hurts looking at them, even after all this time," he says, shaking his head. "Of course, you know what it's like to lose someone close. But suicide!"

"Did everyone blame themselves?"

He shrugs. "I blamed everyone *but* myself, but mostly I blamed him, Jay. I'd have conversations with him in my head saying Jay, you fucking idiot, what have you done to this family?" He takes a gulp of wine, draining his glass, and pours another.

"I was angry. With everything and everyone. I said some things to Mam and Dad that were unforgiveable. Then I walked out."

"What did you say?"

"I blamed Mam for not getting him diagnosed. I probably blamed her for Sara too. Then I said I never wanted to set foot in this house of death again. Mam was in tears. Dad came after me. He was angry too. Told me not to come back till I've learnt some sensitivity."

"And have you?" I say.

He does his sheepish look again. "Maybe!" He sighs. "I've been back since, but it always ends in tears. Even after four years, it's still raw. It's better if I stay away."

It's equally hard, this morning, to drag myself away from him to my room. I feel giddy on so little sleep, the constant flow of wine and talking to someone so intense all night. It's been a long time since I've really connected with someone my own age. Some of the campers are young, but they're here today, gone tomorrow. The conversation's superficial. Adam, like his brother, is different, but unlike his brother, is very real and very male. Again, I re-run the evening, hanging on every word that passed between us.

This time, taking no chances, I get up at eight. He surfaces some time later, yawning, apparently in no hurry to leave. And the magic of the night still hangs around. We fry up the remainder of the whitebait for breakfast, which we eat outside. I feel every second should be savoured. Soon he'll be gone.

He leaves around midday. This time he says goodbye. "Since you are the only person on the planet under thirty with no mobile, I'll do this the old-fashioned way," he says, handing me a piece of paper with his number and email addresses on it. "Come to Nottingham, look me up. I'll show you the college. You'll love it," he says.

"Thanks, I think I will,"

He grabs my shoulder. "I've enjoyed this weekend," he says. "You've been excellent company. I'm glad you're here. Really glad." It is the first time he's touched me apart from that formal handshake when he arrived and when he touched my arm in the pub. It sends electric sensations through my body. He pulls me to him, hugs me quickly then gets onto the bike. I watch him ride up the lane. When he comes to the bend, he turns and waves.

"BEEN COOKING?" TOM looks at the burnt charcoal in the barbecue. Adam said not to tell them anything, unless they ask.

"Uh huh," I nod. "I caught some whitebait yesterday. I hope you don't mind?"

"On your own?"

I don't want to lie to Tom and Rita. "No, um, Adam dropped by. He showed me how to catch fish in the weir."

Tom's expression gives nothing away. "Adam? Well, well! Has he gone now?"

"Yes. He said to say hello."

Chapter Forty-Two

I T'S THE FIRST evening it's been just me and Tom. This could be awkward. I don't know the rules of the game. Who will cook? Having had Adam for company for the past two days, normality is already disrupted. I'm not good at making the rules. I fit in with other people's way of doing things. Judith. Iain. The Carlottis, and now Tom and Rita. Tom seems ill at ease too, shuffling in his great frame. I reflect on the difference between father and son, Adam, utterly at home in his own body, Tom, now he's alone in the house with me, gauche and uncommunicative.

I do something I'm not used to doing. I take control.

"Tom," I say. "I haven't got anything in for tea. Fancy fish and chips?"

"Sounds fantastic."

I take Rita's little van, stopping at the shop to buy some real ale. Tom's not a big drinker, but I've noticed when visitors come he likes a beer or two. I reckon he could use one tonight.

We eat in the living room, putting the telly on to ease the awkwardness.

"How's Rita taking it?" I venture.

"Oh she's bearing up. She's a strong woman."

"You must both be strong given what you've been through."

He nods. "You know Amy, you never get used to the loss of a child. It's the worst thing."

"It must be. And to lose *two* children, I can't even imagine it."

He sighs, his shoulders slumping. "Never a day goes by when I don't think about them. Both of them. Then of course, you feel guilty about the others."

"Adam and Cate are okay, though?"

"Cate, yes, she just gets on with things, but Adam... How did he seem to you?"

"He seemed good. But of course I don't really know him. Shame he doesn't come here more often."

Tom straightens out his back and stretches in the seat. "Adam and Rita wind each other up. Adam gets angry and Rita gets upset. It's best they stay away from each other at the moment."

"Rita doesn't seem to talk about the children who died. I always feel it's a subject I should avoid." I say.

Tom doesn't look at me. He takes a long draught from his beer then says, "After Sara died she talked a lot, and we grieved properly, I think, but Jude was different. She was very, very close to him. And his death was more... controversial. It really cut her up. That's when the arguments started with Adam and it all got very emotional. She needs to come to terms with her grief in her own time. We have to respect that."

"It'll take time, but she'll get there," I say.

"I'll drink to that," says Tom, raising his glass.

Tom takes himself off to bed early, leaving me to ponder. Something is different. I'm not quite sure what, then I have it. I have spent the evening alone in the house with an older man and he didn't come onto me, nor try to take advantage of me in any way.

In this place, at last, I feel safe.

Over the next few days, Tom and I rub along in a companionable enough way, but though I try to steer conversations back to the subject of Jay and Adam, Tom doesn't really respond, and I don't push it.

For the first time since I came to Môr Tawel I feel dissatisfied. The weekend with Adam has made me crave company of my own age. Apart from a couple of middle-aged Germans staying in the caravan there are no other campers to relieve the tedium. I wander around the place, unable to settle to anything. Usually, my jobs absorb my attention. Not now. And the creatures around me seem to pick up on my mood. Rory keeps standing, scratching the earth, rotating multiple times before flopping down again, sighing. The chickens are squabbling. Even the bees seem agitated.

Perhaps it is this restlessness that makes me sign up to an art class at the college in town. When I enrol, I see a purple and white VW Beetle in the car park. I know Lionel Rees Prosser teaches art and I wonder if he will be my tutor.

He isn't. It's a woman called Rhianna, and I look around at my fellow students I see most of them are over fifty. Then in walks Bridget Llewellyn, who's about my age. I've met her before as her dad's a friend of Tom's. We chat as we daub pastels onto paper.

"How's it going at the Lloyd's place?" she says. "I used to go there a lot when I was a kid. I was at school with Jay. You know about him?"

"Yes. Tragic story. What was he like?"

"Gorgeous and very intense. He was an Emo when I knew him, dyed his hair black and gloomed around a lot. We all did, but Jay took it to extremes. He was incredibly, like, moody. Sometimes high as a kite, other times really down. Looking back, you could see it coming. When I heard what happened it didn't surprise me."

"D'you think he was bi-polar?"

"Quite possibly. But it never got diagnosed, thanks to his mam. Don't get me wrong, Rita's a lovely woman but she never used to take the kids to the doctor 'cos she doesn't trust doctors. Rumour has it she even refused treatment for him. I lost touch with Jay in the sixth form 'cos he started hanging round with this arty crowd. They were all a bit up themselves. Not my scene."

I ask if Jay had girlfriends.

"Not as such. He had plenty of girls hanging around him all the time, but I never knew him to have an actual relationship. He was like an honorary girl. Great to talk to. I suppose he might've been gay. A lot of people fancied him. He didn't like people getting close, physically close I mean. He'd have intense emotional relationships but that was all he seemed to be interested in. We called him Jay the untouchable."

"So did you know the rest of the family?"

"A bit. Adam was interesting. Much more of an alpha male than Jay. No ambiguity there! When I was about fourteen I fancied the pants off him but he just saw me as an annoying kid who hung around with his brother."

Chapter Forty-Three

WHEN I GET home, I sit down at the computer and get online. It's a slow, patchy connection. Apart from rare updates to the Môr Tawel social media, I hardly use the Internet these days. I haven't used my Hotmail account since I left Stanlow and I'm not sure it still works, but I want to contact Adam. Logging on, I'm told 'your session has expired. Do you want to re-activate this account?' Answering yes, I'm relieved to see no mail waiting for me. Perhaps the system wipes everything after some period of time.

I type

– Hi Adam. Good to meet you at the weekend. Hope you got back ok. Tom is home now, he asked if I'd had company so I said you dropped by. Hope that's ok. Wondered if you could send me some info about the college you teach at? I'm seriously thinking of taking this gardening thing a bit further.

My words don't do justice to the way I'm feeling. They

sound bland. I start again.

> *– Hey Adam. I enjoyed this weekend. Glad you dropped by. Enjoyed our chats. You helped fill in some of the gaps about your family, which as you know fascinates me.*

No, that sounds creepy. I need to stay casual. In the end I settle for

> *– Great to meet you at the weekend. Hope you and the bike survived the epic journey back. Thanks for taking me out round the island and for teaching me to fish. Now I feel like an honorary Lloyd! Thanks for filling in some of the gaps in Lloyd family history. Your family fascinates me. Tom is back now, he noticed bits of fish in the barbecue so I told him you dropped by. Hope that's ok. Btw I'm interested in more info about your college as I'm seriously thinking of taking this horticulture thing further. Bye for now. Amy.*

I leave it a good twenty-four hours before checking my emails. Nothing from Adam, but my inbox has filled up with stuff going back years. I'm about to trash the whole lot when the words 'Mail from IAIN CARVER' jump off the screen at me. Then as I skim the list of messages and spam, I see there are others. He's emailed me on July 15th, September 12th, November 5th, 10th and 23rd and January 31st. Then there's a gap until April. He's still using the secret Hotmail address he set up just for me. He hasn't fessed up to that one, then. My gut tells me to delete them all, but curiosity wins. I'll just open the most recent message, dated April 27th. It reads.

> *– Amy. I'm writing this in the vain hope it will reach you.*

Judith said you finally got in touch and you're in Wales. I still miss you terribly. My life hasn't been the same since you left. I need to see you, just once, to convince myself you're ok. My job has changed, I'm now on the road a lot more. I could come to Wales to meet up with you – just name the place and time and I'll be there.

I still love you. Please get in touch. Iain xxxx

I feel as though my innards are being squeezed. I pick another at random, November 5th:

– Amy your aunt says you left the family you were living with and she doesn't know where you are. Amy PLEEEEASE get in touch. I'm going out of my mind picturing what could have happened to you.

I feel totally depressed, stuck here, not able to see you, hear your voice, touch you. I miss you TERRIBLY. You don't realise what you did to me, leaving like that. I know I reacted badly when the news came out. I was in a corner and I didn't know which way to run. I was trying to please everyone and ended up pleasing nobody. Worst of all is losing you. Please, please get in touch.

I love you more than I've ever loved anyone and I always will.

Iain xxxx ps if you need money, let me know

January 31st

– Amy, I don't know why I'm wasting my time firing off emails into a void, when I get no word from you. You can be so cruel.

I've heard terrible rumours about you. Is it true you lost a baby? I felt terrible when I heard that, at the thought of you being with someone else. Nobody could love you like I did and still do. You know that don't you? I also heard you're an addict living on the streets somewhere. But I can't believe that, the thought of it kills me. I wish you'd let me look after you. I'll send you money, get you a flat to live in, ANYTHING Amy, just to have you in my life again.

I go through a whole gamut of emotions as I read each one. Anger, fear, nostalgia, but perhaps the strongest, and most dangerous, is curiosity.

He's only a mouse click away.

Chapter Forty-Four

AFTER READING ALL Iain's messages, one after the other, I get up from the computer and move around the house in a daze, his words ringing in my ears. He's still there, waiting for me. He hasn't moved on at all. I feel a certain pride that I can stir such strong emotions in him, to make him carry on sending messages 'into a void'. I remember how I felt, telling Adam about him. How alive, as if recalling the passion, the momentum, the sheer adrenaline of the whole thing reawakened me. And Adam reacted differently to other people I've told. At home, all I got was disgust. I was either villain or loser. "You've brought shame on the family," (Judith), "I can't stand being anywhere near you," (Hannah), "Oh my God, he's ancient!" (girls I'd known at school). Jay listened without much emotion. I knew he understood. I didn't need to spin the story for him. Telling Rita, I felt vaguely apologetic. Maybe I thought she'd judge me. She didn't, but she seemed concerned. With Adam, I flirted with the story. I played the irresistible temptress who had power over a middle-aged man. What if our experiences are only ever what our memories make of them? Maybe by telling them, we can turn them into anything? Could that be the secret to a happy life? Maybe I don't need to look on the Iain Carver period of my life as a failure, and myself a victim. Maybe by putting a different spin on the story I can regain the power.

I KNOW THE sane thing to do would be to bin all Iain's messages, but somewhere in me lurks a desire to screw him over. To send a brilliant, triumphal reply to make him squirm and suffer.

I'll sleep on it.

Rita stays away, nursing her mother through her final days of life. Tom goes about his routine quietly, and I feel frustrated. I am young, healthy, not bad looking, but I'm wasting my life, spending night after night staying in watching TV or reading or surfing the net. Co-existing with a middle-aged man who says little. Where is there to go around here to meet people?

The next few evenings, I check my email. Still nothing from Adam. Why hasn't he messaged back? Maybe I've got his email address wrong? I re-check it, but nothing has come back saying 'undeliverable.' He also gave me his work email address. I decide to try that one, he might look at that more often. Should I forward the exact same message I sent to his other address? I re-read it and cringe. I described myself as an honorary Lloyd. I said his family fascinates me. Maybe I've offended him. Family is a touchy subject.

I compose another, more business-like email:

– Hello Adam. I trust you're good and got back ok on

Sunday. After our chat I've been thinking more about doing some sort of formal horticulture training and wondered if you could recommend anywhere? I tried to look up the college where you teach but couldn't remember what it's called? Thanks, Amy.

Typing out the email address, I realise how lame this sounds. All I have to do is Google NTU horticulture and I get through to information about the Brackenhurst campus where he works. Never mind. I press send anyway, and browse the website, looking in vain for pictures of Adam among the tutors' faces.

Next day, waiting for the antiquated computer to fire up, my stomach leaps as I read the words:

Mail from ADAM LLOYD.

Finally.

But then I read the message. It just says:

– Amy, try these links, then includes a link to the college, and one to the Royal Horticultural Society. It's signed off simply, 'Adam.'

I'm reeling from my disappointment when something else catches my eye. Mail from IAIN CARVER

– Amy, I know I must be stupid clinging to the vain hope you still feel anything for me, even though you haven't replied to a single one of my messages. Your aunt refuses to give me your address or phone number, so all I have is this email and the knowledge that you are somewhere in north Wales.

Amy, I'm heading up to Wales next Friday. Have to see a man about a car just over the Welsh border in the morning, but could head on up to wherever you are

afterwards. Please, please make time to meet me. I just need to see you one more time, to talk to you. To explain. And after that I PROMISE I'll leave you alone. I will walk out of your life forever, if that's what you want.

Amy pleeeeaase respond to this email and tell me where I can meet you on Friday. All my love. Iain xxxxxxxx

Later that day, we get the call to say Rita's mother has gone. The funeral is a week on Monday and Rita comes back to sort out arrangements. Once she's home, the house fills up with flowers and condolences and well-wishers, then two of Rita's sisters and an aunt come over en route to Ireland and stay at Môr Tawel with their families.

There's relatives filling every room. Any campers scheduled to come here have been cancelled. For the first time since I arrived, I feel in the way. So I retreat to my henhouse and my garden and my bedroom and the computer.

I long to talk to Rita. I'm picking up on her stress. I want to be able to comfort her. To give something back. I also know a dose of her wisdom would put all this Iain stuff into perspective. But I can't get near her. In the midst of all this, I discover the fox-mauled remains of two of the hens after one of the kids leaves the henhouse open.

Then on the Sunday evening, the family has some sort of ritual where they sit in a circle with rosary beads, reciting chants over and over. Something about the whole scene unnerves me. I withdraw to my room and sit down at the computer.

– Iain, the reason I haven't replied is I don't want to see you. So stop contacting me. Amy.

"Don't do it!" says the voice inside my head.

Too late, I've already pressed send.

Seconds later a reply pops up. Like he's sitting there, just waiting.

> – Amy, THANK GOD!! You're ALIVE!! I've got SO MUCH to talk to you about. I CAN'T WAIT to see you again.
>
> – Can't you READ? I said DON'T contact me.

But I know as I type it is hopeless.

> – I really didn't know what I'd do if you didn't reply. I accept what you say of course but I need to see you one last time. Meet me in Wales on Friday, Pleeeeeaasse! Then after that I promise I will be out of your hair. I have something to say that can only be said face to face.

Almost simultaneously another message appears. This time from ADAM LLOYD

> – Hey Amy! Hope you're surviving all the pre-funeral chaos. I can imagine what it's like right now. Another good reason for me to stay away, although I'm going over for the funeral of course.
>
> This is a bit short notice but we've got an open day at Brackenhurst next Sat. You can look round and there's demos and things. You could come up Friday and stay at mine? If you get the train to Nottingham I'll pick you up at the station. Once the funeral's over I'm sure Mam can do without you for a weekend. ☺

I email back

> – Sounds good Adam. I'll book a ticket. What time shall I get there?

Chapter Forty-Five

I HAVE TWO appointments for tomorrow, Friday. Two mutually exclusive appointments. Adam Lloyd is expecting to meet me at Nottingham train station. I've booked a ticket on the twelve o'clock train out of Bangor. Meanwhile Iain Carver will be waiting for me in the Garden Hotel, also in Bangor, at twelve thirty.

I go to bed keeping both options open.

I fall into a fitful sleep. Who was it said, 'There is no problem, only indecision'? Whoever it was had it right. Dream layers on dream and I don't know what's real. I'm on a train. Iain is waving. I'm in his arms – Adam's, then he morphs into Iain. Iain is everywhere. I wake, thinking it is done, then realise it's still the night before. There is still the decision to be made. I'm two people. One on a train. One not. So when I see him, shadowy in the half-light of the little room, at first I think this is yet another dream.

Until he speaks.

"Hello, Amy."

"Jay?"

I've been waiting for this moment ever since I first arrived here, I've dreamt it, anticipated it, and more recently, resigned myself to it never happening. But my first emotion now, as I realise I'm awake and this is real, is panic. Not you. Not now. Not when I already have enough to cope with.

"Jay! I don't believe it! What are you doing here?"

"I've missed you too, Amy!"

"Jay – Jude – whoever the hell you are. What are you doing here now?"

"I've come to persuade you not to make a terrible mistake."

"What?"

"You're contemplating meeting Iain Carver in Bangor tomorrow, and I'm saying, don't do it!"

This is all I need.

"What's it got to do with you?"

"I care Amy. I don't want to see you throw your life away again."

"If you care so much, how come you stayed away so long? There's been so many times I willed you to appear, I even tried to summon you up, but you stayed silent when I needed to speak to you."

"I've had… stuff to do."

"Like what? What do *ghosts* do all day, Jay?" There, I've said it.

"I'll explain one day, but for now, I need you to promise not to meet Iain Carver tomorrow."

"Why? What's it to you?"

"My brother's expecting you."

"Adam? He's not interested."

"What makes you think that?"

"He took a week to reply to my email. I thought I'd offended him."

Jay sighs. "Oh Amy. That's because you've grown up with the Iain Carver school of romance."

"What's that, then?"

"You're used to men, older men, who manipulate you till they own you. That's what Carver did. In a world where you craved attention, he gave the little girl what she craved, the little girl who lost her Daddy. He filled that role, got you into a position of trust then abused that trust."

"I see my psychiatrist's back."

"Well maybe, Amy, but I'm right, aren't I?"

"Maybe, Jay, but I had power over him too, it wasn't all one way. He's still pining for me. I've had all these emails."

"Ah, the emails. Yes. 'I had terrible pangs of jealousy when I heard you lost a baby... I've been going out of my mind not knowing where you are...You ruined my life, I can't live without you,'" Jay misquotes Iain's messages. In his long absence I've almost forgotten his uncanny knack of knowing everything about me.

"Have you noticed every single one of Iain's emails makes it all about him? Does he ever even ask how you are? If he cared so much about you he'd stay the fuck away."

"But why keep on and on when he gets nothing back?"

"He can't stand to lose the power game. He wants to control you again, are you so dim you can't see that?"

His words rankle.

"I've got a lot more power than I had. I'm independent now. Look at me, I was only young before. I want the satisfaction of seeing Iain's face when I tell him I want nothing to do with him."

"Amy, that's bullshit. You turn up there you're playing straight into his hands and walking right back into his life. Just like he wants you to. You've got a chance to rewrite the script. To have grown up relationships where you don't play the passive little victim. Iain Carver. Howard Carlotti. Break the pattern, Amy."

"Howard Carlotti? You can't count him. I did *not* have a relationship with him."

"Carver. Carlotti. They're the same. Iain was just a bit more subtle." He moves closer and scrutinises my face.

"Even in Balmoral Street, when you looked like death and went everywhere with your hood covering half your face, men still looked at you. You had this exotic heroin-chic appeal. But now...now you have muscle tone and confidence and you've even got a bit of a tan. Most people who see you will find you attractive. Forget Iain. You can do so much better."

"So how come I'm still on my own?"

Jay backs off a bit and shakes his head.

"Give Adam a chance, Amy. Go to Nottingham tomorrow. He's looking forward to seeing you." He moves towards the door. "Now go to sleep. I'll be back."

My brain races. Adam, Iain, and now Jay. Jay says I hand over power to men but if I do what he says I'll be handing control to *him*. Another man. And one who's not even alive. I need to work out what *I* want. But right now, I haven't a clue.

Something of the excitement I felt in the Iain Carver days is undeniably back. The adrenaline spike as I walked into the showroom in the mornings, knowing I'd see him. The sound of his car outside, the key in the door, the purposeful walk as he came into the office to possess me. And now, my prince is back. Chastened. I've made him suffer for a year, and he's coming all the way to Wales to claim me.

It's no good, I conclude as I roll over to sleep. It's destiny. I have to see Iain. Adam can wait.

When I wake again at four, it's just light, the birds are tuning up, and Jay is back.

"You again?" I say. "You leave me for months, now you can't stay away?"

"Nice to be welcomed in my own home,"

"Well it's always good to see you but couldn't you choose a more social hour?"

I realise this is the first time I've seen him in anything approaching daylight. He looks brilliant, the rays of morning sun framing his blond head.

"I remembered something else I had to say,"

"And it was so urgent it couldn't wait?"

"Amy turn on the computer, go on the Internet. I need to show you something."

"Now? It's four o clock in the morning!"

"Yes."

Heavy with tiredness, I obey, keeping quiet so as not to raise the house. We wait as the computer fires up and the slow broadband does it stuff.

"Key in this address," he dictates a Hotmail address and password.

"This better be good," I say.

"It's enlightening to be able to hack into other people's accounts!" he says.

"Is that what we're doing?"

"Yes. Normally I wouldn't recommend it but on this occasion it might help. Right, you in?"

I gawp at the screen, at what seems to be a script between two people unfolding in front of me. The two characters are called Petrolhead and Girlicious. Then I realise, this is an online sex chat. I read, part horrified, part fascinated. Do people *really* do this stuff?

Petrolhead: *Suck me. I'm hard and ready.*

Girlicious: *Taking you in my mouth, running my tongue over you.*

Petrolhead: *Suck harder. Suck the head.*

Girlicous: *Taking you in deep, big boy.*

Petrolhead: *Sooo good*

"Jay?" I turn round to look at him. "Why do I have to read this? It's like some Z-list attempt at erotica!"

"Amy it's live, it's happening now, and guess who Petrolhead is!"

"No!" but even as I say it, I know it is him. Petrolhead is one of the names Iain used to call himself.

"But it's four-thirty in the morning. How come he's online now?"

"His sweet little Girlicious is in America. He tells his wife he can't sleep and is getting up early to do some work. Or he stays up late. He does this stuff for hours."

"Oh my god! How…"

"Sad? Desperate? Yes it is Amy, but why does it bother you? It's only fantasy."

"But…" I look back again at the screen, where things seem to be reaching a conclusion. Petrolhead is saying – *Take my seed baby. Good girl. Swallow it down.*

I feel sick.

"Seen enough?" says Jay.

I nod. This is the man I've spent most of a sleepless night thinking about, and here he is, playing sex games with some stranger from half-way across the world.

"Hey at least it had a happy ending!" says Jay, creasing with laughter. "Now shut that down, I want to show you something else."

This time he gives me a Hotmail address I recognise. It's the one Iain gave me to contact him on. The secret one he set up years ago just for me. Jay dictates a password. I log into the account.

"Go into messages, look at the inbox."

There's a string of messages, among them, a couple I've sent. There are several from Girlicious, others from someone called Carys. Still more from 'Shewolf'.

"Go on, take a look, you know you're dying to."

I pick one at random. Carys.

[Carys] – *Naughty boy. Give me a buzz when you hit the Welsh border and I'll see if I can fit you in LOLOLOL!!!*

Below it is a message from Iain to Carys:

– I'm heading up to North Wales. Need to be in Bangor for a lunchtime meeting but planning to leave mega-early so can bring you breakfast lol.

I look at Jay. "What's this? He's planning to see this woman *today?*"

Jay nods. "Scroll on down."

I do so until I find a message from Iain saying: *– I have to be in Wales on business next Friday, I could drop by on my way and surprise you.*

"Now look at the message he sent you the same day,"

I go into his sent items and find it. *– Amy, I am heading up to Wales next Friday. Have to see a man about a car just over the Welsh border in the morning, but could head on up to wherever you are afterwards.*

"So," I say slowly. "Carys is the man about the car and I'm the lunchtime meeting." I look up from the screen. "The lying wanker!"

"Precisely!" says Jay. "He's the original Mr Duplicity. Mr *Mutiplicity* in fact. And on the Internet he can be all things to all women. Life must get very complicated. You should feel sorry for him really."

"Why? He seems to be having a nice life with all these women all over the place."

"They're not real Amy. Most of them he's never met. He gets cheap thrills through Internet sex. It's an addiction."

"But this Carys woman, he's actually going to see her this morning. That's not fantasy. That's real."

"True," says Jay, smiling faintly. "He'll park around the corner until her husband leaves for work, then he'll let himself in. She's sent him a key. She'll be wearing her best lingerie. Then they'll get straight down to it for an hour or so before he gets back in his car to meet you."

"Why's he bothering with me if he's got her?"

Jay laughs. "Would you like to see a picture of Carys? Go back into the inbox and scroll down." I find a message from Carys with a picture file attached. It's a photo of a woman in her 30s, bleached blond hair, dark roots, tied back off her face into a tight ponytail. She's sitting on a motorbike, wearing jogging bottoms and a baggy t-shirt. She has a vacant expression in her eyes. But the thing I notice most is her size.

"She's *huge"* I say, looking up at Jay "He doesn't even like big women."

"Or so he told *you,"* says Jay. "Now come out of that, there's just one more thing I want to show you."

"I don't think I can take much more of this."

"This is different. Go into Virginmedia." Jay gives me an email address for Adam Lloyd.

"That's your brother's account!"

"True," he says. "I will show you one thing and you will instantly forget the password."

I open the account and at Jay's instruction, go into draft messages. "There's one addressed to you, open it," I do so. It reads

– hello Amy, good to hear from you, I enjoyed meeting you at the house. Best weekend I've had in ages. You've brought new life to the old place. We seemed to connect.

The email tails off there. I sit back in amazement.

"He intended to continue but he's not great at expressing himself in writing so he left it for later and saved it in draft, then when you contacted him again he thought he'd better respond straight away. This was what he wanted to say Amy. Surprised?"

"Gobsmacked!"

"Now I'll leave you to make up your mind about which appointment to keep!"

Chapter Forty-Six

FRIDAY. TWO MINUTES to twelve. Waiting to depart Bangor Station. Happy in the knowledge that Iain Carver will shortly be arriving at the Garden Hotel, expecting me to dutifully show.

I haven't been on a train since that momentous journey here all those weeks ago. I sit on the side closest to the sea and watch the North Wales coast go by. At Colwyn Bay I note with satisfaction that it is now twelve-thirty. I wonder how long it'll take for Iain to realise I've stood him up. Prestatyn. Rhyll. Light years have passed since I last saw these places. It's a wrench to leave my island paradise, even though it's only for a weekend.

At Crewe I feel a flutter of anxiety. I am heading back to the midlands and passing through territory from my past. Then I remember, I'm going forward, not back, and Adam said he'd meet me at the station. I'm spacey from so little sleep and so much emotion from discovering Iain's lies and seeing Jay, silent for so long, now I know who and what he is. I don't know whether to feel comforted or spooked that he's still out there, watching over me in case I go off course. But again he was, infuriatingly, right. Then I wonder, would Adam want to see me if he knew I spent last night talking to his dead brother?

Butterflies skip around in my insides as the train pulls into Nottingham and I scan the crowds on the station concourse. He's here, resplendent in leather, motorbike helmet in hand.

"Hello Amy."

That voice, familiar and unfamiliar. Like Jay's voice, but with an added something. Sexuality. Danger. Life.

"Hello Adam."

"Good journey?"

"Awesome. I love trains."

"They're ok when they run on time, but they're not as fast as motorbikes," he says. "Wanna go straight home or do you fancy a drink first?"

I know Nottingham a little, having grown up in nearby Derbyshire. We stop at a bikers' pub near the castle. It claims to be the oldest inn in England. Adam leads me upstairs into a cave which doubles up as a bar. We're the only people in here.

"Glad you decided to come to see Brackenhurst," he seems a bit nervous.

"Looking forward to it. Will you be at the open day?"

"I'll be floating around, I've got to give a talk." he looks at me sideways. It's a look I remember from the weekend in Wales. Sitting here, beside him, I wonder how I could have even considered missing this for a shite like Iain Carver.

"So," he says. "What have you been up to?"

"I've started an art class, locally. I met someone who was at school with you and Jay."

"Really? Who?"

"Bridget someone. Said she knew the whole family."

"Bridget Llewellyn. Red curly hair? Never stops talking. What did she say?"

"Said Jay was beautiful."

"What about me?"

"Said nobody could get near you!"

He laughs. "You wouldn't let Bridget Llewellyn near you unless you want your entire life broadcast round the island."

"Sounded like she wanted to get close."

"Really? Well I'm glad the two of you had a nice chat about the Lloyds, and of course, you're fascinated by my family." That sideways look again.

"I thought I'd offended you."

"Nah," he says. "I suppose as a family we are a bit unusual, but so are you. Have you heard from that waster of an ex-boyfriend?"

"Funny you should say that." I tell him the story.

"Weren't you tempted to meet this guy?"

"Nope," I say. "Iain Carver's history." I wonder how long he waited in the Garden Hotel.

We set off for Adam's house, the enormous bike weaving in and out of rush-hour traffic, overtaking and undertaking and leaving the queues behind.

We pull up outside a Victorian terrace, set back a bit

from the road.

"My house," he says.

He leads me into a high-ceilinged living room where a lanky guy with short curly hair wearing headphones sprawls on the sofa. "Amy this is Warren, my housemate." Warren nods in my direction without removing the headphones.

"You hungry Amy? I'll cook something."

In the galley kitchen at the back, I sit on a barstool while Adam rustles up a chilli. He hands me a glass of white wine.

"So d'you own this place?" I say.

"The bank owns most of it."

"You're the only person I know of our sort of age who's got their own house."

"We were lucky," says Adam. "If you want to look at it that way. We got compensation after Sara died. It took years to come through. Mam split it between us and I used my share for the deposit on this place. Picked it up for a song 'cos it was crumbling. I've done a lot of work on it."

Adam cooks with a certain panache, using a meat cleaver to chop an onion. He doesn't measure. He throws stuff in. He swigs beer as he cooks. He produces a mountain of chilli from which he also feeds his house-mate. And later when we go out to the local pub, Warren tags along. Now parted from his headphones, he becomes vocal, and his focus is on me, like he's just noticed I exist.

"So Amy, what music are you into?" "Amy what do you do?" "Seen any good films lately?" "Where will you live if you come to Brackenhurst?"

"Warren, haven't you got an early start tomorrow?" says Adam. Warren doesn't take the hint, and it's well past last orders when the three of us walk back together. Only then does Warren leave our side.

"Coffee?" asks Adam. I follow him into the kitchen. It's here that he turns round and we move closer. "I thought he'd never go," I say, pulling him towards me. We kiss. "Forget the coffee," I say, and start to lead him towards the stairs. But Adam stops. Holds me at arm's length. Studies my face.

"What's wrong?" I'm confused now. What if I've got this all wrong? Misread the signs?

"Amy. I like you. Really like you. But I know what happened to you before. And I really, *really* don't want to be like those guys. So I guess what I'm saying is, you're in control here. We don't have to do anything if you don't want to."

"It's ok," I say. And it is. With Adam I already know it's different.

Adam's bed is a double mattress on the floor in the huge front bedroom. He puts music on. We talk. We kiss. We laugh. We make love. We talk some more. We barely sleep, and when we do, it is wrapped up together and in sync. We wake, tell each other our dreams, then sleep some more. Sleep. Sex. Endorphins. I never want this night to end.

I wake early. Adam's still asleep. I study his face in the morning light, brow slightly knotted as he grapples with some dream. Torso half covered by the quilt, lying on his back, arms out. I admire the contours of his body, his muscle tone. His arms tanned from half way down the upper arm. An oriental bird tattoo on one shoulder. No other body art. He rolls towards me, and reaches out to touch me, murmuring in sleep. Then he wakes, at first disoriented, then, catching sight of me, his face relaxes.

"Good," he says, pulling me close. "You're still here."

I wallow in the luxury of being with someone I can wake up with, spend a whole weekend with. Someone without a wife. I can count on the fingers of one hand the times I actually spent a whole night with Iain. The effort that went into our rare nights away. The planning. The subterfuge. The lies.

This is different. This is how it's supposed to be.

The Open Day doesn't start till ten. That gives us a lazy hour in bed together; an hour of talking, more sex, and of Adam bringing me tea, toast and bananas.

We travel in the van. Adam shares a transit with a guy called Jed who he describes as his 'business partner'. There are dog hairs all over the seats from Jed's spaniel.

Brackenhurst is a wonderful place, stretched out in the Nottinghamshire countryside, built up around a former manor house. It's a sprawling array of beds, greenhouses and polytunnels. A place of growth. Its earthy smell invites me. Adam leads me to a Victorian walled garden, where he's due to give a talk on crop rotation. Someone hands him a mic.

"We can feed the world without herbicides and pesticides," his voice is clear and commanding. People listen.

"If you grow the same crop in the same soil year on year you drain all the natural minerals that pack our food with nutrients. The time for toxic GMOs, nutrient-lacking fruits and vegetables, and the absolute annihilation of the bees that pollinate our crops is over. We don't *need* more processed food – we need *better* food."

He belts out the words, and I learn how intensive farming has systematically stripped the soil of nutrients, but all is not lost. There are areas where people are doing something about this to improve organic matter and soil structure. I learn that people in ancient Rome rotated crops, as did the Egyptians, and people throughout Asia and Europe well before the middle ages. Now I understand why we do it at Môr Tawel.

Adam steps down to loud applause. He comes straight to my side, introducing me to people. "This is Amy, she's come all the way from north Wales for this."

He is clearly liked and respected. The students eye me curiously, jealously.

"Amy come and look at these guys," he leads me away from the crowds to the goat enclosure. I get a flashback. One of those fleeting, vivid memories, locked away until recently, sparked by a smell, a sound, an atmosphere. My parents kept goats. They were my mother's favourites. I wish she could see me now.

Adam has gardens to tend in the afternoon. I go with him, to 'help', but I mostly sit around in the sunshine and look on. In one place, he is building a pond. I watch him dig out a deep hole, admiring the way he shifts the earth and his skill and precision as he cuts out and fits the liner.

Around the corner from Adam's house is an understated eatery simply called 'Kiosk.' Adam tells me it started out as an actual kiosk serving sandwiches, but is fast turning into one of the area's coolest cafés. It boasts a converted shipping container as an indoor eating space. It's still warm, so we sit outside.

"Dude!" Beck, the woman who runs the place greets Adam as we sit down. "Come to admire your handiwork?"

"I designed this garden," says Adam.

I look around me. "Call this a garden? It's a yard!"

"It's an urban garden," he says. "Can't you see what a piece of genius it is?"

Herbs and flowers grow out of unlikely receptacles. A motorbike helmet, an old tyre, a piece of guttering, a hollowed out football, even a cistern. Chives, fennel, oregano, I know them all now. I think of Barnabas and his Scarborough Fair garden, a million miles from here.

After eating we go back to the pub where I meet some of Adam's mates. There's Jed, his business partner, with his multiple body art and long blonde dreads. Jed works festivals during the summer and does gardens the rest of the year. There's Angie, who works behind the bar. She came over from Texas a year ago with just a guitar, and stayed. She's introduced all-American burgers to the lunch menu. Nicko and Ellie are vegans who live above the butchers, and there's Skye, so called because that's where she hails from. She lives on a boat with a woman called Willow who nobody's ever seen. Skye is tiny, even smaller than me, with short pink hair and a habit of sitting next to Adam and stroking his arm. She calls him 'Baby.' They're all in their late 20s, early 30s. They accept me instantly. At closing time the others head off into town to a club, but Adam steers me away. "I want you to myself," he says. Warren has gone away and we have the house to ourselves.

The next day, Sunday, I want more of this. More Adam. More connection. But I've booked myself onto the eleven-o clock train. At the station, Adam pulls a package out of his pocket. "Time you re-entered the twenty-first century."

"A phone?"

"It's for selfish reasons. I want to keep in touch. It's not the latest model, but it'll help us stay connected. There's a bit of credit on there to be going along with. And I've programmed in my numbers."

The train is in. We hold each other, briefly, intensely, then I get on. He's gesturing at me from the platform. Something about the phone. Music? He's put music on there for me. We wave till we're out of sight. I put the headphones on. The playlist is identical to what he'd played that night on the beach.

A few minutes into the journey, I get a text.

<Testing. Testing. Xxxx

<It works. Thank yooooou! ☺ XXXX

<You nearly there yet?

<Haha. XXXX

"How was Nottingham?" Rita asks. "Did you like the college?"

"Good thanks, really good."

"Did my son look after you?"

I'm bursting to tell someone about us, but Adam asked me not to. Not yet. It will make things too complicated.

Chapter Forty-Seven

"**B**ELLA BELLA. *FERMATI*!" I hear Maria before I see her. It's started to drizzle so I've just come in from the garden. Maria has established herself and three children on the decking. She's put the umbrella up. The dog is chasing pebbles on the beach.

"Maria! Didn't know you were here."

"That's ok, we've come to see Rita. She around?"

"She's gone to Llandudno."

"We'll wait."

"She'll be gone all morning."

"That's all right. We're happy here, aren't we kids? *Dan ni'n hapus yma, yn tydan ni, blantos?*"

"I'd better put the kettle on then."

I go inside. Maria's vibe unnerves me. Perhaps it's because she reminds me of some of the characters on Balmoral Street. Or people on the psychiatric ward. I now know the pinprick pupils are due to the prescription drugs

Maria takes to control her mania.

"I've been coming to see Rita for twenty years, you know," she says when I return with tea and juice. "She's a very wise lady, and there's times when no-one else will do."

"I know what you mean," I say. "She gives a lot."

"She's been good to us, hasn't she kids?" Nye nods assent, the others ignore her. The drizzle has eased off and the children disperse across the beach, looking in rock pools.

"I home-school them you know."

I know.

"Boys, are you gonna get the cricket things out?" she calls out. "Rita won't mind if they have a game of cricket on the front field." It's a statement not a question. Two of the boys head for the shed and return with bat, ball and stumps, then the whole troop head for the field, despite the drizzle.

"They used to play cricket with Rita's kids," she says. "My older two and Adam, Caty and Jude. Those were good times."

"Jude joined in?" the conversation is getting more interesting.

"Yes, when he was in the mood. He was very lithe and active you know. A great fielder. He was a beautiful boy, beautiful."

"I know." I say. "But troubled?"

"No more troubled than the rest of them. It was the other one who messed with his head."

"The other one?" I've no idea who she means.

"I saw them you know, that day."

"Who? What day?"

"The day he died. I saw them both."

"Both?"

"Yes. He was with the other one. Bad news that one. Turned the boy's mind."

I'm lost now. Maria lives in a fantasy world peopled by the living and the dead. I don't know who 'the other one' is but suspect whoever she means is not human.

"So did you see him jump?"

"What?"

"Jay. Did you see him jump?"

"Oh no. Nobody saw that. This was earlier. On the bridge."

"Did you tell Rita?"

"Well I tried, but she didn't want to talk about it then, bless her, and now nobody mentions it. The subject is taboo. She ought to let it all out you know, but she won't. It's no good bottling things up."

Maria looks at me now as if finally noticing me.

"And how are you, love? I hope you didn't mind me bringing the Big Issue. I know the young girl who sells it in Menai Bridge. Only about your age. Did you get in touch with the people back home?"

"My aunt? Yes. It was her who placed the ad. There's nobody else."

"So when are you going home?"

"If you mean my aunt's, I'm not. That never really was home. This is my home now."

Maria doesn't seem to hear me.

"I'm always telling that young girl she should go home. Make her peace."

This annoys me. "What if she hasn't got a functional

home to go to?"

Maria isn't listening. "You see all these faces looking up at you from the pages. Missing. Some are only fifteen. I think to myself, that's somebody's daughter, somebody's son. Imagine if any of mine went missing."

I suppress a smile. In Maria's family, it's her who's most likely to go missing.

The rain has stopped. The sun looks about to break through. Maria has finished her tea.

"I'd better get on with some work now, Maria," I say. "Give me a shout if you need anything, but Rita won't be back for a couple of hours."

"Oh we'll stay," says Maria. "The kids are happy here playing cricket."

Next time I look out front, about fifteen minutes later, they've all gone.

Chapter Forty-Eight

I HAVE SPOTTED Lionel Rees-Prosser several times at the college where I do my art class. He's difficult to miss, with his trademark leather trousers or skin-tight red jeans tucked into black leather boots, his voluminous floral silk shirts and leather jacket or military style coat and his flowing blond hair and recently adopted goatee. I saw a feature on him in the local arts mag describing him as 'Steampunk meets Blackadder with a touch of Russell Brand.' Today, the usual teacher is away, and Lionel is taking our class. This should be interesting.

"For those of you who don't know me," he looks straight at me, "I'm Lionel. I teach here and at various other institutions around the area. I'm here to take your class for one night only so make the most of me!"

Bridget, next to me, rolls her eyes.

"I went out on Saturday morning to buy fresh flowers for my apartment. Those of you who know me will know I always like to have fresh flowers in the living room. And as I went out, I was struck by the quality of the light over the sands to the east. I've lived in my prime spot overlooking Menai Bridge for eighteen years now but the changing light and colours never cease to amaze!"

Hhmm. Fresh flowers for a man who, apparently, lives alone? Surely he must be gay.

"He used to teach at the school," Bridget tells me. "I never had him but he was always talked about. He used to take people on trips away to art galleries and stuff. He even took a select little group to Paris!"

Lionel gets us to write our names on a piece of folded up card. As he approaches our table he leans in to read my card then announces to the class: "Now Amy looks like a pre-Raphaelite model!"

"Hey, someone else said that!" I say.

"Not Lizzie Siddal. Georgiana, possibly. Or Jane?" he cocks his head to one side as he studies my face. "Jane Morris. That's you. She could just walk into a party, drape herself over a piano, say nothing at all but fill the room. They were the super-models of their day you know."

Maybe he taught Jay. This is too much of a coincidence.

"But didn't they all die of TB and Laudanum addiction?" I'm now grateful for the knowledge.

"A lot of them came to a sticky end," he winks at me and moves on. I make a mental note to Google Jane Morris when I get back. I don't need to. Later in the session Lionel rummages around in a cupboard at the back of the room then hands me a book about the Pre-Raphaelites. "Take it, you can read about your doppelganger."

"I saw some Pre-Raphs in a gallery in Manchester," I say.

"Stunning, aren't they? And such an interesting back-story. But tell me Amy, where's that accent from?"

"Oh, it's mostly a boring midlands accent," I say. "With bits of Manchester and the south west mixed in."

"Not boring at all, a fascinating fusion." He has a habit of looking directly at me. The sort of look that makes me feel a little giddy. Maybe not gay, after all?

"I'm actually mixed race, though you probably can't tell."

Lionel looks at me with renewed wonder.

"I thought there was something exotic about you. What's your heritage?"

"My mum was half Haitian. I bet none of the pre-Raphaelites were mixed race?"

"Ah," he says, grabbing the book again. He turns the pages to a picture called 'Mulatto Girl'.

"Fanny Eaton. She was Jamaican. She appears in a few of the paintings. They thought her exquisitely beautiful."

"Amazing," I say. "I didn't know back then people thought black was beautiful."

"You're right," he says. "That era was characterised by intense racial prejudice. But the Pre-Raphs were rebels. They challenged societal norms. Take Rosetti. He had links with American Civil Rights activists, and was staunchly anti-slavery."

"Good for him," I say.

"I think you're in there," Bridget says after Lionel moves off. "He used to invite his favourites back to his swanky penthouse. He's got a bit of a reputation."

Later, Lionel approaches again, and asks if I'm a student. I tell him I work on an organic farm down the coast.

"Organic farm? You mean the Lloyd's place?"

"That's right. Môr Tawel. You know it?"

"I went there, many years ago. I taught both the boys."

"Really?"

"Yes, the older one only briefly. But I taught Jude for GCSEs and A levels. He went on to study art, actually. Such a beautiful, talented boy. Such a tragic story."

"I never knew him," I say, "But I heard what happened."

"How's the mother these days? She took it very badly."

"Rita? She's good. But I guess you never get over something like that."

"Can't imagine it, can you? And what about the brother? He was a bit of a hothead, from what I remember." Lionel adds. "You seem too sane to live there. You have to admit, they're an eccentric family. Don't stay too long, you'll get sucked in."

That 'eccentric' comment seems rich coming from him.

Walking back to the car park I ask Bridget if Lionel's gay.

"He's very camp, but he always turns up at places with some glamorous girl half his age on his arm. Never the same once twice."

"Bi, maybe?"

"I think mostly, Lionel's in love with Lionel," she says.

"D'YOU KNOW SOMEONE called Lionel Rees-Prosser?" I ask

Rita later.

"Everyone knows him. He taught the boys."

"Interesting character!"

"Yes." Says Rita. "Quite flamboyant. He was kind to Jude." She then gets up and walks away. Like most conversations involving her dead son, this one ends before it's even begun.

Partly to avoid being overheard, partly to get more than a fleeting signal, I take my mobile a little way up the beach to phone Adam each night. "D'you know Lionel Rees Prosser?"

"Tosser," says Adam.

"I beg your pardon!"

"Tosser. That's what I used to call him. He was so up himself. Is he still around?"

"Yeah, he took our art class. Asked about you, actually."

"Don't tell him anything about me. I don't like the guy."

"Bridget says he was a popular teacher though?"

"He was with certain people. Jay got drawn in. Jay was one of the arty elite that used to hang out at his flat."

Chapter Forty-Nine

J UNE 21st. SUMMER solstice. I wake with the light at four, doze for a bit then wake to a six am text from Adam.

> <Morning. What you up to today? xxxx
>
> <Usual. Rita market. Me here xxxx
>
> <Today's longest day. Wish you were here xxxx

I get on with my day early. Let the hens out, feed them, then set to work in the garden. It's market day in Llandudno so there's veg to be harvested. I pull up carrots and beetroot and lay them out in the yard. Rita likes to take them fresh out of the ground to her stall. There are also gooseberries and rhubarb to separate out into containers, and parsley leaf, fennel and dill.

Together, Rita and I go through everything, shake the earth off, then load up the van. Rita drives off. I'm alone. As I walk up the lane I notice a bunch of bees behaving oddly. I make a mental note to tell Tom. Last week he got called to a swarm in someone's garden. He climbed up a tree to catch them and brought them back, so now we have one more hive. Even stray bees find a home here.

I take the radio with me and set to work in the garden. It's time to muck out the hen-house. My smelliest job.

It's gone eleven when I go back into the house, to discover three missed calls from Adam. I take the phone to my spot on the beach with the best signal and call him back.

"Ame, where've you been? I've been trying to ring you."

"Been working, of course. What's up?"

"Guess where I am!"

"Bit early for the pub, even for you!"

"Cheeky mare. I'm at the end of the lane."

"What? Here? You're in Anglesey?"

"Yeah, came over on the bike. Wanna go for a spin?"

"I'm working. You come here and help me work."

"Nah, someone might see me. I thought we could escape for an hour or two. Meet me at the end of the lane in ten minutes. I'm parked in the lay-by round the corner. You can text Mam, if you must, tell her you're off out for a bit."

"But…"

"No arguing Amy, I'm taking you out!"

The butterflies are back. I feel them doing acrobatics in my stomach as I walk up the lane. Just time to change into something not covered in muck. No time to shower.

"You ready? Christ you stink of chicken shit." He hugs me briefly and hands me a helmet. "Let's get out of here."

This is not the greeting I anticipated. It's been a week and a half since our loved-up weekend in Nottingham. He seems impatient, irritable, wound up. He pulls off quickly onto the coast road, taking the bends too fast. I feel a little frightened, and annoyed. I've no idea where we're going. He takes a side road off uphill and inland. I recognise it as the route the bus goes. Then we wend our way up a narrow lane and stop by a cemetery stretched out across the hill.

"Come on," he says, taking me roughly by the hand. He's barely given me time to take my helmet off.

"Where are we going, Adam?"

He says nothing as he leads me into the graveyard, his face set and stony. Still gripping my hand he leads me up the slope. Although I'm fit these days I'm breathless by the time we reach the top. He stops near two little stones, side by side, too small to be graves. More like memorials to mark the spot where ashes are buried.

"My sister Sara," he nods towards the first one. "It's the anniversary."

"Oh my God!" I read the inscription: Sara Lloyd, 7.10.1991 – 21.6.1999. Much loved daughter, sister and friend. Then some words in Welsh: 'bythol ifanc'.

"It means forever young," he says.

There are fresh purple flowers next to the stone.

"Mam must've been here on her way to market," he says. He then points at the stone next to it.

Jude Lloyd. 7.10.1991 – 20.10.2010. Reunited with his beloved sister. May they Rest in Peace.

I feel a jolt when I read it. Here lies concrete proof that the person I know and speak to is no longer living. I choke up then, with emotion I am not entitled to feel. This is Adam's grief, not mine.

He doesn't seem to notice. He's lost in his own peculiar

mood. I can almost feel the anger seething out of him. He takes my hand again, and leads me to a bench, looking out over the valley. It's an idyllic spot; graveyards can be beautiful places. In the distance, we can see the sea. We sit here, and I wonder what happens next. Then he puts his arm around me, and I feel his tension ebb away as a sort of peace descends. Eventually, he speaks.

"Thank you," he says. "I've done what I had to do. Now we can have a nice time." He stands up and we walk together back to the bike.

We head for the big sandy beach I saw the evening when I first met Adam. We walk along the vast expanse of sand, his mood lifting with each step. Now we are playful again. There are huge red jellyfish washed up on the beach. One has a pebble lodged in the middle of it.

"Aren't they gross!" I say.

"They're a strange life-form," says Adam. "Rory ate one once."

"Oh my God! Did it sting?"

"It made him very ill, very quickly. He sicked up half of it and shat out the rest."

I laugh.

We decide to walk to the pub at the other end of the beach. It's further than it looks, and we joke that it might be a mirage and not really exist, as we never seem to get any closer. It takes an hour and a half to get there, and for the last bit we are wading through clay. We end up covered in the stuff, but it doesn't matter.

"Thanks for coming to the cemetery," he says, "and for putting up with my moods. I can be a grumpy bastard at times."

"I've noticed."

We eat pub food then take a slow stroll back. It is gone five pm when we get back to the bike.

"Wanna go to South Stack?"

"What, now?"

"Yeah, why not. Might as well exorcise all my demons in one day."

Of course. That's where…

It's a fast road out from Menai Bridge and we're here within half an hour. I've seen photos of it, of course, but I'm not prepared for its beauty. The lighthouse on the opposite cliff stands majestic in the early evening sunshine, the rocks dramatic. We walk up a path near a white RSPB observation tower to a part marked 'Perygl, Clogwyni Serth – Danger, Steep Cliffs'. So this is the spot. We stand a while in silence, watching the waves below lashing the rocks, then Adam turns, and leads me away.

"At least he picked an iconic spot to do it," says Adam. "Typical Jay. Home?"

We get back on the bike. He parks it in the lay-by round the corner again. "I'll walk you down the lane."

"What if someone sees you?"

"They won't. I'll hear them coming a mile off and I'll dive into the trees."

"Are you coming to the house? Am I supposed to smuggle you in?"

"No. I want to show you something else. You'll see."

We stop at the sign that says 'Cae Sara,' and he leads me through the gate.

"I've never been here before," I say. "It seems... disrespectful."

"Bollocks, it's just a field. We used to play here as kids."

The field stretches up a steady incline. Adam beats a path through long grass, dotted with daisies, poppies and little pink flowers.

"Mam turned it into a shrine after my little sister died," says Adam. "Since then the field's never been cultivated. Sara loved nature and all the wild flowers attract butterflies and stuff. Mam comes here every now and then to pay homage."

At the edge of the field, the ground drops away abruptly at a cliff edge. Below I see the red stone shapes I saw on the first day with Rita. So this is where we are.

"It's about a thirty-foot drop," says Adam. "There used to be a fence here to stop us falling, but *that* fell over the edge."

We follow the cliff edge round to the far corner of the field, where there's another old caravan and beyond it an old trampoline.

"Ooh a trampoline! Can we go on it?"

"No, it's fucked," says Adam. "It's had a massive rip in it for years."

"Shame. I'm good at trampolining."

"Sara was brilliant at it too, she used to do hand springs and back flips and somersaults."

We approach the caravan. It looks abandoned, its wheels sunk well into the earth. Adam climbs the steps and opens the door. "This was our den," he says. "Hope you're not scared of spiders?"

He pulls a lever in the wall and a double mattress

springs out, along with several spiders. He brushes cobwebs off the mattress then pulls me down onto it. "I've been dying to do this all day."

"Adam, what if someone comes in?"

"They won't."

We have sex in a defunct caravan in a memorial field close to a thirty-foot cliff-edge, the possibility of discovery adding to the thrill. Afterwards we sit, curled up together on the couch, looking out to sea and talking. The wind has got up, it whistles round the caravan and shakes it.

"Summer solstice today," I say.

"Let's stay here and watch the sun go down," says Adam.

"What about Rita and the chickens?"

"Text her and tell her you'll be out a bit later. She'll get the chickens in. She won't mind."

We stay till gone ten, in our bubble. We watch till the mountains turn red with reflected sunset, holding each other as the clouds start to roll in.

"What's that?" I say.

"What?"

"Like a creaking? Can you hear it?"

He listens. All we can hear is the wind. "There's a storm on its way. I'd better get going."

"Are you really going all the way back to Nottingham tonight?"

"Yeah. Working tomorrow. I'll be fine."

"You could stay here and leave really early in the morning. I don't want you riding back in a storm."

"Don't stress, Amy. I've had a fantastic day. I've loved

being with you. And I'll see you really soon."

We part at the gate to Cae Sara. I watch as he walks down the dark path, until he disappears into the gloom. The wind roars through the trees. And still, somewhere around, I can hear the sound of rhythmic creaking. I shiver and walk back to the house. It's gone eleven. Rita and Tom are in bed.

I lie awake, listening to the storm. Rain batters the windows, and the waves crash against the beach. Every few seconds, the room is lit by lightning. The thunder is ear-splitting. I don't rest till I get a text at two am.

<Home. Thanks for a perfect day xxxx

"You all right, Amy?" says Rita the next morning. "Everything okay?"

"Everything's fine Rita, I'm sorry about yesterday," I feel I owe her some kind of apology. "The truth is, I've kind of met someone."

"Ooh, I did wonder!" she says. "Someone local? I might know him."

"He used to live around here and comes back sometimes. It's early days and I don't want to tempt fate by saying too much."

"I understand that, but is he someone your age?" Rita furrows her brow.

"Yeah. Don't worry, he's not another Iain Carver. He's in his twenties and he's not married."

"Well that's exciting," says Rita. "I look forward to meeting him one day."

Chapter Fifty

A LETTER ARRIVES, addressed to 'Amy. C/o Lloyd. Môr Tawel' then instead of an address, it has a description of how to get to the house, and only half the post-code.

Who can this be from?

"Open it, then!" says Tom.

"It's an invitation." I read from the card. "'An evening of champagne, canapés and art.' It's from Lionel Rees-Prosser. It's next Thursday." With it is a note saying, 'I'm having a few art students round, they're bringing some of their work to showcase. I'd very much like it if you could join us.'

"Did you get one of these?" I ask Bridget at art class.

"No. I'm obviously not exotic enough."

"Why did he invite me and nobody else from the class?"

"He must want you to be one of his chosen ones. That's a compliment, he only invites beautiful people. Perhaps he wants you to drape yourself over a piano so he can say he's got a genuine Pre-Raphaelite in his flat," she giggles. "Or maybe he wants you to life-model!"

"Get lost!" I say.

"You should definitely go, just to be nosey, see who's there. But be careful. Like I said, he's got a *reputation.*"

Adam and I communicate by text and secret phone calls. I sneak off up the beach on the pretext of getting a good signal. I wonder how long this pretence has to last. Rita doesn't pry.

"Can I have a couple of days off mid-week?" I ask. Adam's got some time off and has invited me up to Nottingham.

"To see your new fella?"

"Yes."

"Go on then, and have a lovely time." Rita doesn't ask where the mystery man lives.

I arrive in Nottingham on Tuesday evening, late, so we go straight to bed. It's another night like that first weekend, exciting and loved up. Gone is the moodiness I witnessed at summer solstice. Next morning Adam says, "Let's go to London!"

"What, now?"

"Yeah why not? We can go on the bike."

My bottom is numb by the time we reach the capital, despite having two breaks on the way there. We park up outside Catelen's flat in Shepherd's Bush. "This'll keep her guessing when she gets back from work," says Adam, grinning. Then we head into town, giggling on the tube, playing games with the faces, inventing names and back-stories for our fellow passengers.

"That's Frank. He likes to dress in women's clothing."

"That's Imelda. She just said goodbye to her husband, now she's off to meet her lover."

"That old woman used to be a spy. Now she writes erotic fiction under a pseudonym."

We do London in a day, in no particular order. Laughing at the human statues on the South Bank, climbing the lions in Trafalgar, saluting the Queen's guards 'Don't you get hot in that big, furry hat?' No reply but the faintest hint of a smile. Lunching at Covent Garden. Running through the Greenwich foot tunnel, whooping so our voices echo, then getting the docklands train back. We finish off with a drink at Lincoln's Inn. At about six pm, Adam gets a call from Cate, her voice so loud and clear I can hear every word sitting next to him. "Adam, are you in London?"

"Yeah. We'll be round in a bit, if that's ok."

"We?"

"Got a friend with me. You'll see her later."

If Cate is surprised to see me when we turn up at the flat she doesn't show it. Cate, evidently, is allowed to know we are an item, under strict instructions not to tell her parents.

"Are you two staying tonight?"

"If you'll have us, sis."

Cate scowls. "You can sleep on the futon. But I wish you'd told us you were coming."

"We didn't know ourselves, until this morning," says Adam. "It's an Adam Lloyd adventure."

"You're getting like Jay," says Cate.

Adam laughs. "If you think *I'm* spontaneous, Amy, you should've met Jay. Remember the time he hitch-hiked to

Lille instead of going to college?"

Cate rolls her eyes. "He didn't even take a passport. He blagged his way across the channel with a lorry driver then couldn't get back."

"Or the time he landed himself a job with a travelling theatre? Dad had to drive half-way across North Wales to catch up with him."

"Wish I'd known him," I say.

"You'd have loved him," says Cate. "All the girls did."

I remember Bridget describing him as an honorary girl.

"Did he have lots of girlfriends?"

"Only platonic ones, I think. Girls loved him 'cos they could talk to him. He'd listen to all their problems. He could be very caring," says Cate.

"Until you got him on a bad day. He could also be a bitch," says Adam.

I love it when they talk about Jay. I hang on every word. I knew him too, I long to say, but of course I don't.

"He could be incredibly melodramatic," says Cate. "D'you remember, Adam? Telling us the world's going to rat-shit, the whole human race is doomed."

Adam laughs. "When he was on a downer he literally thought the planet was better off without him and everyone else in it. He'd depress everyone, especially Mam."

In the morning, still on the futon while Cate and Robert get up for work, Adam says, "Aren't you glad we're not in this rat-race, Ame?"

Cate is perfunctory. "Let yourselves out, put the key through the door and don't forget the alarm."

"Yes boss." Adam sits up and salutes her.

I GET BACK to Wales in time to get ready for the Lionel Rees-Prosser soirée.

I have no idea what to wear. Champagne and canapés sounds posh.

"There'll be lots of bohemian types there so you won't feel out of place," Rita reassures me.

Lionel's flat is a split-level penthouse, the studio a massive mezzanine space spanning the width of the property, with windows and a balcony overlooking the strait, giving a clear view of both bridges.

I'm served by a petite oriental girl wearing a little black dress. She speaks little English but giggles a lot. One of Lionel's protégées, I assume. The event is to display the work of three art students. One of them, a nerdy boy with an attempt at a hipster beard, latches onto me.

"I had a nervous breakdown and came out painting," he says. "In my darkest days I sought solace in oils." His work seems to consist of vast canvases of abstract splodge, mostly in deep reds and purples. It makes me think of gore. More pleasing is the work of one of the other artists, a young woman from Aberystwyth with jet-black hair in a geometric bob. She also paints abstracts but they look a bit like seascapes and I like the colours. In among Lionel's own collection is an original Ronnie Wood of the Rolling Stones. He also has a Georgia O'Keefe. The other stuff doesn't mean anything to me.

The place is full of beautiful people, mostly twenty years younger than Lionel. I spot a presenter from the regional news. There is also, I'm told, a well-known Welsh poet here. This isn't really my scene and, apart from a flamboyant greeting when I walk in, ('This is Amy, she's living the good life with an *insane* family further down the coast,') Lionel is too preoccupied to notice me, so after about half an hour I make my exit. As I leave I wonder about Lionel. What must it be like to live your whole life like a piece of performance art?

Chapter Fifty-One

I T'S MONDAY, AND I'm out in the garden, doing my stuff, when I hear the landline. It rings for a while, stops, then rings straight back. A few minutes later Rita comes rushing out.

"I've got to go. I've to go to Nottingham. It's my son, Adam. He's had an accident. I can't get hold of Tom. Can you hold the fort here for me, Amy?"

"Oh my God, is he ok?" I feel faint.

"I don't know. He's unconscious. He was knocked off his bike by a car. The bike fell on him."

My heart thumps against my ribcage.

"I need you to take care of things here," says Rita. "I've to go now. Will you tell Tom for me? I can't get hold of him. Now, what do I need?"

"Rita, I'm coming with you."

"No, Amy. Tom will come when he gets the message, and Catelen too, but I need you to be here."

"No, Rita, you don't understand," I grab her by both arms, "It's Adam, your son, who I'm seeing. I need to come with you."

Rita gawps, the words slowly sinking in.

"I'm sorry we kept it from you. Adam wanted to wait before we told you. I'm sorry Rita," I start to cry. Rita hugs me.

"Come with me then Amy, you can keep me sane on the drive over. We'll ask Charlotte to look after the farm. Please God he'll pull through."

Everything seems unreal as we get in the van, bump up the lane then pull out onto the coast road. Rita grips the steering wheel with both hands, her arms taut. She drives faster than usual, spotting a cyclist just in time and swerving to avoid him.

"You ok Rita? You want me to drive?"

I'm not sure I'd be any better than her. I'm in bits too.

"Driving will keep me centred." She says, her arms and upper body still rigid as stone.

"I sometimes wonder if I have a curse," she says. "People in Ireland believe in such things. Amy, I couldn't stand to lose another child. It would destroy me." She chokes up.

I know I have to stay positive, for Rita's sake. I don't know where the calm voice comes from in my head, but I say, "You won't. He's going to be ok. He's alive. He's in the best place, Rita. That hospital in Nottingham has a world-class reputation."

I know my words sound trite, but they seem to help Rita. She relaxes her grip on the wheel a little.

As we cross Menai Bridge I look up, as I usually do now,

to Lionel's flat. He's sitting on the balcony with Aishah, the young Malaysian woman from the party. She seems to be living there.

We drive in silence for a while, calmed by the sight of the sea flanking the road. Then after a while, Rita says, "Amy, will you say a prayer? For Adam? For us?"

"I don't know how to," I say. "I'm not really a believer."

"Doesn't matter," says Rita. "Just see what comes. Do it for me."

I shut my eyes and start to speak. I feel self-conscious at first, then the words begin to flow.

"This is to God. The Universe. Or whatever is out there. Thank you for Môr Tawel and for Rita and Tom and the love and support they give to so many people. Thank you also for Cate and Adam. And I ask you to protect this special family, after all the grief and trauma they've already been through. Please keep Adam strong and safe. Please let him regain consciousness. And thanks also for bringing me to this wonderful family. Help me to repay what they've done for me and to support them, too, when they need it."

"Thank you," Rita whispers, and when I look over at her I see her eyes are glistening.

Optimism doesn't come naturally to me, but I feel a kind of peace. Somehow, I know, it's going to be all right.

The tranquillity of the coastal route gives way to the industrialisation of the Midlands. Bigger, busier roads. We hardly speak as Rita concentrates on her driving.

Rita's phone rings. I answer it. "Mrs Lloyd – it's the hospital."

"She's driving. Can I take a message?" I say.

"Are you a relative?"

"His sister," I lie.

They tell me Adam regained consciousness. He seems to be ok, but they're worried about his leg which got crushed by the bike. They're taking him to theatre now to operate. They hope they can save the leg.

"Please God, they don't have to amputate," says Rita. "I don't know how Adam would cope with losing a leg."

My new, positive voice kicks in again. "Rita, he's alive. He's conscious. He's talking! There's no brain damage. That's all good news. They can save the leg, of course they will, and even if they don't, he'll cope." I tell her about the army guy we knew in Stanlow who came back from Afghanistan with two missing limbs, then ran a marathon on prosthetics a year later.

Once we hit Nottingham, there are roadworks everywhere and the signs are confusing. Satnav tries to take us down a blocked-off street. I know my way round this city a bit so I guide us through the road network. Just as we're walking into the hospital Rita's phone rings again.

"He's out! He's in recovery, and Amy, they've saved his leg! It's broken in several places but it'll heal!" We hug each other and whoop with relief.

I sit in a waiting room, pulling chunks out of a polystyrene cup. I let Rita go in alone to see Adam. At the best of times, this would be an emotional reunion. After about twenty minutes Rita comes out. "He's ok, he's talking, and he's asking for you!" she says.

Adam lies attached to tubes and equipment, right leg elevated in a brace, his face bruised and one eye badly cut and bandaged, but otherwise intact.

"Hello," he says. "Welcome to another Adam Lloyd adventure."

"Thank God!" I say. "You scared the hell out of me. You could have been killed!"

"I know," his grin turns to a grimace.

"Does it hurt?"

"Not yet, but wait till the anaesthetic wears off, and the morphine," then he giggles. "Mam this is my girlfriend Amy, I don't believe you've met!"

"She knows about us now, Adam. It's all out in the open. No more pointless secrets."

"I'll leave you two to have a chat," says Rita, and goes off in search of hospital tea.

"I saw Jay," Adam says when she's gone. "Sat there, where you're sitting, before you and Mam got here."

"You what? That morphine must be good."

"He talked about you."

"What did he say?" my pulse accelerates.

"Said you were a good catch. I should treat you right and hang onto you."

"Sounds like he knows what he's talking about."

Adam shuffles his upper body around on the bed, wincing.

"My leg's full of metal," he says.

"At least it's still there. You nearly lost it."

"So they tell me."

"Can you remember anything about the accident?"

"Not a thing."

Tom arrives later. I go to meet him in the hospital

reception. I spot him, towering above the crowds; he looks lost. He hates busy places and commotion. He hates cities. He scans the massing faces then he spots me.

"Please take me to my son," he says.

Adam is asleep when we walk in. Tom leans over the bed and kisses him on the forehead. Adam opens his eyes. "Hello Dad."

"Hello Adam," Tom reaches across the trailing tubes to grab his son's hand. "Thank God you're alive."

"I know," says Adam. "I'm sorry for everything I've put you through."

"I'm sorry too," says Tom.

Enough said.

When Catelen arrives she books herself, Tom and Rita into a Travelodge and sends me back to Adam's to collect some stuff. Long term, she decides, it's best if Tom and Rita go back to Wales and I stay here to look after Adam. I can even take over some of Adam's gardening jobs while he's recuperating.

"Every crisis needs a Catelen," says Adam, winking at me across the hospital room.

Chapter Fifty-Two

I FEARED BEING out of action might make Adam angrier than ever, but his accident seems, if anything, to have had a mellowing effect. He sees getting back on his feet as a challenge, determined to beat the doctors' predictions. They said he'd be lucky to come out in three weeks in a wheelchair. He's out in less than ten days. already proficient on crutches and in time for his birthday.

"Twenty-eight today!" I say when the day dawns. "That's almost thirty! Happy birthday old git."

"Do you know what twenty-eight years ago today was?"

"Apart from you crash-landing into the world?"

"July thirteenth, nineteen eighty-five. It was Live Aid, Amy. How iconic is that? So while Bob Geldof punched the air and the whole of Wembley Stadium went silent, I was entering the world."

"Better if you were actually born at Live Aid," I say, "like that woman who gave birth at Glastonbury."

"Mam says the nurses were watching it on a tiny telly in the maternity ward. She could hear Freddie Mercury when she was in labour. Said it helped her push! So I was born to a sound-track of eighties music."

"Explains a lot!"

He laughs.

"Reckon you can limp to the Kiosk?"

It's blistering hot as we set off down the street, the sort of heat that wilts the brain. Even the road is sweating.

"It's funny," I say, "I never thought I liked cities, but I like where you live."

"That's because it's an urban village," says Adam. "Everyone knows everyone."

"Hey dude!" Beck clears a space big enough to accommodate us and Adam's crutches. "How you doing?"

"I'm developing big pecs, using these things," he says.

"Cool, I've missed you guys. What can I get you?"

"Beck's becoming a legend," says Adam. "She even got a mention in the Guardian. She's looking for staff you know, you could do worse."

"Me work here?"

"Why not?"

"And live where?"

"I have a big master bedroom."

"You mean, like, move in? With *you*?"

"Why not?"

"We've only known each other a couple of months."

"But it feels like a lifetime," he laughs. "That's a compliment by the way."

I think for a minute. The enormity of this conversation

sinking in.

"I'd miss the sea, and Môr Tawel."

"Oh, that'll always be there. Môr Tawel isn't going to go away. Seriously though Amy, consider it, you could go to Brackenhurst to get qualified, and work here to fund our lifestyle!"

I fall silent. I'm remembering last night. Coming down in the early hours to get a drink of water. The whiff of wood-smoke in the kitchen and then *him*, large as life, leaning on Adam's worktop. How I'd jumped. I certainly didn't expect to see him here, in Nottingham.

"Not got time for your old friend, Amy? Now you're busy playing happy families?"

"Jay, it's always good to see you, I just… didn't expect to see you *here.*"

"Where else can I see you? You've practically moved in with my brother. You need to get back to Môr Tawel."

"I intend to," I said. "I'm just here to help Adam get back on his feet."

"Forget Adam, I need your help and you owe me." I hadn't seen Jay like this before. It was almost like he was jealous.

"What do you want me to do, Jay?" I said, baffled at what he could possibly need from me.

"I need you to solve the mystery of my death."

"What?"

"I don't believe any of the versions I've heard. I need to resolve it before I can rest. I need you to go back to Wales where I can explain properly." He was breathing quickly, talking in short bursts, and getting louder. He seemed anxious, almost desperate.

"Can't you explain now?" I kept my voice down, anxious not to raise the house.

"I can't exactly hang around here while Adam's about, can I? Three's a crowd and all that. Now you'd better get back upstairs, Adam's waiting." There was a cruel edge to his voice.

"YOU OK?" ADAM breaks my reverie. We're back in Beck's garden, melting in the heat.

"Yeah, just hot. Can't think."

"Thought I'd blown it by suggesting you move in. Maybe it's too soon, but I can't imagine not having you in my life now."

That evening, we meet Adam's mates in the pub. The journey that normally takes ten minutes, with Adam on crutches, takes nearly half an hour. When we walk in the whole bar applauds.

I've seen a lot of Jed, of course, as he's been ferrying us around in the transit and taken on a lot of Adam's jobs. The others, I haven't seen since that first weekend here. Nicko and Ellie are here, and Skye, and it's Angie's night off from the bar so she sits with us. There's also a bloke called Chris Koliasnikof, who makes a living busking and carving wooden walking sticks. He presents one to Adam "for when you progress from the crutches, mate." Skye sits next to Adam, stroking his arm and saying, "Baby, we nearly lost you!"

I stand at the bar talking to Nicko and Ellie. "Should I be worried about Skye?"

They both laugh. "Adam always says 'Skye's the limit!'" says Ellie. "No competition there. Anyway, you can tell he's totally into you."

"You can?"

"Oh yeah, much more than he ever was with Beth. He literally never stops talking about you and he's forever texting you."

"Beth?"

Nicko and Ellie exchange glances. "His ex. She was from back in Wales. She was ok but she was a bit neurotic. She used to, like, try and keep him away from us, like she was jealous. Everyone likes you loads better already."

I look over towards Adam. Skye is now caressing his plaster cast.

Later someone suggests we go to town, "It's Adam's birthday. Let's go clubbing."

We pile into an eight-seater taxi to town. It's years since I've been to a club, and this is so different from the meat markets of my teenage years. They play decent music, for a start. I like the place.

"Shall we dance?" I ask Adam, half joking, but he gets up on the dance floor, crutches and all, developing a new routine where he waves one crutch in the air, Sky flutters round us like a moth. When we sit down, Angie grabs one of the crutches and does a pole dance around it, then holds it aloft for Skye to limbo under. Even Warren, Adam's lodger, gets up on the floor.

"That was the best night ever," I say when we roll home at five am, and I mean it.

Next day, I ask him about his ex.

"Beth? I let that drag on way too long. It was a relief to both of us when we broke up."

"How long were you together?"

"A few years. On and off. More off than on. We got drunk together at Jay's funeral. That's how it started."

"So she knew Jay too?"

"She was one of his close mates. I never really knew her till he died. It was a kind of mutual comfort thing, us getting together. Should never have happened."

I pause a moment to digest this information.

"When did you guys split up, exactly?"

"The day after I first met you at Môr Tawel. I kind of knew, you see. When I met you. Something just clicked."

"Really? But nothing happened for ages and we nearly never even got together."

"I know. I was…" he struggles for the words. "After you told me that first night in the pub what happened to you, especially with the guy from Manchester, I was cautious around you. Didn't want to push it. Wanted you to know not all guys are predators."

"I know that now," I say.

IN THE WEEKS that follow, I divide my time between both my places, a week at Adam's then back to Wales. Jed takes on most of Adam's work and I handle those gardens which just need maintenance. Adam's college work doesn't start again until September.

In Wales, I await the promised arrival of Jay, but the longer he stays away, the more I wonder if I dreamt that encounter in Adam's kitchen.

I like my life, alternating between rural idyll and urban bohemia. Adam's friends have become my friends, just as his family has become my family. How things have changed. Less than a year ago I was homeless and friendless in a psychiatric ward. Now I have two places to call home.

Chapter Fifty-Three

"SHALL WE GO to see your aunt some time?" says Adam. "You can drive us while we've got the van."

He's now off crutches, and down to one stick. He's getting restless, and now that he's more mobile, he takes every opportunity to get out while I'm around to drive him. He's not supposed to drive himself yet. The motorbike, of course, was written off.

"See Judith?"

"Why not? It's only down the road. I just thought, now I'm speaking to my family again how about you do the same with yours?"

I make the call, and we're invited to dinner on Sunday.

IT'S WEIRD TO be entering the pristine house, now cleansed of me. Hard to imagine I spent twelve years of my life living here. Stranger still to be entering it with Adam by my side, to be invited into the conservatory, spotless as ever, to sit looking out on the manicured lawn, not a blade of glass out of place, while my aunt mixes us a gin and tonic before lunch. I've joined the ranks of the grown-ups.

Adam behaves impeccably. He makes intelligent conversation with Judith. He stretches his arm out behind me on the sofa and speaks of 'we'. The awkwardness I anticipated is here, but I now realise it comes from having to talk to someone I have little in common with. We talk about science, and landscape gardening, and the resurgence of the Welsh language. Adam and Judith debate the merits of organic versus intensive farming. Adam stands his ground and I'm proud. I'm relieved when we get to the coffee. Soon we can leave and breathe freely again. As I'm counting down the minutes, the doorbell rings. Great, an excuse for us to go. But relief turns to panic when my aunt calls, "Amy, it's for you."

There in the doorway stands Hannah. Fatter, older than I remember her, hair bleached blonde like her mother's, plastered in make-up, but still Hannah.

"Hannah!" I don't know what to say. There's no time to process the rush of emotions charging through my body.

Hannah looks at me then quickly looks away. I sense a subtle change in the balance of power. No longer the stray kitten.

"I'm sorry to call in on spec, it's just, Judith said you'd be here and I wanted to see you."

"Sure," I beckon her in. "Come and meet Adam."

Adam sits at the table, sipping his coffee, a picture of poise and sheer animal attraction. Hannah's reaction is almost comical. Her eyes widen, she stares, then blushes, as

Adam stands up to hold his hand out.

"Shall we go outside, Han?" I say.

We sit on the swinging bench. I feel a surge of confidence. No longer does my former friend have the power to hurt me. I have every right to be angry, but I feel magnanimous.

"Well this is a surprise," I say.

"Hope it's a nice one."

"Depends what you're going to say." The last words I remember Hannah saying to me were 'fuck off out of Stanlow you slag'.

"Don't worry. I just wanted to apologise, really."

"What for?"

"Last time I saw you. Before you left. I was a total bitch."

"True," I say, "But understandable. In the circumstances."

"I let what happened with Dad get in the way of our friendship."

"It must have been a shock for you."

"Too right. But now I know it wasn't really your fault. It was him."

"What d'you mean?"

Hannah looks down at her feet. "I've learnt quite a lot about my dad recently." She kicks absently at a loose piece of gravel.

"Like what?" I say.

"Well he seems to have a problem keeping it in his trousers. He's had other affairs you know."

"Since me?"

"Yes and probably even before." She sits on her hands and rocks the swing. "Mum went through his computer. Since she's had this new job she's got a lot more clued up on IT and stuff. Anyway she found messages from a load of different women."

"Really?"

"Yeah so she hired a private detective to check up on him."

"Wow! And?"

"So he'd been seeing this woman in Birmingham. And now Mum's filed for divorce."

A year ago I might have been shocked to learn all this. Now, of course, Iain's multiplicity is no surprise.

"Is your dad still living at home?"

"He's in the spare room. She told him he's got to leave. He's desperately creeping round her trying to get her to change her mind. It's pathetic."

Hannah sniffs, looking up now and blinking back tears.

"He keeps trying to explain, and it's really awkward. He says he loves Mum and doesn't want to break the family up, which is bullshit. My brothers aren't speaking to him."

"Does your Mum believe him?"

"Hope not. Oh my God I hope she's not stupid enough to take any more of his crap. He's been feeding us shit all these years, Amy. Sometimes I can't even look at him." She looks at me now. Her eyes are swimming. I feel a gulf of experience and maturity separates me from her. She is still that naïve sixteen-year-old I used to know. I feel streetwise next to her.

"I'm sorry Hannah."

"It's not your fault," she says. "But, there's something else." Hannah clenches her hands together.

"What, Hannah? Go on?"

"Remember Sinead?" I nod. "Mum doesn't know this but I think he had a thing with her too. Like, years ago. After you left."

"Sinead?"

"I only think this 'cos I saw a message from her. She moved away from Stanlow. It was a strange message, I didn't really understand it, but why would Sinead even have my Dad's email address?"

"I don't know, Hannah. All I can say is, I'm sorry."

"I think he's always been like this. He's obviously got a problem. Now I realise it was him, not you."

"True."

"So are we friends again?"

"Friends." I say, holding out my arms to hug her. I'm conscious that my body stiffens. I feel absolutely nothing for my former friend. Now we've made our peace, I want to go back to my new life and leave these remnants of my past behind.

"You look amazing by the way," Hannah says. "And where'd you find Adam? He's gorgeous!"

Chapter Fifty-Four

It's now September, and it's Wales week. Adam is back at work at Brackenhurst on 'light duties'. Life is ticking over at Môr Tawel and I'm glad to be here. I like alternating between my two worlds, the tranquillity of the seaside and the buzz of the city. I have, I conclude, a perfect life. The nights are closing in. It's interesting watching the seasons change here, and learning what happens when on the farm. Tom is busy up at Huw's place harvesting the maize. Rita has converted half the games field into a paddock, and bought two goats. I got to name them. I called them Michael and Jeanna, after my mum and dad. We're using them to clear the Himalayan Balsam out of the top field. They're brilliant, they eat everything. I love stroking their beards like they're pets. I love the way they nibble at my clothes, and climb up on everything, the wall, the henhouse, even the van. Life is sublime.

"IT WASN'T SUICIDE."

I wake, disorientated. Is this another dream featuring Jay? I've had a few of those recently. Dreams where he's trying to say something, something urgent, but I can't make out the words. I dig my nails into my arms to wake myself up. But this is real. He is here.

"You took your time," I say rubbing the sleep from my eyes.

"I've been busy," he says. "And I've had trouble getting through to you. But there's no time to lose. I know it wasn't suicide."

"What was it then? An accident, like Rita said?"

"I don't know. Bits of memory have come back, and I know I didn't jump. I remember falling. I remember the surprise. But I can't remember the stuff that happened in the lead-up, or what I was doing there. Why was I even at South Stack? How did I get there that day? Amy, I need you to talk to people who were around at the time. Do some investigating. Help me piece it together. Talk to my friends. I had friends. Their names escape me now but Adam will know. Track them down, ask questions."

I feel uneasy. How can I explain to people around here why I want to rake up a past that doesn't even belong to me? I stretch myself up from the pillow and lean against the wall.

Jay stands by the bed, hands on hips. He looks more brilliant than ever; hair glowing, face flawless. I find myself comparing his physical features to his brother's.

"Please Amy, I know this is awkward for you, but you

owe me," he says.

"I want to help, but I don't know where to start."

"How about you start by getting your boyfriend on side."

"Adam?" I say. "I can't tell him! He'll think I've lost the plot."

"You're gonna have to tell him sometime. About us."

He makes it sound like an affair or something.

"Why does Adam have to know?"

Jay moves closer, leaning in towards me as he speaks. "You're in a relationship with him. You're practically living together. Don't you think he'd want to know you're in touch with his brother's ghost? Shouldn't he know the real reason you left Manchester? Isn't my role in your life important enough to tell the man you're sleeping with?"

I stare at Jay. The jealousy I'd witnessed in Adam's kitchen is back.

"Adam doesn't believe in anything supernatural. He'd think I'm crazy. Why don't you tell him yourself?"

"I managed to get through to him once, at the hospital, when he was drifting in and out of consciousness. Now he thinks it was a morphine-induced hallucination." Jay moves back and rests against the window sill.

"Well try again, Jay. It would make my job a whole lot easier."

"I'll have a go," says Jay, "But in the meantime you need to start making enquiries."

"Ok, I'll see if I can broach the subject with Adam when I'm back to Nottingham tomorrow, it's my week there. When I'm next in Wales I'll start asking around."

Chapter Fifty-Five

R ITA'S VOICE ON the phone sounds different. Hesitant.
Perhaps it's because we're not used to speaking on the
phone. She sounds more Irish, and rather dour.

"Amy love, is Adam around? I've tried his mobile but
I'm getting no answer."

"He just hobbled round to the shop. He's left his phone
here. He won't be long. Everything ok?"

"Not too bad, Amy, I need to talk to Adam when he
comes back. Is it best if I phone back later?"

"I'll get him to ring you. Is something wrong, Rita?"

There's a pause on the line, long enough to make me
think we'd lost connection. A disconnect.

"Rita?"

"I'm sure I'll be fine, Amy, but I've to go into the
hospital for an operation."

"Really? Is it serious?"

"I hope not, love. I hope they've caught it early enough.

I've to have a breast removed."

"Rita, no! So it's …"

"Yes it's cancer, Amy, but that's not such a scary word these days. They confirmed it today. They've been great at the hospital."

"But when did you suspect, Rita? I wish I'd known. I could've stayed in Wales. I could've come with you to the hospital."

"That's very kind Amy but Tom came with me and now Cate's here too. The operation's next week."

"Oh my god Rita! It's not fair you of all people should get it," I hope she can't hear the break in my voice. This is a time I need to be strong; for Rita, for Adam, for everyone.

"But life isn't fair, is it Amy? And there are people much worse off than me. Now would you get Adam to call me when he comes back?"

"FUCK, FUCK, DOUBLE fuck," Adam thumps the work surface. "Just when things in our family were starting to get back to some semblance of normality, *this* has to happen."

I've learnt to let him release his anger. I leave him in the kitchen to calm down, knowing he'll come to me when he has. When he does, his eyes are wet. He stretches out his arms and I run to him.

"It's not fair, Amy. It's not fucking fair."

Cate phones later. Adam puts her on speaker-phone so I can hear too. Cate has been Googling all things breast cancer.

"At her age, it's likely to be hormone related, so it's treatable. There's an eighty-four per cent survival rate. That's bloody good." She reels off a list of women she knows who've survived the disease with no recurrence.

"But look at Moira," says Adam. "She didn't survive, did she?" Moira is Rita's cousin who died of secondary breast cancer last year.

"That was different," says Cate. "Adam, you've got to focus on the positive, for Mam's sake."

"I've lost two siblings Cate, I couldn't stand losing my mother."

"Well this may come as a surprise to you Adam but those siblings were mine too and she's my mother too. I don't want to lose her any more than you do, but we have to be positive."

Later, in bed, we hold each other like people in a shipwreck. I say, "Adam, I know what it's like to lose someone. I'm here for you and Rita and Tom, you're my family now."

Chapter Fifty-Six

IT'S NOT UNTIL the rest of the family have left the hospital room that Rita drops her guard and her eyes start to swim. It's the day after her operation.

"It's ok to be upset. I'd be devastated," I say.

"I feel vulnerable," says Rita, "and guilty."

"What for?"

"If I die I'll be letting everyone down. This family's had enough tragedy."

"It's not your fault you got cancer," I say.

"But, I could have found it earlier, I never used to check. I didn't show up for screening appointments."

I reach through trailing wires to hold her hand. "You found it when you needed to. No point in having regrets."

"I'm scared, Amy. What if I? What if it's spread? They can't tell yet. I don't want to die."

"Rita you're not alone," I squeeze her hand more firmly. "You have us and we all love you. We all want you to live.

And… what about your faith, Rita? You have something you believe in."

"I know, but when it comes to the crunch, no matter how much faith you have, you're still facing a void, and the scary thing about death is you go there alone."

I don't know what to say, so I just sit close and hold Rita's hand. Then the memory of a car journey comes back to me, a desperate journey with so much at stake.

"Rita, would you like me to pray?"

I haven't prayed since that day. I tried, once or twice, to get back into that flow, but it didn't work, so I retreated to my own brand of agnosticism.

Now, I shut my eyes and, still holding Rita's hand, let the words pour out of me.

"Thank you for Rita. For all the good things Rita does, the people she helps. Thank you for her family, all reunited now; for the way you've helped everyone heal from the bad stuff. The way Adam's accident brought everyone back together. Please be with Rita now, give her strength, bring her back to health. Please give her peace, and take away her fear." I stop, eyes still shut. We stay like that for a moment, then Rita squeezes my hand.

I open my eyes to see Adam sitting silently opposite. "I didn't want to break the spell," he says. I feel a surge of pride and warmth as I look at him. He is mine.

"When you come out of hospital I'll be back at Môr Tawel full time," I tell Rita. "With Adam back on his feet he doesn't need me so much now."

Rita smiles. "I bet you didn't think when you showed up here in March you'd turn into Florence Nightingale? You might not have walked down the lane if you'd known."

"Walking down the lane that day was the best thing I ever did," I say.

PART THREE

Investigations

Chapter Fifty-Seven

"SO," SAYS JAY, rousing me from sleep. "What have you done today, Amy?"

I murmur.

"Didn't quite catch that, or are you too tired to talk to me these days?"

"I'm sorry, Jay. It's just, you don't half pick your moments." I sit up to squint at the time on my phone. "It's half past three in the morning!"

"Amy, you know I don't have the luxury of sleep. And I don't pick my moments. I have to catch you when you're most receptive, it's not like I can walk up to you on the street or meet you in the pub, is it?"

He's standing by the bed leaning in towards me.

"Ok Jay, I'm sorry. I'm awake now. What did you want to talk about?"

"Progress check. What progress have you made in your investigations?"

"You asked me that yesterday."

"And I wasn't very satisfied with the answer, so I'm asking again today."

"I told you I'd drawn a blank, didn't I?"

He starts to pace around the room. "You'll have to try harder, up the ante, step up a gear. Christ!"

He whips round to face me again, pointing at me as he says, "You *owe* me, Amy. We've got an agreement. I didn't pull you out of Manchester purely for your own wellbeing you know."

"No. It was for the wellbeing of your family. And it's come good. I've proved myself. I've helped Rita. I've helped Adam. Whatever I do, you want more. I've helped the whole family reconcile after the mess you left when you jumped off that fucking cliff-top."

"How many times do I have to tell you? I. Did. Not. Jump."

He's raising his voice. I hold out my hand to quiet him, not wanting Rita and Tom to hear voices.

"Ok, ok, you didn't jump."

He sits down on the computer chair, hugging his thin body with both arms, rocking backwards and forwards.

"I know I'm unreasonable, Amy. But this is an unreasonable position to be in. Why do I have to prove the truth to my own family before I can move on? And it's so frustrating because I haven't got the tools to do it by myself so I need help. And the only people who can assist are you and possibly my brother because you're the only ones I can communicate with."

"Ok, but you have to be patient."

He stands up and starts to walk around the room again, clenching and unclenching his hands. He speaks in quick bursts. "I've got the feeling that time's running out. My mother's ill. We don't know if she'll make it. It would comfort her to know I didn't kill myself. It would prove she was right."

I think for a moment, pulling my knees up towards me and hugging them. "It would help if there was something, *anything* about that day you can remember. Like what were you doing immediately before finding yourself on the cliff. Shall we start at the beginning? What happened earlier that day? Just tell me what you can remember."

Jay pulls the computer chair close to the bed. He shuts his eyes and I study him in the half-light.

We sit like this for some time, Jay in a position of repose, me propped up in bed, struggling to keep awake. It's four am. In another hour it will be light. Another night wrecked. Rita's noticed, recently, the dark circles under my eyes.

Eventually he opens his eyes and starts to speak. "It was a Saturday. I'd come over by train from Manchester that morning." His speech now is calm and measured. "I got here in time for lunch. I was feeling upbeat. Cate was up from London. Adam was floating around, he was living back here then. Mam cooked a meal. Dad came in from the fields and we ate. And I remember it being ok, quite convivial really. Mam was in a good mood, asking me lots of questions. We had a bottle of homemade red with the meal."

He stops.

"Go on," I say, "This is all good. What happened next?"

"After lunch, Adam made himself scarce, so did Dad, and I sat around with Cate and Mam in the kitchen for about an hour drinking tea and chatting. Then I had to go."

"Back to Manchester?"

"No. Don't think so. I had somewhere to go but I was planning on spending the weekend here. I had to go and see someone, possibly a few people."

"Where?"

"Beaumaris? Bangor? Somewhere like that."

"And did you see them? Was it old mates from school or something?"

"That's the bit that's gone. It's all a blank. I remember walking out of the house and up the lane. I don't remember anything else until I stood on the cliff-edge."

"What time was it, when you left the house?"

"I think it was late afternoon, three or four-ish."

"And the time of death was about seven pm?"

"Apparently so."

"So we need to account for a few hours?"

"I know, Amy," he says, sitting on his hands and swivelling round in the chair. "That's what's so fucking frustrating. I just can't."

"Would you have told someone, Rita or Cate or anyone, where you were going?"

"Don't think so. I've got the feeling it was kind of bad. Like I wasn't looking forward to it, wherever I was going. Like I had unfinished business somewhere. I wouldn't have told Mam. I used to keep anything unpleasant from her."

"Can you remember anything else about being on the cliff? What was it like? Were there people around?"

He leans forward, forehead creased in concentration. "Don't remember any walkers or tourists or anything like that. It was getting dark, and it was cold and just starting to rain. I remember looking over at the rocks and the lighthouse. We were on the south Stack."

"We?"

He sits bolt upright. "Yes! Me and …. *someone.*"

"Someone who saw you fall? Or even pushed you?"

"Possibly."

"Whoever they were, they will have information. And they never came forward?" Then I remember something. "What about Maria?"

"Maria?"

"Yeah. Do you remember someone called Maria? Manic woman. Lots of kids. Comes to see Rita."

"Mad Maz? What about her?"

"She said something about seeing you that night. It didn't make much sense."

He creases his brow.

"I don't remember her being around."

"Maybe it was her?"

He thinks for a moment. I can almost see the cogs of his brain whirring.

"It wasn't her," he says at last. "But she might have information, I suppose, if you can get any sense out of her."

Chapter Fifty-Eight

I NEED ADAM on side. I need to tell him everything. But opportunity after opportunity passes me by, until I feel like I'm almost choking on the information. He's my boyfriend, isn't he? I ought to be able to share intimacies with him. So what's holding me back?

I'm back in Anglesey permanently now, looking after Rita as she gets weaker with the chemo. My contact with Adam is limited to phone-calls and weekends when he can get the van to come over. Often, others intrude on our time. Adam helps in the garden when he's back, so when we go to bed he's dog-tired. No time to talk. He's asleep within seconds.

I try a couple of times to bring the subject round to Jay, but it always feels inappropriate. Insensitive even. The closest I get is when Adam's on the computer in my room and finds a folder with some of Jay's paintings in it.

"Hey is that your brother's art?" I say, looking over his

shoulder. "Wow he was good."

"Yeah," says Adam. "Artistic temperament."

"D'you think that contributed to his death?"

Adam looks up and frowns. "Dunno." He says. "Why?"

"A lot of artists kill themselves. And musicians. A higher proportion than the general population." I quote something I once read.

"Maybe. Who knows?"

"What if he didn't do it?"

Even as I say this I know it sounds strange.

"Do what? What are you on about, Amy?"

"What if he didn't kill himself. If it really was an accident after all? What if he didn't jump…"

I can't bring myself to say it. *What if someone pushed him*?

Adam looks at me with narrowed eyes. "Not you as well."

"What d'you mean?"

"A few people said that at the time. And I don't mean just Mam. Certain people obsessed over the whole thing. Started spouting conspiracy theories. It wasn't helpful." I get the feeling he's referring to his ex. "How come you're so fixated on him anyway?"

I wasn't aware I was.

"You said yourself you didn't talk enough when it happened."

"Well now's not the time. We've got enough going on with Mam's cancer. What happened, happened. And I don't think you should dwell on it Amy. It's morbid." He turns back to the computer, closes down Jay's art file and pushes the chair back.

"I thought when you came here it was a fresh start for everyone. Someone who never knew my brother. But even though he's dead he seems to have got to you. Whatever you do, don't bring the subject up around Mam."

Drawing a blank with Adam, I start to think who else I can ask about Jay. Maybe someone less emotionally involved.

A SURPRISE OPENING arises when Eirwen, the little white hen, gets ill. She's had the runs for several days and she's looking very sorry for herself. Rita has to avoid infection so I take the hen to the vets. As I negotiate my way through the door with Eirwen in a cat basket I see Bridget in the waiting room with a collie dog.

"Didn't know you had a dog," I say. "What's his name?"

"Dylan," she says, pulling the dog away as he starts sniffing round Eirwen's cage. "And guess where he came from? We got him from the Lloyd's place. Rita got him as a puppy after Jay died, but he didn't get on with Rory so we rehomed him."

I'm thinking quickly. Here's a rare opportunity to talk about Jay's death. "So did they get the dog, like, as therapy?"

"Something like that. Didn't work though. Just caused more grief."

"What was the version you heard about Jay's death?" I ask. Bridget raises her eyebrows slightly, then moves closer and lowers her voice.

Bridget tells me all she knows, which isn't much more than I've already heard. Jay came home from Manchester.

Went off to South Stack and never came back. Someone spotted the body from the opposite cliff. The rest is history.

"How did he get to South Stack? Did he drive? It's some distance from Môr Tawel."

Bridget looks at me oddly, like this question has never occurred to her. "By bus I s'pose. It'd be two buses. He never drove. Or he could have hitched a ride. He used to hitch places."

The vet calls Bridget and Dylan in for their appointment. As she stands up I ask, "D'you think it really *was* suicide? I was originally told it was an accident."

She leans in towards me. "I think the accident theory was just a line to keep Rita happy. If you knew Jay you'd know how manic he could be. Didn't surprise me at all when I heard. Doesn't matter now though, does it?"

Except it does.

Jay's visits are increasingly disturbed and disturbing. He's taken to appearing at three or four am, waking me from deep sleep, and agitating. Gone is the calm counsellor of Balmoral Street. This is a person on the brink.

"We've got to solve this one, Amy. Please just get on with it. Can't you see I'm in pain? This half-life is nothing but a waking nightmare and you, Amy, yes you, the person I pulled out a Diazepam-induced purgatory, are the only person with the power to do anything about it. We *have* to get some answers."

"I've tried, Jay, but I'm hitting a brick wall. I don't know who to ask. I don't have the contacts."

"Well as I keep saying, get your boyfriend to help you. He's got the contacts."

I sigh. "But as *I* keep saying, if I tell Adam the whole story he's gonna think I'm crazy! He already thinks I've got a morbid obsession with you."

"Just bite the bullet. Please! Do something proactive for my sake," and with that he is gone.

RITA IS ON chemo cycle three. They've changed her drug, and since her last infusion she's spent four days wrapped in a fleece blanket, shivering.

"How are you?" I ask.

"Not bad for someone who's being systematically poisoned."

We had to bully her to have chemo. It was only when Cate presented her with the odds, eighty per cent chance of survival with, sixty per cent without, that she agreed. And it's not just the chemo, it's all the other stuff that goes with it. Anti-sickness drugs, steroids, painkillers; her herbal shelf now looks like a pharmacist's.

"Is this the medical world getting back at me, after all I've said about them?" Rita asks.

She's barely recognisable. Her hair, mostly gone, is shaved close, but apart from the baldness, her skin has taken on a deathly pallor, her face drawn. She's hardly eating. She looks like someone from a concentration camp.

She has to take her temperature every morning. If it goes up beyond thirty-eight degrees, we should phone the hospital. So far her temperature is teetering just below the danger zone, but I'm worried about her. Having kept her strength up for the first couple of rounds, the new drug seems to have floored her.

"Amy, can you Google the side-effects of Docetaxel?"

Flu symptoms, restless legs, shivers and shakes, disorientation, 'chemo-brain', Rita has the lot, but should it really be going on for four days or more?

"Please, Rita, let me phone the chemo-clinic. They might say to come in for a blood test."

They do, so I drive her to hospital. Still wrapped in her fleece, she can hardly stand. We wait for a doctor in a side-room where Rita lies on a couch, shivering. The doctor pronounces her neutropenic, with a white blood count of zero. "No wonder you feel ill," he says, and admits her. Tom comes straight over, so I head back to the farm to await Adam's arrival. It's a Friday and he's got off early to come up to Wales.

Chapter Fifty-Nine

ADAM IS ON edge, worried about his mother. He paces up and down, wanting to go to the hospital, then we get a call from Tom. "She's responding to the antibiotics and her blood count's started to creep up. I don't recommend anyone visits today. I'll stay with her for a few hours. She's going to be ok."

Adam relaxes, and I sense my moment. The group of Aussies who've parked their motor home on the beach have taken themselves off somewhere, so Adam and I have some precious time to ourselves. We sit opposite each other at the kitchen table, as we did when we first met.

"What shall we do this afternoon, Ame? Dad won't be back till much later."

"Fancy going out? We could go for a drink in Beaumaris?"

"Or we could just stay in. It's not often we get this place to ourselves," he reaches over to me, his eyes laughing, suggesting. How easy it would be to have a loved-up afternoon with him, crack open a bottle of wine, eat and then sleep, but I have a feeling it's now or never.

"Adam, I need to tell you something."

He drops my hand. "Sounds ominous!"

"It's not. Not really."

"You're not dumping me?"

"No."

"Or proposing?"

"God, no!"

"Pregnant?"

"No! Now shut up and listen. This is going to sound well weird and I need to know I can trust you."

"Course you can. You can tell me anything, Amy." He leans forward. He looks sincere.

"When I came here it wasn't by accident."

"Meaning?"

"I was kind of sent here."

He leans back a bit, eyes narrowed. "Meaning?"

"This is going to sound crazy."

"Try me!"

"Well, you know when you were in hospital after your leg operation, you said you saw Jay?"

"When I was off my face on morphine, yes."

"I saw him too. In Manchester. Night after night. Only I didn't know who he was then."

Adam sits bolt upright. "You're fucking kidding me. You said you never knew him."

"I didn't. Not while he was alive. I couldn't have. But I swear I saw him. He came to my room when I was dosed up on Diazepam. He listened to me. He got me to stop taking the tablets and start talking to people. He helped me out of a dark place. And he sent me here, to Môr Tawel."

Adam says nothing. He hunches his shoulders, which makes him look small, and a little afraid. I can't tell what he's thinking.

"So I came," I continue. "He gave me instructions how to get here, right down to what bus to get and what to say when I got here."

Adam pushes his chair back.

"And I didn't have money for the trip but he told me not to worry and the next day the money was there because the purse I'd lost got handed in and…"

Adam stands up and holds his hand out. "Whoa. Let me get this right. You're telling me my brother's *ghost* told you to come here?"

"I know it sounds mad."

He glares at me as if I *am* mad. "A ghost? That Diazepam must be strong stuff."

"D'you think I'm making all this up?"

"I don't know what to think. It's completely fucking mental," he starts to pace around the kitchen.

"It's important you believe me!"

"I'm trying, Amy. I'm trying to suspend disbelief but this is just so fucking…"

"He said he could get through to me because of my state of mind at the time. He appeared to you in the hospital for the same reason. You were susceptible. He says he could only get through to you that once."

Adam stops, and stares at me. "Hang on a minute. You

mean you're *still* seeing him?"

"Yes, sometimes at night, mostly here, but once at your house. But recently he's come more and more often."

"Bloody hell, Amy!" Adam slumps into the chair and holds his head in his hands.

"After I moved here I didn't see him for ages. Then he showed up the night before I went to Nottingham for the open day. That night I was toying with the idea of going to meet Iain Carver instead of coming to see you. Jay persuaded me to choose you."

Adam looks up again. His eyes have darkened. Sometimes they're almost black.

"So I have my dead brother to thank for us getting together?"

"Well, yes. Sort of."

"And what's he like, my brother? Give me your impressions of him, Amy. It's important to me." There's an edge to his voice I can't quite interpret. An irony. A bitterness.

"He's beautiful, of course, and kind of, you know, spiritual."

"He would be. He's dead."

"When he first appeared in my room in Manchester I couldn't see his face because he wore this big Parka with the hood up. Then he started getting clearer. He's got big brown eyes and a wide face. He's like you but thinner, and taller. He's got an innocent air about him, like a child. And he's kind of androgynous."

Adam nods. "All this you could have got from photos. Tell me something you only learnt from talking to Jay."

"Shit, Adam. Do I have to prove myself to you? You said you'd trust me!"

"I said *you* could trust *me*. That's different." Adam stands and walks out of the kitchen.

"Ok," I follow him, racking my brains for something. "He said he stole your girlfriend. When you were fifteen and he was thirteen. You brought some girl here. She was supposed to be with you but Jay reckoned he charmed her. In the end you went out and left them to it."

"Bronwyn," he says, turning back towards me.

"So it's true?"

"Jay seduced her with poetry. But he didn't do anything with her because he was gay, or asexual, or whatever he was. He only ever got emotionally close to people, never physical. If they wanted more, he ran a mile. They called him Jay the untouchable."

"But I couldn't have known about that girl, could I?"

"Hmm. Maybe you found one of his old diaries or something. He wrote everything down. Maybe you've been snooping round talking to locals. Who knows what your game is?"

His words cut through me like a razor.

"Adam that's not fucking fair. I've been up and down between here and Nottingham working my socks off to help you and your family."

"So we're all supposed to be grateful? Maybe that's all part of some sick plan to make yourself indispensable," Adam is pacing again. It reminds me of the first evening together when he told me about Jay's suicide. "Nobody asked you to do all this, Amy. We were fine as we were."

He winces as his leg pain kicks in.

"*He* did, Adam. Jay. Jude. Whatever you want to call him. He asked me. I've got no reason to lie."

Adam grabs his jacket, slung over the back of a chair. "Listen Amy, I can't handle this. I'm going."

The door slams shut. I hear the van start up then drive off up the lane. I wonder if he'll go all the way back to Nottingham today, or just to the pub and reappear later.

Chapter Sixty

I SIT ON the decking, shivering in my coat, cursing Jay. "I told Adam, and look where it got me. Now he's gone, and I don't know if he'll ever come back."

Rory lies stretched out under one of the chairs, chest rising and falling, feet occasionally twitching as he chases rabbits in dreamland. As I look at him he opens his eyes. I can just see the whites. He seems to know when I'm watching him. He also knows when I'm about to get up, and braces himself for action, even when I haven't yet made a move.

He's watching me intently now, picking up on my distress. He rouses himself, comes over, nuzzles me and rests his head on my knee, looking up at me with big, bloodshot eyes.

"What would you do about it, Rory? What would you say, if you could speak? You'd have all the answers. You'd be the only one that made any sense."

It's early evening and still light when I hear the campers coming back. They're heading for the beach. I'll be required to be sociable. I don't feel sociable.

"Come on Rory, let's go for a little walk."

I need to be alone, just me and the dog, somewhere I can think. I know just the place. I head off up the lane.

I stop by the gate to Cae Sara, and hesitate. Although Adam said it was ok to come here, it still feels like intruding, and I've never ventured through this gate since that midsummer night. But the field with its grasses moved by the breeze seems peaceful and inviting. I go in.

To my surprise, Rory doesn't follow, but lies down at the entrance. "Rory, come on!" I try to entice him in but can't persuade him to enter the field. Maybe he was trained not to come in here. Out of respect.

Memories, bittersweet, flood in as I walk up the slope. The place has changed since the solstice. The flowers have died down, but other vegetation has grown up. I have to stamp it flat as I beat a path to the cliff, each step heavy and sad. This is so different from the first time I came here, when things with Adam were just beginning. Now it seems, suddenly, cruelly, they are ending. I stand at the cliff edge, silent tears running down my face. I look down at the cove below. It beckons. Here lies peace, it says.

For a few seconds I stare into the void, then step back. I don't want to go there.

Now I hear the creak, creak, creak that I heard here before. But this is a clear calm day, with no storm brewing.

I turn towards the sound. I'm not alone in the field. There's someone on the trampoline.

Strange, Adam said it was broken.

The person on the trampoline is jumping high, doing back-flips and belly flops and somersaults. A small person. Very agile. Some kid from the neighbourhood? I start out towards it and the figure takes shape. A little girl wearing denim dungarees with purple flowers embroidered on the legs. A little girl with dark curly hair and enormous brown eyes.

This is no child from the neighbourhood. I know exactly who this is. As I approach, drawn by some irresistible force, the girl stops jumping, and sits on the trampoline with her legs stretched out in front of her. She is clutching a purple toy elephant.

"You should've jumped, stupid. Why didn't you jump off the cliff?"

I say nothing.

"You couldn't do it, could you? You didn't have the guts?"

I open my mouth to speak, but no words come.

"He didn't either. My brother. He didn't jump. Someone pushed him, see. And you've got to find out who." She takes a piece of hair and twirls it round her finger, staring at me.

"I'm trying," I have a voice, at last, but it's weak.

"Why did my brother have to get someone so stupid to help him, Christopher?"

"Christopher?"

"Christopher's my elephant, stupid," says the little girl. Then she jumps off, still clutching the elephant, and runs off in the direction of the caravan. Only now do I approach the trampoline. It's exactly as it was when Adam and I were here, shabby and neglected, a massive rip right down the middle. I press on it and my hand goes right through.

My head rushes. I have to get out of this place. It's now almost dark. I run, stumbling on hummocks in the long grass. And there, by the gate where I left him, Rory stands, trembling.

We've just got back to the house when I hear the van. Adam steps out. "I'm sorry," he says, holding out his arms to me. "Amy, why are you shaking?"

I sob.

"Amy. I'm sorry I'm such a shit. I just couldn't handle it."

"I'm scared," I say. "Hold me."

"Come inside," There's alcohol on his breath. "Now tell me all about it."

"I… went to the field…" I say between sobs. "Cae Sara… Where you took me… I saw a little girl… On the trampoline… She was bouncing. High."

"Amy, no-one's used the trampoline for years!"

"It was your sister… Sara." I then sob uncontrollably. "It scared the hell out of me. Adam, I'm frightened!"

"Now listen," he draws me closer, but even as he does so I sense him distancing. "I don't know what happened up there but it must have been some kid messing about. Or maybe…"

"Maybe what?"

"Your mind plays strange tricks, Amy."

He sounds calm, rational, and I know I'm losing him.

"It *was* her. You've got to believe me. There's no point if you don't believe me."

"Ok," he says, still calm. "What did she look like?"

"Little and dark with huge eyes and she was wearing denim dungarees with purple flowers on them."

Adam pulls back, that intense stare is back.

"She was jumping on the trampoline, doing back-flips and somersaults like you said she used to. She was kind of showing off."

"Okay," he says. "What else?"

"She had this big stuffed toy elephant. Purple. And she kept twisting her hair round her fingers, and she kind of sucked in her cheek on one side."

"And did she say anything?"

"She called me stupid. She asked why I didn't jump off the cliff. She said Jay didn't jump, he was pushed. She kept calling me stupid. And she talked to the elephant. She called it Christopher."

He turns away. Finally, I know, I've got through to him.

"I need a drink," he says.

We drink until the alcohol numbs our senses and lulls us into a dream-like state. We drink some more, and forget to eat. "Let's go to bed," he says. "We can talk about all this in the morning."

We lie entwined in the little bed. I barely sleep. Thoughts pervade my brain. Thoughts that don't even seem to come from me. Of life. Of death. Of beyond. And somewhere in the distance is the rhythmic creaking of a child jumping on a trampoline.

Chapter Sixty-One

I N THE MORNING, Adam draws me close and kisses me. I pull him into me, our bodies connecting with silent intensity. Everything feels unreal. Afterwards he gets up and pulls his clothes on.

"Where are you going?"

"Just out, for a bit. Need to get my head together. Don't worry, I'll be back." He kisses me on the head, then leaves.

This time, when he returns, there's no anger. He takes me by the hand, his touch gentle. He leads me out of the house and along the beach a little, just beyond the bend, out of sight of the house.

His voice almost cracking, he says, "I'm sorry Amy, I can't handle this any more."

I stare at him. "Can't handle what? You mean us?"

"I can't be with someone who talks to ghosts. I'm sorry. It's too much."

The tears smart in the back of my eyes, stinging as I

push them back. I choke up, unable to speak.

Adam turns away.

"This isn't fair!" I find my voice, but it comes out strangled. "I never asked for any of this. They're not even my ghosts. They're *yours*!"

"I know, Amy. I know you never invited them in, it's just… you seem to be a captive audience. And I can't handle it." He looks at me now, his eyes are glistening too. "I know this is all tied up with my family, but I have to get out." He starts to kick at the shingle. "I should have stayed away, not got involved. I can't be dragged back into the past. I have to move on. I'm sorry."

I look at the sea, at the swell and the ripples and the constant, lapping movement. It's benign today. I want to run into it, add my tears to that great body of salt water and let it swallow me up.

Neither of us speaks for a while, then I say, "I think I'll leave Môr Tawel. There's nothing here for me now. I think I'll go away."

"No!" he says, grabbing my shoulder. "Stay, Amy. *I'll* go away. I'll go back to Nottingham and not come here anymore. I can do that. I've done it before. Please stay here, they need you."

"Who? Your ghosts? Great!"

"My parents need you, especially Mam, right now. They'd be devastated if you left. You're one of the family now."

"And what about you, Adam, now you've decided to smash us apart for no good reason. Will you be devastated too?"

"You've got no idea how hard I'm finding this, but I have to get away from this place. There's too many memories. There's too much stuff from the past hanging around here, and being with you is just dragging me back. I'm sorry. It'll drive me insane if I don't get out. I have to get my head back together again."

He turns and walks away, still limping from his injury. I watch him round the bend. I can still hear the crunch of his boots on the shingle as he walks out of my life.

"He'll come round."

A different voice. One I have never heard before outside, in daylight. A voice that, right now, I don't want to hear.

"You?" I say, looking around. I can hear Jay but not see him.

"He'll come round, Amy. You just need to give him time."

"This is all your fault," I turn to the disembodied voice. "You just couldn't leave me alone, could you? You and now even your sister – what next?" I begin to wonder if I am, indeed, mad. Hearing voices. Seeing things.

"You're not going mad," it's like he's read my mind. Maybe he *is* my mind.

"Well fucking go and convince your brother of that," I shout. "Go and reveal yourself to him. Stop offloading all your shit on me."

"I *have* been to see Adam," says Jay, "But I can only get through to him in dreams. And it's me that's doing his head in, not you, Amy. He thinks if he runs away again and stays away from this place he'll be left in peace. But when he gets back to his house with only his monosyllabic lodger and the cat for company, when every room he walks in smells of you, when every paving stone in every street and every bar he ever goes in reminds him of you, he'll realise he can't live without you."

"You reckon?"

"Trust me."

I sense the voice has gone. Now it's just me and the sea. I've no desire to go back to the house yet. I walk towards the shapes, through the arch, where I went that first day with Rita. Drawn towards the cave, I keep walking. I look up at the graffiti high in the cave roof. JAL, SCL. Of course! Jude Alun Lloyd, and Sara Ciara Lloyd. I hear the plaintive cries of the seagulls up above, and I feel that same pull I felt the first time I came here, as though the cave is calling to me. I enter, crouching, and sit back against the soft stone. I pull my hood up over my head and shut out the world. "Should've jumped, stupid, why didn't you jump? You didn't have the guts." The child's voice from yesterday resonates in my head, cruel and insistent. I feel that same sense of disassociation I felt when I first came into this cave, the seagull cries muted. I sit, curled up, hugging my knees. Closing my eyes, I shut out the world.

RORY TUGS AT my sleeve, growling. "Rory what are you doing? Why are you wet?" His fur is damp. Is it raining outside the cave? It was clear earlier.

Then I remember. Something Rita said that first day when I ventured into the cave. You can get cut off here at high tide. The tide was coming in when Adam left. Shit. I jump to my feet. "Come on Rory let's go."

Water lashes round the entrance to the cave, the beach beneath the arch completely submerged. The waves, now close, are huge, crashing against the rocks. I'm in up to my waist, and a wave drenches my chest, the cold shock squeezing the breath from my lungs. Rory doggy-paddles in front. Another monster wave knocks me off balance, I grab at a slime covered rock, but lose my grip as some force in the water pulls me under. I taste salt water. My ears fill. There's an eerie quiet. *Is this it? Am I drowning?* My body slows. Then from somewhere a calm voice takes over. I still my breath and let my body rise until my head shoots up above the water and my ears fill once more with sound as the wave subsides.

I can now feel the ground beneath my feet but I'm stumbling on the stones. Rory has reached dry ground. I flail towards him. *Wait, Rory, Wait!* Another wave propels me forward, onto the shingle. I pick myself up and stumble forward to put distance between me and the waves, my body soaking. Rory shakes himself.

We've made it. I hug him, and let him lick me all over.

"HAS ADAM GONE?"

I've been sitting on the living room sofa, arms around the dog, weeping into his fur. Thankfully nobody was around to see us arrive back, dripping. Now I've changed, Rory's dry and we're warming up in front of the woodburner.

"Yes, Tom we, er, we had a bit of an argument."

"He'll come round."

Nice that Adam's family have such faith. I don't share it

as the hours, then the days go by with no word from him. No text, no call; just a big, fat absence. Just a longing. Just a wrench.

"He'll come round," Rita this time, back from the hospital, immune system, for now, restored.

"Give him time," Jay again, back to bother me, disrupting my sleep.

"How much time? It's been nearly a week."

"D'you want some intervention from me?"

"Haven't you done enough damage already?"

"I can sometimes get through to him in dreams. I can also reach him when he's very, very drunk, and I can assure you Amy, since he split up with you he's been bladdered every single night."

Chapter Sixty-Two

SATURDAY. A WEEK since Adam left, and no word. I've been strong, not texting him. Getting my phone wet in the sea didn't help. But now it's dried out and apparently functional. Still no word.

I'm sitting on the decking, reading, in the late afternoon sun, with Rita's blanket wrapped round my shoulders. Although it's now October I still find it comforting to sit outside, drinking in my view of the mountains.

The Aussies are still with us. They're building a fire on the beach. One of them, Jake, brings a can of Stella over to me. "What you reading?" he says. I show him. Weirdly, Adam's leaving seems to have unlocked my reading ability. This is the third novel I've devoured since he left.

Jake shrugs. "Join us for food?" he asks. He's tall, blond, muscular, tanned. He's most people's definition of drop dead gorgeous. He does nothing for me.

"I might come over in a bit," I say. I catch the smell of

meat cooking on the barbecue. There are five Australians. James and Rochelle ('Shell'), appear to be a couple. Then there's a woman called Marlie, who seems to go off on her own a lot, and two guys, Seb and Jake. Apart from Marlie, who's a bit older, they're all in their mid to late 20s.

The beer warms my innards. Catching Jake's eye, I raise the can to him. He brings me another, seating himself opposite me on the decking.

"So how long have you guys lived here?"

He's from Melbourne. He's been working in a bar in London for six months, now he's joined up with the others to travel. He asks a lot of questions. It's easy, and as the Stella slips down smoothly I wonder what it would be like to kiss him. Could an encounter with an attractive visiting Australian be what I need to get over Adam?

We join the others for food. I'm one bite into my steak bun when Rita comes out, head covered in a scarf. "Visitor for you Amy," she says. Behind her stands Lionel Rees Prosser.

He's dressed differently from his usual signature attire. More normal looking. Wearing jeans and a long black coat, hair tied back. He saunters over to join the party at the barbecue.

"This is Lionel, everyone," I say.

"Beer?" asks Jake. Lionel declines. I sense them sizing each other up. I have a glorious feeling of being in demand.

"Nice to see you, Lionel. Don't think you've ever visited before. What brings you here?"

"Can we talk?" says Lionel. I lead him away from the others, back to the decking. I take my lager with me.

"I saw you in town today. You looked like something was wrong. And Bridget told me you missed the art class. I wanted to see if you're ok?"

"Me and Adam broke up," I say. "I've been a bit emotional, but I'm over it now."

"Poor darling," he says, putting his arm round me. "Let's take a walk."

We walk along the beach in the opposite direction to the shapes.

We round the corner. We can see Beaumaris further along the shoreline. Lionel keeps his arm around me. Is this a friendly, comforting gesture? Or is he hitting on me? I've seen him be demonstrative with plenty of people, women and men. But today he seems different, more real, more substantial. I don't know what I expected, but his body next to mine feels all male.

"There's something you should know about that family," he says. "They're as dysfunctional as they come."

"Aren't all families?"

"The Lloyds especially." He turns towards me, lifts a stray hair out of my face. "You want to watch you don't get sucked in. I've seen it happen. I was worried about you when I heard you lived here."

"But I love it here, Lionel. I belong here."

He links arms with me and we walk some more.

"Before you know it you've got no life beyond this place. Their values become your values. Their problems your problems. I'm concerned that's happening to you." He pulls me round to face him. He strokes the contour of my cheek with his finger. His touch is delicate. An artist's touch.

"You're beautiful, Amy. You have such potential. Don't let that family mess you up."

We've reached the bit where a stream crosses the beach. To get over it you have to climb up to the road.

"I have to get back," I say. "I'm looking after the campers."

Lionel sighs. "Do they even pay you, Amy? I'd put money on it that they don't. Think about it. You're wasting your life here. You're better off out of it."

We start to walk back, arms linked.

"Want to come back to my apartment tonight? I'll serve you champagne on the terrace, looking out over the Menai Straits. You can watch the lights reflecting off the water. Beats drinking canned lager on the beach with a bunch of Australians, surely?"

I'm tempted. I find Lionel attractive, especially tonight. There's more to him than Jake with his animal attraction. There's a depth. A desire to know me.

But then I check myself. I've felt this way before. Fallen for the same techniques. The person who remembers everything you've ever told them. The one who makes you feel like you're the only person in the room. The Iain Carver techniques.

I also know about Lionel's lifestyle. His penthouse never empty of beautiful people. You couldn't live with someone like that. You couldn't trust them. And I wonder about his aversion to the Lloyd family. It seems uncalled for. What have the Lloyds ever done to him?

I think of Adam, and my stomach twists. Adam didn't like Lionel. Called him 'Tosser'. For a nanosecond I wonder if it would be worth sleeping with Lionel just to get back at Adam. For a nanosecond only.

But the main thing I know, as Môr Tawel comes back into view, is this: however much of a fuckwit Adam has been, however hard I work for not much money, however much I've sold my soul for this family, my place lies here. With Rita. With Tom. With Rory. With the hens and the goats and the plants I've tended and watched grow. This is my place. My Môr Tawel.

"My car's round the back," says Lionel. I walk him to it.

"Sure you won't come?" he says.

I shake my head. He draws me close. I look up at him. I'm looking at an enigma. We kiss. We part. He gets in his vintage VW and drives off, giving three short toots of the horn as he goes.

I don't go back to the beach to join the others. I need to be alone.

I go to bed, but sleep eludes me for several hours. I half wake, sense Adam beside me, shift towards him, then wake fully, remembering Adam's gone. An icy spike shoots up my spine. The person in bed next to me is his brother.

"What the...?"

"Don't freak!" says Jay.

"What are you doing in bed next to me?"

"Nothing. I was just cold. And lonely."

"What the fuck, Jay? You don't feel the cold. You scared me."

"Don't cause a scene Amy. Please, please just give me peace." I look at him now. He's shaking under the duvet.

"I'm fading, Amy. I can't stand this much longer. This

half-life. I don't know how long I've got. Please, please help me soon."

I turn towards him. He's brilliant against the sheets. A vision of perfect beauty. I'm overcome by a sudden urge to hold him.

"Don't touch me!" he sounds in pain. We lie side by side.

"I used to sleep like this sometimes, with girls. Just lying next to each other, talking into the night."

Jay the untouchable. It must have frustrated the hell out of them. I long for Adam's sexual presence. Eventually, I sleep.

When I wake, Jay's gone.

Chapter Sixty-Three

"**C**AN YOU COPE without me on Friday, Rita? I want to go over to Nottingham."

"To see Adam?"

"To get my stuff."

"Still no word? My son can be very stubborn."

I time it so I'll arrive while Adam is out. I know his last session at the college on a Friday finishes at three, but my train is late and it's gone two-thirty by the time I reach Nottingham. No time to lose, but the bus takes forever and, as always when you're in a rush, there are people in the way, dawdling, people with all the time in the world. It's three fifteen by the time I turn the key in Adam's door. The place is a mess. Unopened mail in the hallway. Beer cans everywhere. Dirty plates in the sink. No time for sentimentality. I gather up my belongings, mostly clothes, cram them into my rucksack, and go. Time for one last look round? No, I'll only cry. Get the hell out before he comes back.

Outside, I bump into Angie from the pub.

"Amy! You guys back together?"

I shake my head. "Just been to get my stuff. Not stopping,"

"Shame," says Angie. "He's been in every night since you split, drowning his sorrows."

"That's his choice," I say, hailing my bus.

I have a bit of time to kill before my train. Now out of the danger-zone, I can afford to amble through Nottingham's streets. I move in a sort of trance, emotion suspended. It's getting dark as I walk past the brightly lit shops and the pavement cafes, wending my way though the thronging masses, people leaving work early on 'poet's' Friday, heading for the city's bars and restaurants. Their weekend starts here. Yet again, Christmas has crept up on me without me noticing. Though it's only November, the tree and the lights are up in the square. We used to come to Nottingham as teenagers to see the lights. For old time's sake, I take a detour through the Christmas market.

"Amy!"

It takes a few seconds to recognise him. Seconds of adjustment. He's the same, but different. Hair shaved short, beard gone, but it isn't that. He seems diminished, smaller, and an awful lot older than I remember him.

Iain Carver, perched on a bar stool, drinking alone at one of the Christmas market outdoor bars.

"Amy!" he stands up and grabs my arm. "I can't believe it's you."

"Iain," I say, shaking free. "What are you doing here?"

"Just, you know, having a drink after work." I wonder if he's had a few already.

"Join me. Let me buy you a drink." He's in his overcoat and work suit, tie slightly askew.

"I've got a train to catch."

"What time's your train? You must have time for a quick one?"

It's not so much the thought of spending time with Iain that draws me, more a kind of morbid curiosity.

"I've got fifteen minutes."

He dives into the bar and returns with a mulled wine. He hasn't even asked me what I want. I notice he gets served quickly, although the bar is busy.

"Cheers," he says raising his glass. "Just like the old days."

"Not really," I say. Now I've joined him I'm wondering what to say to him. I keep noticing how small he is. "So how come you're in Nottingham when you work in Stanlow?"

"I left."

"You left the garage?"

"Yes," he says. I sense he's hiding something, but I really can't be bothered to draw it out of him. Then he says, "A lot of things have changed in my life, Amy, and I'm so glad I've found you again. I live on my own now."

"Yeah?"

"Yeah. Got an apartment in Derby. And I'm doing a sales job in Nottingham at the minute."

"D'you drive here?"

"No, I get the train."

Iain Carver on a train. Something's definitely not right.

"Actually, Amy, I wasn't going to tell you this but you know I never could keep anything from you. I lost my job because I lost my licence."

"Drink drive?"

He nods. "I was only just over. I was unlucky. But they come down hard on you these days. It was all part of a downward slide that started the day you left. I went to pieces when you left me, Amy."

"Right." I check the time on my phone and drain my glass. "Well thanks for the drink, Iain, I'm off."

"Amy, you can't go! I've got so much more to tell you. You can get a later train, just stay for one more drink. Please! I can take you out for dinner later, just the two of us. My life is different now, I have no commitments."

Just then his phone buzzes. He reaches for it but not before I have time to read the name flashing upside down on the screen: Lisa.

"Someone wants you," I say, standing up.

"That can wait. This is more important. Don't you see, Amy? This is destiny, us running into each other. We're fated to be together."

"Bullshit," I say, picking up my rucksack.

"At least let me walk you to the station,"

"Goodbye Iain."

"At least let me have your number…" his voice tails off as I blend in with the crowds. He doesn't try to come after me.

On the train, I bask for a while in the empowerment this encounter has given me. I walked away from Iain Carver. I walked away and didn't want to stay.

I'm glad of the chance meeting, actually. It distracts me from the ton of grief I still feel over Adam, the weight of the rucksack now evidence to the ending of the best relationship I've ever had.

Time to sit back and let the weariness come. Time to wallow. Headphones on, music for the journey, music to exorcise my demons. The only problem is it's all Adam's music now.

My phone buzzes. Adam. I ignore it. A shot of adrenaline shoots through me. So much for a relaxing journey. He calls again. I ignore it again. The third time, I answer.

"Amy, this is Adam."

"I know."

"You've been back to the house. Your stuff's gone."

"I know."

"Amy, why?"

"It's what you wanted, me out of your life. You can have your life back now."

"Amy, where are you?"

"On a train."

"Where?"

"Just leaving Nottingham, on my way back to Wales."

"Amy listen," the line cracks as the train picks up speed. He rings back, but I ignore it. He can leave a voicemail if he's got anything to say.

Now it dawns on me, I feel good. Apart from a faint curiosity, and a tinge of pity, I felt nothing at all for Iain Carver. I saw him as he really is, a child in a forty-four-year-old's body. Stuck on the same old treadmill, finger on the self-destruct button. But crucially, someone who no longer has any power over me.

As for Adam, he can go back to his life, and I, right now, am going back to mine. I have a home waiting for me, people who love me, something to do that I'm good at, a place I belong. I, Amy Blue, am good enough, strong enough, entirely on my own. I am enough.

Derby station hoves into view. I have a fifteen-minute wait before the train to Crewe. Time to go to the loo, get a takeout tea and browse the book stand. I arrive at my platform just as they announce the train.

"Amy!"

He's running awkwardly on his still-gammy foot, wincing at each step, face screwed up with concentration, sweat dripping off his forehead.

"Amy, thank God! I thought I'd miss you."

"Adam that's my train. It leaves in three minutes."

"I'm coming with you."

"Don't be stupid."

"I'm not letting you out of my sight."

"Whatever." I turn towards the train door.

"Amy, I fucking love you." He follows me on.

He hasn't got a ticket. He got Warren to drive him to Derby and jumped the barrier. "Jed's got the van and I had to bribe Warren to drive me and he drives so fucking slow."

I smile. "Guess who I bumped into in Nottingham."

"Who? Someone I know?"

"I did bump into Angie, she said you were a mess, but someone else."

"Who then?"

"My ex, Iain Carver."

"Fuck," said Adam.

"He bought me a drink."

"You let that arsehole buy you a drink?"

"You got a problem with that?"

"Nothing that wouldn't be solved by me knocking the shit out of him."

"Yeah, right."

I'll let him squirm a while before I tell him that Iain Carver means no more to me now than the coffee stain on the Formica table in front of us. Let him stew before I tell him that I love him.

"I came back with more than I bargained for," I say as we both walk into Môr Tawel.

"Thank God!" says Rita. "See, I told you he'd come round."

Chapter Sixty-Four

"IT WAS HORRIBLE without you," Adam concedes later. "Like I'd lost my soul-mate. Like I'd even lost part of myself. Like you're now an extension of my brain. It's been doing my head in."

"So why didn't you contact me?"

"It was like, I was trying to prove something to myself. Trying to prove I could live without you. Then today at work, another day when everything reminds me of you, and everyone asks about you, I just thought, what's the point in torturing yourself, just admit you fucking love this woman. I've been a total idiot Amy. You and me, we're meant to be together."

"Interesting," I say. "That's what Iain Carver said."

Adam creases up his forehead. "Fuck him," he says. "The difference is I mean it, and I'll prove it to you, if you'll have me."

"Ghosts and all?"

"Ghosts and all," he says. "I've seen Jay too, you know, since we broke up. Every night. He wouldn't leave the fuck alone."

"So you believe me now?"

He nods. "The sooner we sort out this mess the better. Come on, we've got to lay our ghosts to rest."

THE NEXT DAY, we start to plan our strategy for helping Jay. We begin by looking up news reports from the time. What coverage there was in the local paper isn't much help.

"When Sara died, it was a big national story. We had TV crews coming to the house. Thankfully for Mam, they left us alone when Jay died. I don't think they made the connection between the sibling deaths. I just remember a short piece in the local paper. Suicides don't normally make the news."

We find the piece. It describes Jay as a hiker whose body was found at the bottom of a cliff. It does say the Police weren't looking for anyone else in connection with the incident. Subtext for suicide.

There's another short article after the inquest, 'hiker's death ruled accidental.'

According to Adam, the Coroner gave that verdict to spare Rita's feelings.

"He knew Mam from years back and was just being nice, I reckon. It should really have been at least an open verdict."

"So who found Jay?" I ask.

"Some twitcher bloke with binoculars spotted the body from the opposite cliff. They had the lifeboat out but it couldn't get close enough so they abseiled down to pull him out."

"So that guy, the bird-watcher," I say. "D'you know his name? Could we talk to him?"

"It'll be in the inquest notes."

Then I remember something.

"What about Maria?"

"Who?"

"Mad Maz." I tell him about Maria's cryptic comments about seeing Jay with someone the day he died.

"Her? She's fucking mad. Not exactly a reliable witness. What did she say?"

I rack my memory for the words. What exactly had she said?

"The other one," I say. "She said she saw Jay with 'the other one' the day he died."

"Who d'you think she meant?"

Thoughts race through my mind. I remember what Charlotte said about Maria – she talks to the dead.

"D'you think she meant your sister?"

"Cate?"

"No, Sara. Maria's a medium. She conjours up dead people. Maybe she thought she saw Sara with Jay."

"Or made it up. She was trying to get Mam to have a séance you know. Anyway if that's who she meant that's not gonna help us. Sara cannot have killed Jay."

"How about, what's his name, Bramwell?" I remembered the weird scene I'd witnessed in the dining room in the middle of the night.

"Who?"

"The guy who built the wigwam? He knew Jay, apparently."

"He's weird enough," says Adam. "But the timing doesn't fit. Maria saw whoever it was the day Jay died. That guy didn't turn up at Môr Tawel till about two years later."

"Well I guess we'll have to track her down and ask her."

Chapter Sixty-Five

MARIA IS NOT at her house, and the children we find there say she's working at the Bridge café. The Bridge is a dry house for addicts and alcoholics. Apparently Maria is a volunteer counsellor there.

"Bloody hell!" says Adam. "Who counsels who?"

But when we get to the Bridge they say she's gone.

"Did she say where?"

"For a walk."

"Great!" says Adam. "She's only the fucking walking woman of North Wales, she could be anywhere."

We're just about to head for home when we hear a familiar "Bella Bella," and there she is, dog on lead, two children in tow. She's wearing a shapeless shift which almost touches the ground, a shaggy fur jacket over it, and big sunglasses.

"Maria we've been looking for you. Can we talk to you please?"

Maria huffs. "You'll have to walk with me, I've got things to do."

Maria, despite her dodgy foot, walks at pace. Adam, with his gammy leg, can't keep up. I run alongside. We're heading towards the suspension bridge.

"We're trying to find out about the night Jude died," I say, breathless. "And I wanted to ask you about something you said, about seeing him that day, with someone?"

Maria quickens her step and shrugs her shoulders. "So you want to talk to me now, do you? I tried to tell people at the time but nobody would listen, dim na fyddent? I'm not sure I can remember now."

"Maria, please, it's important."

"Funny how all of a sudden people want to talk to me." She turns away as she speaks, looking out towards the strait, we are now half-way across the bridge. The wind almost drowns out her words.

"Maria, I'm sorry nobody listened then, but I'm listening now. Please tell me what you saw."

She stops and turns towards me, her long dress billowing in the breeze. The sunglasses are heart-shaped. She looks like some throwback from the sixties.

"He was there on the bridge," she gestures to the other side. "They seemed to be having some sort of disagreement."

"Who, Maria? Jude and who?"

"The other one of course, there were raised voices, and some choice language."

"What other one, Maria? I don't know who you mean."

"That one of course," she nods her head heavenwards. She must mean Sara after all.

"You mean the sister who died?"

"No!" she says. "You know the one, lives up there in the big house. The arty farty one."

I follow her gaze. Lionel Rees Prosser's flat is directly in our line of vision.

"Lionel Rees-Prosser was on the bridge that day, arguing with Jude? Did you hear what they were arguing about?"

"I heard nothing apart from the swear words, which I'm not going to repeat in front of the kids. I've told you all I know now, we have to go." She grabs the lead from the oldest child and scurries off in the direction of Bangor. I walk back to Adam.

"Tosser saw him the day he died, and he never came forward, never told anyone?" says Adam. "Bloody hell, I want a word with him." He makes as if to climb the steps to Lionel's flat.

"Wait," I say. "We need to think about this. You can't go up there accusing him of stuff."

"You have to admit it looks suspicious."

I look up at the apartment, with its sweeping terrace. I think of Lionel, flouncing around in his leathers. Exhibitionist, yes. Drama-queen, yes, but murderer? I can't see it.

Then I remember how he was the other night. The night he tried to persuade me to come with him to his flat. The night he tried to turn me against the Lloyds, and I wonder.

"Let's just hang on a minute. We should wait until we've gathered more evidence."

"How we gonna do that? Ask Jay next time he decides to

put in an appearance?"

"Let me think," I say, then I remember something. "You said he used to keep a diary."

"Yeah, he always did. Like a journal. He used to fill it with poetry and drawings and stuff."

"Maybe he kept one when he was in Manchester."

"We picked up his stuff from that flat, I don't remember a diary, and if there was it'll be long gone."

"Not necessarily," I say, remembering the pile of books stashed away in the fireplace, hidden by the chest of drawers. A copy of *War and Peace*, some Plato, an art history book and a notebook. I remember flicking through the notebook on my last day, not understanding its contents, and replacing it in the alcove.

"Did it have poems in it?"

"Yes, I think so."

"Worth a trip to Manchester then?"

"Yup."

Chapter Sixty-Six

THE KNOT IN my stomach proves that I dread this trip back to my past, as Adam and I rattle up the motorway towards Manchester in Rita's little van. Heading east from the city centre I see the familiar outline of the Pennines in the distance and I'm struck by how beautiful they are. How could I have missed this beauty while I lived within sight of them? I know how, of course, I had an altered perception then. I couldn't see beyond my own misery.

As we get closer to Balmoral Street the knot tightens. The hills may be beautiful, but the streets we are entering are still dire, though not quite as grim as I remember them. Perhaps it's the weather. I was here in the bleakness of last winter. This year it's much milder. And today is bright sunshine. Nearing Balmoral Street, I see a sign which says: 'East Manchester Regeneration Project'. I remember being told they got money to spruce the place up. There are now splashes of colour. Some of the houses have hanging baskets.

Others have new fences. There's less litter on the streets than I remember.

No problem getting into the property; the front door is wedged open, there are workmen in. This in itself is bizarre. The hallway, which used to be yellowed with age and nicotine, has had a fresh coat of magnolia. The shabby sideboard that housed the junk mail's gone, replaced by a neat row of lockable mailboxes. There's even new carpet on the stairs.

We climb up to my old attic room. Again the door is open for us. I gasp as I walk in, it's barely recognisable. The painters are in, giving it a last lick of emulsion. A new skylight window replaces the broken one. The furniture has been cleared out.

"Can I help you love?" says a man in paint-splashed overalls.

"Er. This used to be my room. I think I left some books behind."

"Everything's gone to the skip."

"The one outside?"

"Yeah but there's been eight skip-loads since we started," says the other man. "You'll be lucky to find anything."

"Good to see you doing the place up," I say.

"Needed it," says the older of the two men. "I'm the new owner."

"You bought it?"

"Yeah. Council want to spruce up some of these old properties. Giving out grants. I've got three of these houses."

"Are any of the tenants still here?"

"Oh yeah. I bought it with sitting tenants and honoured

their agreements. This is the only room that's been empty for ages."

"People say it's haunted," says the other painter, "Other tenants have heard voices."

"Careful," says the landlord. "She might want her old room back!" he winks.

Outside, I climb into the skip.

"Like looking for a needle in a fucking haystack," says Adam, as we sift through rubble and bits of furniture. "Anything you recognise from the room?"

I shake my head. I spot the remnants of the old hall chest, but the other items are all unfamiliar. I suspect the rotting remains of my old room are long gone.

"Wonder where the tip is," I muse.

"I'm not searching the entire neighbourhood for this thing," says Adam. "If it's not here, we're going."

There could have been an argument if it hadn't been for someone calling out: "Ames! What you doin' here?"

"Tania!" I hardly recognise her, she's so smartly dressed. Her hair's cut short and streaked with blonde.

"Just looking for some stuff I left behind."

"You'll be lucky, they've gutted the place. I've got a fab new room, come in and see and I'll make you a cuppa."

If Adam feels embarrassed in this boudoir full of bondage gear, he doesn't let on. Tania has been allowed to choose the colour scheme, and she's gone for a deep tantric red.

"What stuff you looking for?"

"A book."

"*War and Peace*?"

"No, it's like a diary."

Tania shakes her head. "The only thing I remember is *War and Peace*. I think Barny took it."

"Barny?"

"You know, from Flat Five. He's always scavenging through the skip. Rooting around to see what people have chucked out."

"Oh Barnabas?"

"Yeah. Might be worth you seeing if he's got it. If I see him I'll ask him. You don't want people reading your diary, eh Ames?"

"It wasn't hers. It belonged to my brother," says Adam. "He lived here a few years ago, young blond bloke, art student, did you know him?"

Tania thinks for a minute. "A lot of people come and go in a place like this. I'm the only one left from when you were here Ames, apart from Barny who's been here forever."

"What happened to Psycho-Boy?" I nod my head in the direction of the floor above.

"Oh they busted him. It was soon after you'd gone. He moved his mates into the two empty flats. None of them paid any rent, including him. Anyway Ames, tell me what you've been up to. Did you get to Wales?"

We go round the back to Flat Five and knock. Nobody answers, so we sit outside in the yard in the sunshine. The plastic table and chairs look like they've had a wash. The windows and patio doors look new. The plant pots are still lined up outside.

"That's Barnabas's Scarborough Fair garden," I tell Adam.

"Parsley, sage, rosemary, thyme. Very clever. But where is he, this Barny bloke? We could be here hours!"

Just then the patio door opens and he appears, wearing a purple striped towelling robe.

"Sorry, I've been asleep," he says. "Can I help you?"

"Hi Barnabas, it's me, Amy. I used to live here."

He scrutinises me for a few seconds before recognition.

"I remember you," he says slowly. "You sat in my garden, I made you tea, then you disappeared."

"Yes, I left in a bit of a hurry. No time to say goodbye. I left some things behind actually, books and stuff. Tania said you might have rescued them. Not bothered about the books but the thing I'm really looking for is a diary."

Barnabas motions for us to come in.

"Do sit down," he says, clearing books and papers off an aged sofa, then disappears into the back of the flat.

The place is like an antique shop. Dusty pot ornaments and brass objects cover every ledge, the walls are lined with shelves stuffed full of ancient books. A sword hangs above the doorway.

Barnabas returns, having changed out of the robe into faded, misshapen jeans and a t-shirt. He has an electronic cigarette in one hand and a hard-backed A4 notebook in the other.

"Is this what you're looking for?" he says, drawing deeply on his device. Adam grabs the notebook.

"Sorry. Barnabas, this is Adam," I say. Barnabas studies him.

"You look familiar too, Adam. Did you live here once?"

"No but my brother did, and he looked a bit like me.

Maybe you knew him?"

"Ye…es," says Barnabas, sitting down opposite us on a well-worn armchair. "I think I may have done. Art student. It was a good few years ago now. He was interesting. He used to sit in the garden sometimes and we'd chat about art and philosophy and put the world to rights."

"Sounds like Jay," says Adam.

"That's right, Jay, it's all coming back. He disappeared too, rather suddenly. He told me he was going back home for a few days then he never came back. I'm thinking it must be three, four years ago now. Funny how time marches on. Do you two fancy a brew?"

It seems impolite to refuse, and I'm keen to get him to talk more about Jay.

Adam doesn't join in the conversation, he's busy leafing through the notebook. Barnabas can't remember much more about Jay, even though I push him. He seems flustered by my questioning, drawing repeatedly on his e-cig and wiping his hands on his jeans. Now I have a nagging feeling about him. I remember his reaction when I first talked about Jay. "I never thought he would come back," he said, like he knew Jay was dead. Could he be a suspect? I'll mention this to Adam. But how could Barnabas have been in Wales the day Jay died? I'm not cut out to be a detective. You start to suspect everybody.

Barnabas looks relieved when we drain our mugs and stand up to go.

Walking to the van, I see a once familiar figure approaching along the street. He walks with a jaunt to his step, almost like he's dancing. He's wearing a bright orange puffer jacket. His face cracks into a smile. I realise I can't greet him by name as I never knew it.

"Ah Pixie!" he holds out his arms. His embrace is warm. "I never thought I'd see Pixie-girl again, and you looking so good!" he turns to Adam. "And you with your young mon too. Dis a happy day."

"He thinks you're Jay," I whisper to Adam.

"Life treat you good Pixie girl I can tell. I'm good too mon. Everything change around here. Tings good around here now."

We don't stop and chat. Adam seems impatient to go, but as we head off in the van I feel a warmth for the people of Balmoral Street I never thought possible.

"Sorry to drag you away," says Adam, "but I want you to take a look at what's in that diary. I think it's all a load of incomprehensible bollocks but you might be able to make sense of it."

The page falls open at the same page I'd seen back in March. I read aloud.

A suicide stood naked at the dawn
Of understanding, wondering if he could
Compare those he was about to leave forlorn
A suicide stood

"But," I say, "this suggests… it sounds like…"

"Say it," says Adam.

"He really did it! Killed himself, I mean."

"What's the date on that?" says Adam.

"No date."

"Read some more, have a look at the stuff before the end."

I flick through the pages.

Your face.
In the window.
Watching, wanting
Yearning for lost youth.
Face at the window
Of opportunity.
While we are young enough to be your fools
While we are sick enough to think you're cool
Games at the window.

"What's that about?"

"No idea. Have a look at the last entry."

This is more like a journal entry. It reads: 'Been in touch with Glyn and Iwan and they say I'm the only one who can do this. The only one he never had power over. Got my ticket. Tomorrow. I'M GOING IN.'

"Huh?" I say. "What does he mean, 'I'm going in?' and who are these people, Glyn and Iwan …?"

"Oh they were mates of his at school. People he used to hang with."

"Are they still around Bangor?"

"Dunno. Beth might know, I suppose."

"Beth? You mean… your ex?"

"Yup," says Adam. "She was one of that crowd. But they all had some kind of falling out after Jay died, so she might not know where they are. There was some bad scene involving them all. Don't know the details. She didn't like to talk about it."

"Could you ask her?"

"I'm not contacting her. Not if I can help it."

"So how do we find this Glyn and Iwan then?"

"Maybe it's time to go back on Facebook."

Chapter Sixty-Seven

A DAM AND I have something in common. We feel it a distinction *not* to be on Facebook. Me because of the cyber-bullying I experienced after Iain. Adam because he finds the whole thing vacuous and inane. He's even got a t-shirt with the slogan: 'I'm not on F***ing Facebook.'

It doesn't take long, through the world of the Internet, to track both boys down, although Iwan gives his hometown as Boston Massachusetts. Adam also, through trawling through their friends, draws up a list of a few others who might be able to help. He sends them all a private message, composed and dictated by me, which says:

'Hope you don't mind me contacting you, but I know you were friends with my brother Jude (Jay), who everyone believed committed suicide in 2010. Well, some new information has come to light suggesting there may be more to it than that, and we understand he was on his way to meet someone that day, but we're not sure who. I'm writing in case you have any information about what that meeting could have been about. If you know anything, it would help our family massively if you'd be prepared to speak to us. Anything you say will be treated in strict confidence of course. You can reply to all, message me separately or phone me.'

A few minutes after we've pressed send, a reply pings into Adam's inbox from Iwan Pryce, now living in America, but as luck would have it, back for a month visiting family. It's a bit cryptic. It says:

"Pleased you're doing this Adam. It's played on my mind ever since Jay tragically left us. I'm glad someone is grabbing this by the balls. Suggest we all meet up to discuss. Am in Wales for three more weeks."

There are no more responses.

Chapter Sixty-Eight

I'M SITTING IN Lionel's mezzanine living room, looking out over the Menai Straits. We thought it would seem more natural if I came here alone. Adam dropped me off before meeting up with his ex-girlfriend Beth, Iwan and Glyn.

To my surprise, Lionel offers me a vodka and tops up a glass he's already almost finished. I've never seen him drink before. Even at his party he stuck to sparkling water. I take a little to keep him company but I want to keep a clear head.

"So why the vodka? You celebrating something?" I say.

Strange to celebrate alone, at one o' clock in the afternoon.

He shakes his head. "Just needed something to steady my nerves." He's looking a bit dishevelled.

"Why? What's up?"

"Nothing for you to worry about. Just some people I thought were friends getting the knives out. I've had a few nasty comments on social media about my new exhibition."

He has his tablet in his hand and he's scrolling through messages.

"That's bad. Ignore them Lionel. They're just trolls. Probably jealous of your success."

I need to keep Lionel sweet to get him to trust me.

"Ah, Amy you always make me feel so much better," he says, relaxing a little into the leather armchair opposite, but still with half an eye on his tablet. "So lovely to see you, my little English rose. What's been going on with you?"

I talk about neutral things before bringing the subject round to Jay. I try to do it seamlessly. Even so it sounds like a bolt from a blue when I say. "I think there's a lot of mystery surrounding Jay's death, don't you? Didn't you say you saw him the day he died?"

Lionel looks up. "I never said that, did I?"

"I thought you said he came to see you. Or maybe someone saw you together… yeah that was it. Someone said they saw you together earlier that day."

"Hmm," says Lionel, draining his drink. "It was a long time ago Amy. I may have seen him. Come to think of it, I think he did come to see me around that time. He used to pop in when he was passing."

"Did he say anything? I mean, was there any indication of what he was planning to do? Why did he come to see you?"

"My goodness, Amy. How am I supposed to remember what some boy came to see me about years ago? Probably his art. His art project for Uni. Yes, it's coming back to me now. He was back from university in Leeds…"

"Manchester," I say.

"Was it? Well, he was back from wherever and he dropped round. A lot of former students get in touch when they want my advice. He couldn't decide what to do for his dissertation. He *was* a bit agitated, come to think of it, but he was a very intense kind of boy. Why does it matter to you, anyway?"

"I've got this theory it might not have been suicide. And from what you're telling me he doesn't sound like someone planning to take their own life."

"Not that old chestnut," says Lionel, standing. "There were people at the time, mainly the mother, who didn't think he'd done it. But if you ask me, that's just denial. If you knew Jay you'd have known he *was* capable of suicide. His mood could plummet so quickly. He was a very volatile and insecure person. Now let's talk about more cheerful things."

Perhaps it's the vodka that clouds my judgement, but I can't let it rest.

"So did he just come to see you at the flat then leave, or did you go somewhere together?"

Lionel tips up his glass to drain it then says, "What is this? The Spanish inquisition? Like I said he dropped by the flat then went away again."

But Maria saw them on the bridge, arguing. So Lionel's lying.

"I'm sure someone said they saw you talking to him on the bridge," I say.

Lionel moves towards the drinks cabinet, reaches for the vodka bottle then hesitates as we hear the front door open downstairs and the sound of singing as his Malaysian lodger – or whatever she is – drifts up the stairs.

Lionel moves towards me, touches my arm then says, "I'd like to talk about this some more but not here. I need to go to Beaumaris so I'll take you home. We can talk on the way." He lifts his military coat from a hook near the door then leads me down the stairs to where his car sits in the car port.

"Are you ok to drive?" I know he's had at least two vodkas.

"Never been better," he says, opening the passenger door of the Beetle and almost pushing me inside.

Chapter Sixty-Nine

I T MIGHT BE the unfamiliarity of sitting on the wrong side in the left-hand drive car, where the driver usually sits, that unnerves me, but as we pull out of the car port onto the street Lionel's driving seems erratic and jumpy. There's a painting wedged in behind the back seat and the car smells of linseed oil. The car has long ago lost its suspension and I feel every jolt as we go over bumps in the road.

My phone, which is on vibrate, starts to buzz repeatedly. I pick it up. Adam.

"You in Tosser's car?" He's talking fast, and it's hard to hear over the noise of the engine.

"Yeah, just coming home."

"Don't look now but I'm following. I'm about four cars behind."

I glance in the wing mirror and see Adam's van above the traffic.

"Everything ok?" I say.

"Spoke to the twitcher," he says, his voice barely audible. I lose him for a few moments then he comes back. "Tell you later, but be careful."

I try to phone back but I've lost signal.

When we clear Menai Bridge, Lionel doesn't take the route to Beaumaris but speeds off on the fast road towards Holyhead.

My heart rate accelerates.

"Where are we going? Thought you were taking me home?"

"I will but not yet. Please Amy, can we just go for a drive first?" He's acting weird, but the traffic is fast moving and there are no opportunities to jump out. Behind, I see the Transit still following. There's only a couple of cars between us now and I can just make out someone on the passenger seat beside Adam.

I tell myself it's all ok. This is Lionel Rees Prosser, not some psychopathic maniac. He's just a bit upset and wants to talk. I've been to his flat several times and it's not the first time he's given me a lift. Everything will be fine. But my pulse continues to pound.

"Lionel I need to get home," I say. Trying to keep it calm, trying to pretend everything's normal.

"I wanted to talk about this Jay business a bit more," he says. "But not at the flat with Aishah there."

"Oh right," I say. This could be important. "So there's more?" I have to raise my voice to be heard over the sound of the straining engine as Lionel pulls out into the outside lane of the dual carriageway and steps on the gas.

He doesn't answer. I try to read his expression but his face is set. I look at my phone, still no signal. I check the mirror, Adam's still following.

We eventually slow down a little, and Lionel speaks.

"It'll do me good to get it off my chest. It's played on my mind since that day, but I blanked it all out, bottled it up."

"What has, Lionel?"

He swears as the car in front brakes suddenly.

"Jay did come to see me that day and we did go for a walk to get some air. I was trying to calm him down, you see. He was very agitated. He'd just come from his family. He'd had a horrendous argument with them."

"Really?" This is not the version I'd heard.

"Amy if you really want to know what pushed him over the edge you should look no further than that ex-boyfriend of yours."

For a second I think he means Iain. Then I remember that the last time I saw Lionel I told him Adam and I broke up. He doesn't know we're back together.

"There was huge sibling rivalry you know. Adam was jealous of his younger brother. Jay was so much more beautiful and talented. If anyone drove him to suicide, it would have been his big brother."

"You mean literally drove him there? I did wonder how he got all the way to South Stack." As I say this I realise we're approaching Holyhead. The car slows as we enter the town. I consider jumping out, but I'm on the driver's side, I'd be in the path of oncoming traffic. We speed up again and the moment is lost.

Lionel takes the bends too fast, and blasts his horn at a lorry about to reverse out of a driveway. We swing past it, but I see in the mirror Adam's got stuck behind the lorry and I lose sight of him.

I see a sign for South Stack and the lighthouse, then I realise where we're heading. "Why are you taking me to South Stack?"

"I haven't been here since," he says. "I used to bring students here to paint, because of the views and the lovely light, but after what happened... after I heard what happened, I..." His voice trails off as we pull up in the lower car park, but instead of getting out he grips the steering wheel then buries his head in his arms.

"Lionel are you ok?" I say and he looks up at me, his eyes wet, his face ashen.

"I loved Jay, you know. In a platonic, paternal kind of way of course," then adds very softly. "I would never do anything to hurt him."

A message from Adam flashes up on my screen. <Twitcher says LRP VW @ S Stack that day.>

Lionel opens the car door. "Come with me?" he looks vulnerable now, his eyes pleading. "I want to see the spot where he died. But I can't face this alone."

As I get out of the car I look around for Adam but there's still no sign of the Transit. Lionel links his arm though mine and we start to walk along the path, but this is not like our companionable stroll along the beach from Môr Tawel, his grip is a little too forceful and his pace too fast. As we walk towards the white observation tower I see the van swing past, heading for the top car park. Thank God.

Adam's here.

Lionel releases my arm as we pass the tower and head towards the cliff, looking out at the lighthouse on the facing rocks. It's been a clear bright day but the winter sun has dropped behind low cloud and the light is failing. The whole scene, beautiful when I last saw it, now has an air of melancholy. I'm only wearing my light jacket and I shiver as a blast of wind hits me. We stop by the cliff edge, where I stood with Adam on Solstice day, the sign 'Perygl, Clogwyni Serth – Danger, Steep Cliffs' marking the spot.

A bird flies up from the cliffs below, almost close enough to feel the beat of its wings. Startled, I step back, but Lionel grips my shoulders with both hands and propels me forward. I look up at him. Gone is the emotion of earlier, his face is stony. "Be careful now," he says, and there's a touch of menace in his voice. "We wouldn't want you to slip here and take a nasty tumble."

"Lionel!" I try to break free, to push back from the edge, but he's got me in a tight arm lock.

For a second, I stare into the abyss. I see the rocks and the swirling waters below, I glimpse what Jay had seen, and then:

"Let her go, Lionel."

Adam's voice cuts in from the top path. We look up to see him running towards us, then curse as he stumbles on the rough ground as his weak leg gives way, but it's enough distraction for Lionel to loosen his grip and for me to get away.

Adam picks himself up, hobbles towards us then stands between me and Lionel.

"Were you about to push her off the cliff like you pushed my brother?"

"I didn't push anyone," says Lionel.

"So how d'you explain this?" says Adam. "You were seen arguing with Jay on the bridge the day he died. You never came forward."

"Seen by whom?" says Lionel. He looks to me for help.

"Lionel," I say, "you told me earlier that you saw him that day, so why didn't you say anything, after his death? Why didn't you speak at the inquest?"

"I… I didn't think I had anything to add. The boy was depressed. He took a tumble, and that's all there is to it, really, now if you don't mind." He turns back towards the path to the car park.

"I *do* mind," Adam blocks his exit. "Because that's *not* all there is to it. Your car was seen at South Stack."

"What?"

"Very distinctive it is. Not many people have a purple and white convertible VW. The bird-watcher who spotted Jay's body also saw your car in the lower car park about half an hour before Jay died."

"Well why didn't they say so at the time?" Lionel's eyes flit from side to side as though looking for someone to rescue him. "What's the point in dragging all this up now? Haven't you got anything better to do than rake up the past?"

"We've just got unanswered questions about why Jay did what he did," I say. "And since you were probably the last person to see him alive, we think you may have some answers. What were the two of you arguing about?"

"It's none of your business," he says, and once more turns to go. Adam jumps in front of him. Lionel tries to sidestep but a large boulder blocks his path. Lifting his hands, he attempts to shove Adam out of the way but Adam, by far the stronger, pushes him back. Lionel stumbles against the boulder.

"Did you have an inappropriate relationship with my brother?"

"That's outrageous!" says Lionel, straightening.

"Like you did with Glyn Evans and Iwan Pryce?"

I gawp at Adam. This is new.

"Stop right there."

"*And* Beth Rowlands?

Beth too?

"Did you, Lionel?"

"That's enough. I'm going. Get out of my way."

Adam doesn't budge. "Would you prefer we got the Police to ask these questions?" he says, "because if you walk away now, that's where I'm going."

"And say what? They'd laugh you out of the Police Station."

"That you were at the scene and never told anyone. That you lied about it. I think they'd be very interested. Particularly with the other allegations stacking up against you. If you run away now you won't do yourself any favours."

Lionel shrugs, then wraps his coat around him against a sudden gust of wind. Again he looks around as though summoning help from an unseen public.

"So Lionel," I say. "Seeing as we're here, how about you

walk us through what really happened."

"What is this? A re-enactment?" he says.

"Jay came to see you at the flat. You went for a walk. You argued. You drove the two of you here. Then what?"

Lionel looks at me as he says. "We walked up to the tower. He was still agitated, see. Talking like he did. About how pointless it all was. How humanity was a drain on the planet, how his family didn't understand him, you know, like he used to."

"Like he talked when he was about fifteen," says Adam. "He'd moved on from all that."

"Not that day he hadn't. Anyway we walked over to the cliff edge to get a look at the lighthouse." Lionel waves in the direction of the lighthouse. I notice it's half obscured by cloud.

A foghorn sounds.

Lionel starts to snivel. "I tried to stop him," he sniffs. "I grabbed his hand, to stop him from jumping, but he broke free and it was too late." Lionel slumps down onto the boulder, head in his hands.

"My heart bleeds for you Lionel." A different voice from the upper path, a man looms over us, silhouetted against the sky. A tall, thin man about my age with a deep tan and hipster beard. The passenger in Adam's van, presumably. Adam nods at him as he walks down the path towards us.

Lionel jumps up.

"Remember me, Lionel?" The stranger has an American twang to his once Welsh accent. "Iwan Pryce. Don't look so surprised. I know I've changed a bit. No longer the pretty boy you abused when I was fourteen."

Iwan and Lionel stare at each other for a few seconds. Their eyes lock. I sense an invisible power struggle. Iwan looks down for a minute, his shoulders starting to slump, then he straightens up again, looks Lionel in the eye, and says: "We nearly brought Glyn with us too, but he couldn't stand seeing you again. Said the thought of what you did to him makes him sick."

Lionel looks up towards the top car park as if he's worried there might be others.

Adam starts again: "First you say you weren't here at all, then you say you only came here to talk, now you concede there was a struggle. You have to admit it's not looking good. If your version's true why not come out and say it at the time? You'd have been hailed a hero for trying to save him."

"I was a teacher. I had a reputation. I didn't need the publicity, and what difference would it make? It wouldn't have brought him back."

"Publicity!" says Iwan. "You're *so* about to learn the meaning of publicity." I sense a subtle shift in power between the two men.

"Me, Glyn, Beth. How many of your little elite did you have sex with, Lionel? Boys *and* girls. And we all thought we were the only one. Until we compared notes years later. Jay came to see you that day to out you, didn't he?"

Lionel's eyes dart from one to the other, like a wild animal cornered.

"On the back seat of your car. On the overnight sleeper to Edinburgh. In the hotel room in Paris," Iwan continues. "And later in your apartment that time with the cocaine."

"You could have walked away," snaps Lionel. "Nobody forced you. The truth is, you wanted it. You all did. You weren't complaining then. It was consensual."

"Consensual, Lionel? How can it ever be consensual between a fourteen-year old boy and a thirty-two-year-old man? I didn't know that then. I was naïve. But I know now. It was abuse."

"Well why didn't you report it? Why wait all these years? You liked it, it gave you status."

"Sure," says Iwan. "Try explaining that to the cops. I've just been having a nice chat with them. Know where they are right now, Lionel? They're at your flat, having a good old look around."

"You…"

"Nothing to worry about," says Adam. "I expect they're just admiring the art."

"You bastards, all of you, ganging up on me. What did I ever do to you?"

"What did *Jay* ever do to *you*?" says Adam. "I think we've got all we need for now. Shall we go, Amy?" he takes my hand and starts to lead me away, nodding to Iwan who follows.

"That won't stand up in court you know, any of it," Lionel calls after us. "It's a lie you cooked up between you."

"Whatever, Lionel, but we've got enough. You've admitted you had a relationship with Iwan."

"I'll say you made it up. You had a grudge, a vendetta against a former teacher. I never admitted anything."

Adam turns round and laughs. "What century do you think we live in, Tosser? There are three of us and we all have mobile phones. This entire conversation is on record," he holds his phone up, waving it at Lionel.

"You scheming, bullying bastards," Lionel shouts as we walk away.

"Shouldn't we stay with him?" I ask. "What if he tries to cut and run, gets in his car and escapes by ferry or something."

"It's ok, cavalry's coming," says Adam, just as the cop car creeps over the hill.

I don't know why we all turn round at that moment. A second later we'd have missed it. One moment Lionel is there, silhouetted against the cliff edge, the next he is gone, and a deep, guttural, animalistic cry pierces the dusk.

Chapter Seventy

THEY TAKE STATEMENTS from the three of us at the police station. Iwan is in there ages. A lot to say, presumably.

Since watching Lionel jump I've been shivering uncontrollably. I'm still shaking as we wait in reception. Adam holds me close to warm me up.

While we wait for Iwan, Adam tells me more about what happened earlier. Seems Lionel abused Glyn, Iwan and Beth at different times. But they didn't know about each other until they all met up a few months before Jay died.

"They started talking about Lionel then they all had this 'me too!' moment." says Adam. "So they decided to confront him."

The plan was to secretly record Lionel, so they'd have evidence.

"The three of them were supposed to go with Jay, who he never abused, but not for want of trying."

"Jay the untouchable," I say.

But on the day, one by one they dropped out. Couldn't face it. So Jay went alone.

"So why didn't they say anything after Jay died?"

"They didn't realise Jay had actually gone to meet Tosser. They thought he really did kill himself. They all felt like they were to blame because they'd let him down. Wimped out. Then they all fell out with each other. Glyn had a bit of a breakdown. Iwan moved to America. Beth always had her doubts about Jay's suicide, but I wasn't prepared to listen at that point."

I think for a moment, absorbing the information.

"So did you know about Beth and Lionel? Is that how come you hate him?"

"One of the reasons," says Adam. "I never liked him. Beth did tell me a bit about what happened, but the details were hazy. She'd had a couple of lines of coke at one of Tosser's parties and woke up in his bed. She was seventeen."

"So not underage?"

"No, but she was one of his students so it could've got him fired. She did try reporting him to another teacher but was warned off. They said draw a line under it. She wouldn't want her parents finding out about the cocaine, would she?"

I shake my head. "That's so wrong!"

It'd be different now. With all the stuff that's come out recently about people in power abusing their roles, people are finding the courage to come forward, even after years. And they're finally being listened to.

"All that stuff about the police searching his house was bollocks," says Adam. "That was just to call his bluff. But it worked."

"So how come the Police came to South Stack?"

"Iwan stayed behind in the car park to phone them. Told them a man was threatening to throw a girl off the cliff." He hugs me closer. "I seriously thought Tosser was going to push you over. Thought history was going to repeat itself."

IT'S LATE BY the time we get back to Môr Tawel. Rita looks up from where she's resting on the sofa.

"Mam, we have something to tell you."

Her body stiffens, her eyes, enormous in her hairless face, widen. How can somebody look alarmed but hopeful at the same time?

"It's nothing for you to worry about," I say. "It's ok, really, but it might be a bit of a shock." I hold her hand under the fleece blanket she's wrapped in.

"Listen Mam," says Adam. "Lionel Rees-Prosser is dead. He threw himself off South Stack cliffs today."

Rita gasps.

"But before he did he admitted he was with Jay the day he died. They were both at South Stack. There was a struggle, and Jay went over the edge. We don't know if Lionel pushed Jay or if it was an accident. But the police are taking Lionel's suicide as an admission of guilt."

"Oh Lordy!"

"The Police are searching Lionel's flat. It looks like he was a paedophile, which some people suspected anyway. We've been in touch with people he molested. Anyway it seems Jay was planning to confront him the day he died."

"Did he… did that man… with Jude?"

"No, Mam, we're pretty sure he didn't abuse Jay. He wanted to. He and Lionel had this kind of psychological battle of wits, but as you know Jay wouldn't let anyone touch him."

There are tears rolling down Rita's face.

"So," I say, squeezing her hand, "when you thought Jude's death wasn't suicide, when you felt it in your bones he didn't kill himself, you were right, Rita, you were right."

"So this is also an apology," says Adam, moving forward. "I refused to listen. I was bullish and insensitive, and I'm sorry."

Rita shuts her eyes. "Please God," she whispers. "May they rest in peace."

POLICE SEARCHING THE home of art teacher Lionel Rees-Prosser have found over three thousand indecent images of children on his computer along with other evidence that he abused students in his care. Since our earlier report when we gave the news of Rees-Prosser's death at South Stack, several more people have come forward claiming they were abused by the teacher. It's now thought he could have abused more than thirty students over a ten-year period.

"But not Jude," Rita says to the television news.

"Not Jude," says Adam.

Chapter Seventy-One

F IVE MONTHS HAVE passed since the events of that day
on the cliff. Five months of healing, and a slow return
to normality.

The aftermath of that day was tough, but we got
through it together, as a family. They called me, Adam and
Iwan as witnesses at Lionel's inquest. There was a mass of
media attention. After Lionel died other people came out of
the woodwork, claiming they'd been abused by him. But
because of his death they never got their day in court, unless
you count Coroner's Court. There were a lot of angry people
at the inquest. The coroner had to keep reminding them
what the purpose of an inquest is. "This is not a free for all.
Lionel Rees Prosser is not on trial here. We are here to
establish how, when and where he died." he said. But he
recorded a 'narrative verdict', where details surrounding
Lionel's activities did come out. So they got closure. Sort of.

Cate, with her legal brain, talked us through all the

possibilities beforehand. There might be angry Rees Prosser family members there. We might feel as though *we* were on trial. They sent Police officers to keep the two sides apart, if necessary, but in the end the only person there for Lionel was his mother. She cut a lonely figure, sitting upright and immobile in a fur coat, even though it was a warm spring day. Her face was as white as her hair. She clutched a framed photo of her son throughout.

Lionel's family's solicitor quizzed us on exactly what happened in the run-up, the suggestion being we'd goaded him into committing suicide, but the Police testified they'd seen us walking away before Lionel jumped and they played the audio evidence from our phones.

It was the same Coroner who did Jay's original inquest. He asked the Lloyds if they wanted to squash the original one and hold a new one, but Rita said no. She didn't want to drag it all up again. They wouldn't be able to prove anything after all this time so it could only ever be an open verdict. I'm glad Rita was spared that ordeal.

We spent Christmas together, all the Lloyds, for the first time for years, and me with them. I think you can say I am indisputably an honorary Lloyd. We even invited Judith, but she'd booked herself on a cruise.

In March, we had a party to celebrate Rita finishing treatment, and the anniversary of me coming to Môr Tawel – Rita kept a note of the date I arrived – 12th March 2014. Some of our friends from Nottingham came down and stayed in our new log cabins. Bridget Llewellyn also came, and Iwan, who's moved back from the States. Môr Tawel's the perfect place for a house party.

Now it's May, and I am alone at Môr Tawel. It's a warm clear day. I stand at the steps, leaning on the wall, looking out over the changing landscape. I feel a strange kind of peace, mixed with nervousness and nausea.

They've gone to the hospital, Adam and Rita, for Rita's final follow-up appointment. The prognosis is hopeful. She's still weak, and can't do much, so Adam is back here full-time for the summer to help out. Since Rita's cancer we've made some changes around here. Cate's taken control of the finances. Adam's doing most of the work in the garden while I look after the new campsite and the Alpacas. Yes, we have Alpacas! I'm busy halter-training them.

There's even talk of Adam moving back permanently, of us having the house and taking over the business, and converting one of the outbuildings for Rita and Tom to live in. We'll see.

Now I have the place to myself, it is time. Time to confirm what, deep down in my psyche, I already know. I have felt this way before.

I know, even before those two little blue lines confirm it.

I have time to compose myself before seeing Adam. How will he react? Will he bolt? Explode? Reach for a drink? The old Adam could have done any of those things, but he's mellowed. Since the truth about Jay came out, he's been a different person. Still spontaneous, still fun, but a lot of the anger has gone, he goes days without drinking, and he now treats me like the most revered person on the planet.

Something draws me to the room with Rita's paintings, and what I now know to be Jay's A-level artwork. I still have the Pre-Raphaelite picture of me, framed, on my wall, but the style of his earlier work is very different. I flick through the canvases. They are wild, garish, abstract. Some look disturbed.

In among them I find a line drawing by a different hand. It's of Jay as a teenager. In the corner are the initials LRP. I think of Lionel, and I shudder.

A surge of nausea brings me back to the present and the new life I'm nurturing inside me. I go outside for some air and sit on the decking. I feel the calm I always feel when I look at the view across the strait.

The sea is quiet today. Living up to its name, Môr Tawel.

Tom, back from inspecting the bees, comes to join me on the decking. We watch the shadows shift across the mountains on the shoreline opposite as clouds chase each other overhead.

"Even though I was born here I still think that's the best view in the world," says Tom.

"Funny to think of all those generations of Lloyds looking at that same view," I say.

"Yes," he says. "That view remains more or less the same as it was in my father's lifetime, and my grandfather's before that, and it'll still be there in your children's lifetime."

It's almost like he knows.

"FAN-FUCKING-TASTIC!" SAYS ADAM without hesitation, when I break the news. "We're gonna be parents. I'm gonna be a dad! I can't believe it! Aren't we clever Ame?" He lifts me up and spins me round till I think I really will be sick. "Let's go and tell my parents."

"No, Adam. Not yet, we have to wait."

"What for? You're not thinking of…you do want it, don't you?" his brow furrows.

"Of course Adam, it's just… What if… What if I lose it again? Like the last one?"

"You won't lose this one," says Adam, his eyes narrow and dark.

"How can you be so sure?"

"Because it's wanted. This baby is *ours*. Things grow here now Amy. Nothing dies here anymore."

Then he hugs me. "And even if we do lose it, we'll get through it together." I melt into his warmth, his strength, and I know he's right.

We're in the room Adam shared with Jay when they were boys. We've cleared out most of the furniture and we've started stripping the wallpaper. The room is draped in dust sheets.

I spot a bee trapped between the two panes of the old sash window, which is jammed half open. I move over to the window and start grappling with the heavy frame.

"What are you doing?" says Adam.

"There's a bee. It's stuck. I can't get to it."

Adam looks round. "It's only a bumble bee."

"It's beautiful. We have to rescue it."

"Don't try and lift the window in your condition, I'll do it."

He lifts the frame just enough for me to reach in and coax the insect out. It flies out then comes to rest on the outside of the glass.

"Stupid thing," says Adam, returning to work, "Now it's

got its freedom it doesn't want to leave."

I pick up a colour chart from the work bench and hold it up against the wall. "What colour shall we go for?"

"You can have any colour you want as long as it's magnolia," he says.

"Boring. Can't we have purple pout or tangerine twist?"

"Blue."

I gasp. It's not Adam speaking.

"Amy Blue. The colour suits you."

It's the voice I haven't heard for so long, the one I thought had gone. I sit down heavily on the bench. Adam turns, says nothing, and joins me.

"I've come to say goodbye." That voice, so musical, so rich, so heavenly. I don't see him now, just sense his presence. Adam feels it too.

"Not just goodbye. Thank you and goodbye. The future's yours now."

It's like those very early days in Balmoral Street, before he took shape. But this time there's a feeling of calm, of resolution. I sense him slipping away.

I whisper, "Goodbye Jay." Adam squeezes my hand.

We look up at the window. The bee, which had been hovering round the glass, finally takes flight.

"Goodbye," I say again.

Epilogue

March 2019

"STORY, MUMMY,"

Tamara Rita Lloyd Blue has eyes the colour of crystal, and my curls, but her hair is fair, like Adam's. She's in her bed in the little room at Môr Tawel.

"*Another* story? You've already had two!"

"One more Mummy!"

"One more, if you promise to go to sleep afterwards." She's nearly asleep now. Her eyelids are drooping. It takes a tremendous effort of will to keep them open. But my daughter already has her father's stubbornness.

I flick through the storybook. I've read each one so many times I know them all by heart. "Let's have something different. This is a story from Mummy's head," I say, then I begin.

A long time ago in a far-off land in the east, there lived a girl called Pixie. She was under the spell of an evil wizard who kept her in a box and only let her out to play when he felt like it.

One day, Pixie escaped from the box and ran away from the wizard, heading west, and the further she got from the wizard the less power he had over her and the more he shrank. But the journey was very dangerous and she got lost and hurt along the way and ended up in the attic of a big, dark house in a cold, rainy place. The girl was very lonely and very frightened because there were monsters downstairs. Then an angel started appearing at the end of her bed at night, and with the angel there she felt safe.

The girl found a hiding place in her room where she discovered the secret diary of a beautiful boy who used to live there. There were poems and pictures in the diary as well as other pieces of writing. And as she read it the boy came to life for her and she felt like she had known him for a long time already. Inside the diary she found a piece of card with an address on it and a picture of a place by the sea. Pixie decided to go and look for this place. It was a long journey to a different country even further west, but it was worth it because once she got to the place by the sea the people welcomed her. And the people and the animals there became her friends. And the spell the wicked wizard had put on her was finally broken, and the wizard shrunk even more till he was tiny and shriveled and had lost all his power.

Some of her new friends were sad because the

beautiful boy whose diary she'd read had died. Pixie, who knew the boy well because she'd read his diary, didn't believe he'd jumped off a cliff like everyone thought, so she turned into a detective to find out what really happened. She discovered there was a wicked wizard of the west, too, who held a lot of people in his spell. The beautiful boy tried to fight this wizard on the cliff top, but the wizard pushed the boy over the edge. When the girl told everyone what really happened they realised how evil the wicked wizard of the west really was and discovered all the bad things that he'd done. The wizard, rather than face their anger, jumped off the cliff himself. After that everyone who'd been under his spell was free. And they all lived happily ever after.

Tamara's been asleep since the first line. I move to kiss her forehead. I breathe in the smell of her peachy skin. "Sweet dreams, little darling," I whisper, like my granddad used to say to me.

"I'm not asleep," she says, opening her eyes. "I listened to the whole story. Mummy, what's an angel?"

"It's a good spirit who watches over you," I say. "Now go to sleep. You promised."

"I will but I'm waiting," she says. "I'm waiting for the angel. The one who sits at the end of my bed."

Acknowledgements

I have so many people to thank, from the early draft readers who took the time to read my embryonic work, to my tutors, classmates and fellow writers who helped me knock it into shape, and those who let me into their worlds for research purposes, and of course my publishers, who believed in the book enough to bring it to publication.

This is a long list:
To Kate Fletcher; John Perkins; Peter Smith; Di Peasey; Rob Edwards; Janet Davies; Joy Mitchell; Linda Metcalfe; Karl Dent; Ann Lawrie; the Nottingham Trent University Creative Writing MA class of 2014; Andrew Taylor; Graham Joyce (RIP); William Ivory; Georgina Locke; Tell Tale Writers; Makeshift Authors, Nottingham Writers' Studio; my friend the poet – author of 'A Suicide Stood'; Mark Barry; Phil Pidluznyj; Scotty Clark; Anne Marie Egbokhan; Brigid Girling and Graham Dempsey from The Weir; Vivienne and Graeme Matravers from Manor Organic Farm; Jane Masters from The Field, Woodborough; Marie Langford, bee-keeper; Emma and Roger Pugh; Anne Goodwin; Chris Breen; Nigel Chapman, Nottingham Coroner (retired); Eurig Williams; Bettina Benski; and to Sara-Jane Slack and the team at Inspired Quill.

Thank you!

About the Author

Clare Stevens grew up in the wilds of Somerset where she was weaned on cider and fed a daily diet of ghost stories cooked up in her older sister's imagination. This fostered an early love of storytelling long before she could read or write.

Her favourite writing time is first thing in the morning when she's still half in dreamland. She also writes in cafes and other public spaces, drawing inspiration from the unlimited supply of human interest.

When not writing or working, Clare can be found walking Max, her inexhaustible springer/pointer cross, heading off for weekends in Whitby (her spiritual home), or trying to learn piano. She runs a half-marathon once a decade.

Find the author via her website:

clarestevens.com

Or tweet her: @ClareWynStevens

Lightning Source UK Ltd.
Milton Keynes UK
UKHW011009140622
404410UK00002B/146